The Sheik's Ruby

by

Jennifer Moore

This is a work of fiction. Names, characters, places, and incidents are either the product of the author's imagination or are used fictitiously, and any resemblance to actual persons living or dead, business establishments, events, or locales, is entirely coincidental.

The Sheik's Ruby

COPYRIGHT © 2015 by Jennifer Moore

Cover Art by *Tina Lynn Stout*

The Wild Rose Press, Inc.
PO Box 708
Adams Basin, NY 14410-0708
Visit us at www.thewildrosepress.com

Publishing History
First Sweetheart Rose Edition, 2015
Print ISBN 978-1-5092-0132-7
Digital ISBN 978-1-5092-0133-4

Published in the United States of America

"Does your father know you're asking me?"

Hakim gazed over her shoulder and took a deep breath. "He knows."

"But he doesn't want me to come, right?"

"I will bring a companion of my choice tomorrow." He locked his gaze onto Shelby's and leaned toward her. "*You* are my choice. Will you please come?"

The Sheik apparently doesn't buy into the whole "guests are gifts from Allah" idea. "Of course, I would love to come." She smiled, but knew it didn't appear convincing. She hated feeling like she was the source of their discord.

"You are nervous. Please do not feel uncomfortable."

"I'm worried I'll say or do something stupid." She winced. "I'm not exactly a refined debutante who knows how to act in formal situations. I don't want to embarrass you, Hakim."

"I do not want you to be a refined debutante. I have spent enough time with those people to know they are not what I want." Hakim maneuvered his horse until he faced Shelby and their legs were nearly touching. He leaned closer, his gaze earnest. "What I want is you, Shelby Jo." He cupped her cheek in his hand.

Shelby felt her heart flutter and her nerve endings tingle as she lost herself in the deep brown pools of his eyes.

His thumb stroked her skin, leaving a trail of heat in its wake. He slid his hand into her hair and drew her closer, his lips covering hers.

When she drew away, Shelby inhaled deeply and grinned. "Hearing you put it that way, how could I possibly refuse?"

Dedication

For Josi and Nancy, my besties.
You always believe in me.

Acknowledgments

This is the first book I ever tried to write, and when I started six years ago, I had no idea what I was doing. I'm so thankful to the people who took the time to help me research, as well as improve my craft.

Thanks so much to the Harris family who let me come down to their branding weekend, to Brent Hardy for giving me a tour of his company jet. Thanks to my husband, Frank, for taking me to the Middle East where I completely fell in love with the culture and the people. To my dad for teaching me to ski, to Dr. Jeff Gardner for answering crazy medical questions.

And thank you to Gary for inviting me to join your critique group and for Angela, Chelsea, Chris, Cindy, Gaynelle, and Susan, for reading chapter after chapter and helping me get it just right. Josi Kilpack and Nancy Allen, I couldn't ask for better critique partners and friends. Thank you to Jacob Roundy for accepting the manuscript and helping with my preliminary edits. And so many thanks to Leanne Morgena for hours and hours and round after round of edits. You have been so patient with my questions and mistakes, and easy to talk to, and an absolute dream of an editor.

Mostly, thanks to my super supportive husband and sons for giving me the time to do what I love. It's a sacrifice for everyone whenever a mom takes time away from her family. And I love you for all the times you've pitched in around the house and never complained when dinner was cold cereal.

Chapter One

Shelby gazed at the fifty-foot drop below. Her exhilaration sent a thrill skittering over her skin, leaving tingles in its wake. She rode the ski lift alone, reveling in the freedom of flying through the frigid mountain air. Snow fell the night before, blanketing the Rocky Mountains of Colorado in a soft powder. Today, the sky shone clear and bright—the kind of day skiers called "bluebird."

Her legs, heavy with their skis, swung back and forth, as the bright sun streamed on her face and cold bit her freckled cheeks. The smell of mountain snow carried on a frosty breeze awakened her senses and ramped up her impatience to get on the slopes while they were still pristine. Tourists usually slept in for a few more hours before swarming the slopes and churning the perfect powder.

She neared the summit. The runs had been groomed into neat corduroy lines, which Shelby planned to avoid as she stuck to the powder on the fringes. Moguls covered the first fifty or so yards— carved over time as skiers followed the paths, executing their turns. Skiing on moguls was especially difficult, even for the most experienced skiers, and Shelby smiled in anticipation of the challenge. Sliding off the chair, she strapped her poles to her wrists while she glided the fifteen yards to the crest.

When she arrived at the summit, she saw someone already there. A small pang of disappointment washed through her at not being the first one on the fresh powder.

A man crouched down on one knee, checking his bindings.

The idea of flying past him and beating him to the untouched snow flitted through her mind. She pursed her lips as her sense of fair play and skier etiquette squelched the thought. *He* did *get here first.*

"Looking for a good line?" Shelby raised her voice to avoid catching him off guard. Based on the way he started, he hadn't heard her approach. Since she hadn't seen him riding the lift, she figured he arrived via the lodge lifts connecting to the network of slopes crisscrossing the resort.

He stood and motioned with his pole toward a more gradual incline to their left. "I'll traverse the summit and start down farther that way. The slope is a little less steep over there."

She noticed as he rose that he was close to six feet tall and had a slight accent she couldn't place. Shelby let her gaze dart over him as she assessed his expensive equipment and all-black designer ski clothes—probably the self-heating kind. His perfect posture, tan skin, and strong cheekbones made him look like a model from a ski catalog. *Wintersports*, the magazine she worked for, had done a story about that apparel line a few years back. *I'll bet that jacket costs more than all my equipment put together.*

She had seen plenty of these guys, completely obsessed with their image, but never as talented as they appeared. Shelby employed every ounce of her self-control to keep from rolling her eyes. She couldn't wait to breeze past him in a shower of powder. "Yes, that should be easier for you." With an arched brow, she studied the path he indicated.

"Easier?" He lowered his chin and raised his brows.

"Yeah, and if you started over there, I'd have all this sweet powder on the moguls to myself." She gave him a mischievous smile. "Unless you beat me to it."

When he saw her expression, the stranger grinned. His teeth shined white against his cinnamon-colored skin.

Shelby's heart skipped when she saw his smile, but she credited it to the waiting powder.

"You're looking for a race then?" He lifted his chin in the direction of the run.

"Oh no, I wouldn't want to embarrass you." She flipped a braid over her shoulder to show she was teasing.

"Hmmm…" The stranger tapped his gloved forefinger on his chin and widened his smile. "I accept your challenge." He slid his expensive goggles down over his eyes, turning her way and tipping his head toward the slope.

"I'll wait for you at the bottom." Shelby pulled on her own goggles and adjusted her ski cap.

Simultaneously, they pushed off over the edge and began carving parallel paths through the moguls. Shelby couldn't help but grin as she flew through the bumpy mounds, leaving behind a spray of snow. Adrenaline spiked through her veins as she pushed herself even faster. She darted a glance at her companion. She could tell he wasn't accustomed to skiing at such a break-neck speed. One bad judgment or delayed reaction would cause him to over-correct and lose his balance. She smirked. No way would she let this "pretty-boy" with his fancy gear and perfect teeth beat her down the mountain.

To his credit, he skied pretty well. But this was her home territory. She'd been skiing these mountains since she was a little girl, and he didn't stand a chance. Shelby could feel him watching. Keeping her upper body stationary, leaning forward, while her knees moved to the right and left, Shelby rode over the bumps in the snow with a blinding speed. Each movement appeared fluid and effortless, and she knew it.

Shelby caught a glimpse of her companion and saw his lips were pressed together into a tight line, as if he were concentrating.

Their gazes met for an instant. The quick glance lasted just a split second too long, and the tip of his right ski veered the smallest bit off course. This mistake cost him, and he was forced to lean into the mountain to catch himself. Sliding twenty feet on his right side, he managed to stop and re-align his skis, and then pushed himself up.

"Are you all right?" she called from where she stopped farther down the slope. Her breath came in quick gasps that sent out mist clouds.

"Yes," he yelled back, shaking his head. "I am just trying to make you overconfident."

"I guess you've had enough, then?" The concern in Shelby's voice was replaced by teasing. She bent forward, ready to set off again down the slope, and looked over her shoulder.

"Hardly." He brushed the snow off his jacket,

snatched up his poles, and pushed off.

This early in the morning, the run was nearly empty. Shelby noticed only one other skier on the entire slope. Near the bottom of the hill, additional trails merged together. The pair adopted a more leisurely pace as they passed more skiers.

At the bottom of the run, Shelby spun to a stop, sending out a spray of snow with her skis. "Who shall we declare the winner?"

"Hmmm." He tapped his finger on his lips. "A rematch is the only fair option."

She considered for a minute. He assumed a lot. Should she do another run? He was charming and handsome, but more than that, he was intriguing—unlike the typical ski guys she usually met on the slopes. *Maybe I'll let this play out a little longer—see what happens.* After a moment, she gave a nod. "Agreed." Tugging off her right glove, she held out her hand. "By the way, my name's Shelby Walker."

"I am Hakim Khalid. It's nice to meet you, Shelby Walker."

The warmth in his dark eyes surprised Shelby. When they shook hands, she was very aware of his skin on hers. In spite of the cool air, heat rushed into her cheeks. She pulled away her hand and occupied herself with replacing her glove.

They chose another run, this time a double black diamond trail, and headed to the chair lift for the north face of the mountain. The chair scooped them up and carried them toward the borders of the resort. Although more skiers arrived as the day progressed, this lift line was one of the least crowded. Shelby knew the run was quite challenging, even for expert skiers, and they had the quad chair to themselves.

Shelby leaned back in her seat, gazing up at the majestic view above the Colorado Rocky Mountains. The updates the resort had made improved the ski experience, and she was excited to try all the new runs. "So, where did you learn to ski like that?"

"Various places. New South Wales, Austria, Oslo." He shrugged. "I have skied since I was young. We also have an indoor ski resort near my home."

"Indoor skiing?" She jerked her head around and faced him with widened eyes. "Where is home?" If he'd skied in all those places, he wasn't as inexperienced as she'd thought. And *indoor skiing*? That would be an excellent angle for an article. Hakim might just be someone she wanted to get to know better—*for his ski experience, not his dark eyes and white smile.*

"Khali-dar. You have probably never heard of my small country."

Again, she detected the slightest hint of an accent. Something about the way he pronounced "*h*" from the back of his throat. Shelby nodded once. "On the Arabian Peninsula near Qatar and the United Arab Emirates. I *have* heard of it."

His eyebrows arched. "I have spoken with few Americans who knew of my country."

"I'm not like most people. I really like geography. When I was a kid, I spent hours poring over my dad's atlas." Shelby glanced at her companion. She estimated he was not much older than she, although discerning his age was difficult with his ski hat. Thick lashes ringed his deep brown eyes. He had a thin mustache. A well-trimmed beard just covered the tip of his chin, and a small triangle of whiskers sat right below his bottom lip. *Like a goatee with no sides.* But what drew her gaze were his straight, white teeth. When he smiled, his top teeth overlapped his bottom teeth perfectly. "Hakim Khalid?" Shelby broke the silence. "That's not your full name, is it?"

He studied her for a moment, squinting. "My proper name is Hakim Abdal-Salam bin Rashid Al Khalid. In my experience, Americans tend to shorten names. But, as we have established, you are not like most people."

"So, your father's name is Rashid?"

"From where does this knowledge of foreign name dissection derive?" A smile quirked at the edges of his mouth.

"I took a Middle-Eastern culture class in college."

"Is Shelby Walker *your* full name?"

"I guess my proper name is Shelby Jo Walker," she mimicked his manner.

"And your mother is named Jo?"

"No, my mom is Debbie. Jo is short for Josephine. That's my grandma." Shelby slid her poles beneath her knee to hold them in place on the swinging lift chair and pressed down between her fingers to push her gloves on tightly.

"Where is your home, Shelby Jo Walker?" He shifted in the seat, holding on to the bar over his head.

"I'm from a small town in Southern Colorado called Culver Springs. You've probably never heard of it."

"No, I have not," he admitted.

"It's about a five hour drive from here. I still consider it home even though I don't live there now. I moved to Denver for college and stayed."

The conversation tapered off as they neared the top of the lift. They each busied themselves adjusting gloves and pole straps until the time came to slide off the quad chair.

Unlike the first run, this one was not a wide, open track, but a series of "chutes"—trails leading through trees and around rocks. Knowing how difficult chute skiing was, Shelby didn't mention a rematch. She set a fast but not deadly pace, free-styling through the trees, rocks, and powder on the steep, un-groomed trails. Glancing back from a parallel trail, she noticed his eyes were squinted, and she smiled. He was a pretty good sport. Again, Shelby saw only one other skier on the hill. The new runs had certainly cut down on the crowds. She'd have to remember that for her article.

A cat track sloped at a gentler incline, linking them to another run. The two slowed their pace and moved to the lift line.

"What is indoor skiing like? How is it even possible?" Shelby pushed up her goggles. *This could be a perfect angle for my next story.*

Hakim slid forward on his skis as the line moved. "The runs are rather limited, obviously. The snow is man-made. A ski-lift conveys you to the top of a slope inside a giant, refrigerated dome. The ceiling is the stage for a fantastic lightshow. The major advantage, of course, is that the weather is not a factor. No snow falls in Khali-dar, but one can ski any day of the year."

"That's amazing!" Shelby made a mental note to look up indoor ski slopes on the internet when she got home. "How did anyone ever dream up that idea? Let alone afford it?"

"Khali-dar is an amazing place," he answered.

For the next few hours, they took turns choosing different runs. Shelby picked a lift that led to another, higher up the mountain. Weaving back and forth over the network of trails, the run took much longer than the others. By the time they reached the bottom, the time was nearly noon, and Shelby's stomach rumbled. "Can I buy you a cup of chili?" she asked, when they stopped in front of the snack shop.

"That is not necessary."

"Are you just saying that to be polite, or do you hate chili? Or do you have other plans for lunch?" She stepped out of her ski binding.

Hakim's silence stretched for several long seconds. He rubbed the back of his neck with his gloved hand, his brows furrowed.

"Hey, don't worry about it." Shelby knelt and pretended to adjust her other ski to conceal the color spreading over her cheeks.

He cleared his throat. "Shelby, I do not wish to offend you—"

"Oh, no, I understand. Not a big deal." Shelby tried to keep the embarrassment out of her voice and turned to leave.

He touched her shoulder. "Wait, please let me explain myself. Where I come from, gender roles are much more...traditional. For a woman to initiate something like this would be almost forbidden. I was just surprised for a moment and unsure how to respond. Please allow me to try again." Taking a deep breath, he smiled. "Shelby Walker, I would love to have lunch with you." His gaze held hers. "I apologize for acting rudely."

Relief washed over her. "You weren't rude. That's

something I should have remembered from my college class. But, just so you know, things are a little different here. And I don't really go for the 'gender role' thing." She saw the sincerity in his face, and her smile returned then she picked up her skis and poles.

They deposited their equipment on the outside rack and made their way toward the crowded restaurant.

Stuffing her gloves into her pocket, Shelby turned to Hakim. "How about since I asked you to lunch, I'll get the food, and you get us a table?" She spoke with a light tone, but her gaze searched his expression for any sign of discomfort.

He nodded and turned to scan the room.

Waiting in the line, Shelby gazed around the little snack shop. She liked the rustic log cabin look. The decor was much nicer than the snack shops at most resorts. Filling the air was the familiar noise of conversation and ski boots clomping around on the rubber floor mats. The line was long, but fast moving.

Shelby put two bowls of chili on her tray and grabbed some breadsticks and bottled water. She carried their lunch toward the cashier. While she waited, she turned her thoughts to Hakim. Was he spending the day with her because he couldn't think of a polite way to get out of doing so?

Throughout the years, she had met plenty of skiers. Hanging out with a stranger for a run or two was not unusual, but she even surprised herself with the amount of time she was spending with this man. She felt such a comfortable easiness while they were together. Maybe because he was an out-of-towner, she knew no pressure existed to make a friendly day of skiing into anything more. But that did little to explain the way her heart thumped every time he smiled.

Shelby slid her tray in front of the cashier, pulled her wallet out of an inside coat pocket, and paid for the meal. Once she spotted Hakim on the other side of the crowded dining room, she picked up the tray and clomped toward him in her stiff ski boots. As she got closer, she realized he spoke with another man. With all the noise in the snack shack, she couldn't hear what they were saying, but by the cadence of their voices, she could tell they weren't speaking English.

When Hakim saw her, he waved and both men stood. "Shelby, I'd like to introduce you to my friend, Nasir." He gestured to the man next to him.

Shelby recognized him as the other skier she had seen on the slopes that morning. Nasir was a goliath. Hakim stood close to six feet tall, but Nasir loomed above him—at least a head taller. Large muscles bulged under his ski parka. He sported a dark goatee and piercing eyes that didn't quite look directly at her.

"Nasir, may I present Shelby Jo Walker?"

Shelby resisted the urge to cringe from the large man and extended her hand.

Nasir put his hands together and inclined his head. "*Ahlan wa sahlan.*"

"Nasir says he is pleased to meet you," Hakim translated.

Yeah, right. Nasir's stony expression did not change, and his gaze was severe. Pleased looked like the farthest thing from the man's mind, but Shelby put her hands together anyway and gave a little bow, "*Ahlan wa sahlan, Nasir.*" She hoped her pronunciation sounded even close to correct.

He tipped his head forward, his gaze focused on

something above her head.

Shelby wondered if he spoke English, but she didn't like the idea of engaging this intimidating hulk in conversation. Instead, she turned and spoke to Hakim. "I'm sorry...I didn't realize you were here with a friend. Here, you two eat these, and I'll run and grab another bowl of chili."

"Thank you, but no," Nasir stated in a heavy accent. "I will leave now."

The two men spoke for a moment in what Shelby assumed was Arabic.

Then, Nasir again put his hands together and bowed in her direction. "It was a pleasure to make your acquaintance, Shelby Jo Walker. I hope your day is enjoyable."

"Nice to meet you, too, Nasir." Shelby smiled.

Once more, Nasir glanced around the dining room, and then strode out the door, turning heads as he passed.

He was obviously accustomed to the attention his size attracted. *Wow. He didn't spare any of the gawkers a single glance.*

Hakim held the back of the wobbly metal chair and waited for Shelby to be seated before he sat on the other side of the small table.

"Hakim, I'm sorry." Shelby set their meals and utensils in front of them. "I didn't know you were here with someone. Am I keeping you from your friend?"

"Please do not apologize. Nasir prefers to ski alone."

"What about you? Am I monopolizing your time today? Would *you* rather ski alone?" She chewed on her lip and stirred her chili.

Hakim unwrapped the plastic spoon, and then set it down next to his foam chili bowl. He lifted his gaze and met Shelby's. "Today, I prefer to ski with you."

"Oh." Her heart skipped a beat, and her ears got warm.

After a moment, Hakim opened his paper napkin and spread it over his lap. "Tell me, Shelby Jo Walker, do you have a job you are escaping today, or are you a professional skier?"

Before answering, she swallowed a bite of her breadstick. "Actually, I'm working right now. I write for a sports magazine called *Wintersports*. Basically, I travel around and stay at different resorts, demo new equipment, or interview athletes for research."

"And do you enjoy this job?"

"It's fine. I've worked there for three years. Since my senior year in college." Shelby sipped from her water bottle. "This job isn't what I want to do forever. I mean, sports reporting doesn't exactly change the world."

"You intend to change the world?" Hakim asked.

She couldn't tell whether his question was asked out of amusement or curiosity, but based on his sincere expression, he didn't intend it sarcastically. "I want to advocate for an important cause, or write stories that cause people to change the way they think...or brings an issue to their attention." She leaned forward. "Something that makes a difference. Writing for a sports magazine is fun, the pay is ok, but this position's not where I want to be in five years." After twisting the lid onto her water bottle, she sat back, realizing she'd been speaking too passionately. *I need to calm down before I scare this guy away.* "What about you? What type of work do you do?"

He chewed slowly then swallowed, his eyebrows crunched together. "I work for my father. I am expected to take over the family business someday."

"That's great. What's the business?"

"Consulting, as well as real estate and horse breeding."

"My dad raises horses, too. What kind of horses do you have? Oh, that's a stupid question. They're Arabians, right?" Shelby wiped the breadstick grease off her hands with a napkin. *How crazy that this man from the other side of the world and I share such common interests.*

"Yes, most of our horses are Arabian. I am here in the States to meet with a business associate and tour some land in Kentucky my father hopes to purchase for horse breeding. I arrived a week early to ski. I will fly to Kentucky on Friday." He smiled, but his eyes remained serious.

His mannerisms were stiff, and the way he spoke was guarded. Shelby tried to read him, but struggled. She wondered if he simply had a lot on his mind. Once they'd finished their lunch, she stacked their bowls on the tray.

Hakim took the tray and emptied it into the trash on the way out the door.

Shelby walked outside and squinted at the brightness of the sun on the snow. She followed Hakim to the ski rack.

He grabbed their equipment. "Now, may I choose the run?" He planted their poles before he tipped her skis toward her.

She nodded and concentrated on separating her

skis. *He wants to spend the rest of the day with me?* Her chest felt light and her fingers a bit shaky as she laid the skis in the snow, and then pushed her toes into the bindings and stepped down on her heels.

"I hope you are not too disappointed if I choose a less difficult hill. After all, we just ate." Hakim stepped into his skis and clicked his boots into place.

"Sounds good." Shelby hoped her tone didn't convey more than basic friendliness. *Stop acting ridiculous.*

Later in the day, the shade of the pine trees covered more of the slopes. Soon, the bright patches of snow peeking through the shadows would be gone. As the day had progressed, Shelby became more comfortable with Hakim, not feeling the need to fill the silences, but enjoying their time spent together. She wondered if he felt the same.

Shelby made sure she tried out every one of the lifts, especially the new ones that opened this season, gaining plenty of material for her article. The hours passed quickly. Acknowledging her tired muscles, she rested her head on the back of the chair. Today had been a long one. She turned her face toward her companion, who leaned back on the seat with his eyes closed. *Is he tired, too?* "This will be my last run. I'm trashed."

Turning his head, he smiled. "Yes, I also feel tired. I have felt quite challenged at keeping up with you today."

"I don't think so. I'm pretty sure you've been holding back to keep pace with me."

"Don't underestimate your talent. You are an exceptional skier. And I will be sorry to lose your

15

company."

His words caused her stomach to flutter. "Thanks, Hakim. I've had a great day, too." She paused, chewing on her lip. "Hey, I was wondering…I mean, I hope this isn't too much, and I totally understand if you can't or you don't want to or whatever, but I'm coming back up the canyon in a few days to do a story on a snowmobiling company. They're just a few miles away. Anyway, the guy told me to bring friends, but finding people who have the whole day off in the middle of the week is hard. So, do you want to come with me?" she finished in a rush. Why did she always wave her hands around so much when she was nervous?

"Thank you for the invitation." He inclined his head forward. "I would be delighted to go snowmobiling with you."

If she didn't know better, she would have thought he was being cynical. *Or maybe that was just his formal way of speaking.* "We're meeting at the Canyon Rim Lodge at nine-thirty, day after tomorrow. You can bring Nasir, too."

"Thank you."

The last lift line was nearly as empty as the first had been. Shelby found a trail through the trees with small jumps.

At the end of the run, they continued down the slope, past the lifts.

"The parking lot is totally out of your way. Aren't you staying at the lodge?" she asked.

"It is not far. I will see you safely to your vehicle."

Shelby raised her eyebrows, touched by his chivalry. "Thanks."

After taking off their skis, they walked the short

distance to her compact car in silence. Shelby rested her skis and poles against the driver's side door and removed her gloves. Hakim helped her strap the equipment to the ski rack on the roof of the red car. She popped the trunk, then grabbed her sneakers and hopped for a few steps while she replaced her ski boots. Shelby fished her keys out of her pocket and turned toward him.

He clasped her hand in both of his.

"So, I'll see you Thursday, right?" Shelby asked.

"Yes. Until Thursday, Shelby Jo Walker."

"Until Thursday, Hakim." She climbed behind the wheel. As she drove into the winter evening, her hand continued to feel the warmth of his touch.

Chapter Two

Hakim watched Shelby drive away and considered what intrigued him about the American woman. He was astonished to realize the answer—she simply treated him as a friend. He tried to remember ever being treated that way before. There had been tutors and playmates, under obligation to associate with him. Later, college classmates and women sought his attention and attempted to impress him. None of them ever regarded him as an equal.

That was the curse of his birthright—the inability to fully trust any relationship. The fact that this confident, lively woman was the only person who had befriended him without knowing the truth amazed him. For the first time in his life, someone knew him as Hakim, the *man*, instead of Hakim, the *prince*. He wondered how she would act if she knew his true identity. Selfishly, he hoped she would never find out.

Still lost in thought, he walked toward the resort, hardly noticing Nasir waiting at the edge of the parking lot. Both men re-attached their skis and made their way to the special lift that would take them back to the lodge.

The lift swung into the air. Hakim knew by Nasir's silence he disapproved of the prince spending the day with a stranger. At lunch, Nasir had tried to convince Hakim that Shelby was a safety risk. How could they be sure she was who she claimed to be?

Hakim had insisted he was safe, but Nasir had still tried to persuade him to follow procedure which involved a background check, extra security, and perhaps even a polygraph test. Hakim had flatly refused.

Nasir had left the restaurant after giving his word not to let the prince out of his sight.

Hakim rubbed his palm over the back of his neck, bending his head from side to side. His frustration continued to build. He knew Nasir was only doing his job, but Hakim disliked being treated like a child, unable to make his own decisions and constantly suffocated in the name of safety.

"Nasir." Hakim let out a cold breath as he turned to the larger man. Without the sun, the breeze had a distinct chill. "I have accepted an invitation from Miss Walker to accompany her on a snowmobile excursion Thursday at the Canyon Rim Lodge. Please see to the necessary arrangements."

"Your Highness, this leaves me only one day to plan for your security. I need to organize an advance reconnaissance investigation at the Canyon Rim Lodge and the surrounding area. I will also need to run complete background checks on anyone who will be there." Nasir removed his gloves and pushed them into his coat pocket.

Hakim blew out a frustrated sigh. "I am traveling anonymously. This snowmobile trip is merely a friendly excursion, not a trap set by an assassin. As far as Miss Walker knows, I am just a businessman on vacation. Please allow me to enjoy myself as such."

"I understand, Your Highness. As I am charged

with your protection, I must insist on providing what security measures I deem necessary. However, at your insistence, I will do my best to use discretion."

"Thank you, Nasir."

The ski valet met them as they arrived onto the lodge porch. He wore a dark green ski coat with the Bear Creek Lodge insignia above a name tag that read, "Brent." Hakim judged Brent to be in his early twenties.

"How was the snow today, sir?" Brent asked in a polite voice.

"Very nice, thank you," Hakim replied as he removed his skis. Although the motion was subtle, he noticed Brent's eyes narrow when he heard his accent.

Nasir picked up both sets of skis and poles and handed them to Brent.

The valet strapped them to a rack and ducked into the back room, returning with the men's shoes. "I'll get those waxed up and ready for you tomorrow morning.

Nasir handed him a tip.

"Thank you, sir." Brent slid the folded bill into his pocket.

Nasir held the door open and followed Hakim into the main lobby.

The large area was tastefully decorated with a rustic American western feel. Chandeliers made of antlers hung from the ceiling, casting interesting shadows on the high walls. Leather couches and brightly upholstered lodge pole chairs formed small sitting areas between the pool table and bar. The space was warm and inviting after the cold darkness outside.

Hakim was aware of the looks the other guests gave him. The instant distrust in people's faces when they saw his dark tan skin and heard his accent. He often wondered how these same people would treat him if he revealed who he truly was. He loved the anonymity of traveling in the United States, but the discrimination often unnerved him.

As Hakim rode the penthouse elevator, his thoughts turned to Shelby. He was still surprised with himself for not dismissing her outright as soon as she spoke. Not out of arrogance, but because of his lack of social experience. But something about her had intrigued him. Was it her easy smile? Or her competitiveness? Or the way she chewed on her lip when she was thinking?

The elevator doors opened, and the penthouse butler stood in the suite entryway. The butler wore white gloves and an immaculate suit bearing the hotel crest on his lapel. "How was skiing, sir?"

"Very nice, thank you." Hakim turned to allow the butler to slide his jacket off his shoulders.

"The chef has informed me supper will be ready in half an hour."

Hakim nodded and took a moment to admire the view of the darkening mountain from the penthouse window.

The western décor theme carried throughout the lodge and into the guestrooms. A stone fireplace with a crackling flame was the focal point of the main area of the penthouse.

Hakim waved a farewell to Nasir, who retired to his own room, and then the prince stepped past the rustic planked dining table set for one and into a hall leading to the master bedroom, so he could shower before dinner.

For a few hours the next morning, Hakim skied, but found the activity wasn't as appealing as the day before. Memories of the previous day distracted him. Every other thought was of Shelby—her smile as she raced him down the slope, their conversations on the lifts, the way she removed her gloves with her teeth, and chewed her lower lip when she was thinking. After a few runs, he returned to his suite, unable to concentrate.

Shelby was, as far as he could tell, a fairly typical American woman—average height and build. Pretty, though not stunning, more of a natural beauty. His gaze had been constantly drawn to her face which was so full of life, although something else, an aspect he couldn't quite put his finger on, attracted him. She exuded confidence—a different kind of self-confidence than he was accustomed to—a type of poise which didn't come from beauty, money, or status. She was honest. Competitive, yes, but not in an attempt to impress him. She seemed so open, yet not naïve. Simply comfortable being herself. And for reasons he couldn't understand, she seemed comfortable being with him.

And did he ask too much, wanting the experiences of a regular life? To enjoy himself, to make friends, and to not worry about the finality of his future? He would be the Sheik soon enough, and such decisions would be made for him.

Dressed in a cashmere sweater and jeans, Hakim sat in front of the massive fireplace attempting to distract himself with a book.

"Excuse me, Your Highness." Nasir entered the room with quiet footsteps. "I have the background check information for Miss Walker."

Hakim put down his book and rolled his finger, indicating for Nasir to continue.

"Shelby Jo Walker, age twenty-four. Born in Culver Springs, Colorado. Parents are Burke and Deborah Walker. Brother is Chet Walker. None of her family has traveled outside of the country or had contact with any person or groups of interest." Nasir spoke in a modulated tone, skimming his gaze down the page for pertinent information.

"Aside from one speeding ticket, Miss Walker has no criminal record. She is the registered owner of a 2005 economy compact car. Attended Culver High School, degree in Journalism from the University of Colorado, where she lived with three roommates. None of whom cause any suspicion. Employed by *Wintersports* magazine. Currently a resident of Washington Park, where she has lived for the past seventeen months. Miss Walker was issued an American passport and traveled to Vancouver, British Columbia in April of last year. As far as we can tell, she is no threat to your safety or the national security of Khali-dar."

"Thank you." Hakim took the papers from Nasir. He read over them with interest until his personal assistant, Shanayze, interrupted him with documents to sign. The prince set down the papers and resigned himself to conducting regular business matters.

An hour later, Shanayze stood to leave.

Hakim cleared his throat to stop her. "Shanayze, I would like you to do me a favor."

"Of course, Your Highness."

Shelby had over shadowed his thoughts all day. Had she been thinking about him, as well? American women were baffling to say the least, and he had no idea what sort of things might please this one. He looked to where his assistant waited. "Would you please speak to the concierge and arrange a floral delivery?"

****

Shelby stared at her computer screen. The words just wouldn't come. Her mind wandered again to the events of the previous day. *Come on, concentrate. Remember, here in reality, there are deadlines and no handsome, exotic stranger to race down the mountain.* She tucked her wavy hair behind her ears and leaned back in her chair, allowing her gaze to travel around her workspace.

A crowded main floor office was the home of *Wintersports* magazine. Mismatched tables and chairs served as desks for the journalists. Shelby was the only employee sitting on the writers' side of the office today. She heard voices in the conference room as the next month's magazine was being laid out. The constant sound of the printing press rattled and hummed in the basement, making the floor vibrate. The walls in the office were papered in typical fashion with magazine clippings, pictures, comic strips, and photos of loved ones. Shelby only had two pictures on her desk. Her family smiled out of one frame. She studied their faces and felt the familiar twinge of homesickness.

A snapshot of Shelby's best friend, Lacey, holding her brand new baby, rested against the family picture. Shelby had always been a little jealous of how beautiful Lacey was. Lacey's grandfather was Navajo, his genes evident in her gorgeous hair, tan skin, and dark eyes. Undoubtedly the prettiest girl in school and

Homecoming Queen their senior year, Lacey turned heads. Growing up, Shelby had felt awkward around boys. Her curly hair and freckles didn't help her self-confidence much, especially when all males drooled over her best friend. She had usually been shy and insecure anytime a situation required her to interact with a member of the opposite sex. Luckily, Shelby had discovered sports and writing, giving her the confidence she needed. But this unfortunately resigned her to the role of a "guy's best friend."

That was what made yesterday so unique. For some reason, Hakim was different. She had no problem challenging him on the mountain, and amazingly, he continued to spend the day with her. She was delighted to feel so at ease with and so attracted to a man she'd just met.

The day was more than half over, and she knew she needed to at least start her article about yesterday's skiing. Especially since she'd be snowmobiling all day tomorrow. But when she began to type, she was distracted by the image of dark brown eyes and a white smile. Closing her laptop, she sighed and wandered through a door on the back wall into her boss's office.

"Hey, Xan! Wanna grab a late lunch?" She leaned her shoulder against the doorframe.

"Love to." He smiled, tossed aside the magazine he was reading, and sprang out of his chair. As he grabbed his coat from a hook on the wall, the phone rang. He glanced at the caller ID screen and winked. "Sorry, gotta take this real quick."

Shelby sat in a soft chair to wait. Although she had been in Xan's office hundreds of times, she shook her head as she gazed around. Had a room ever so perfectly reflected its owner? Hanging on the walls were pictures of skiers and snowboarders flying through powder, signed photographs of Olympic athletes, and posters for Warren Miller movies. She rested her gaze on Xan.

He rolled his eyes as he pointed at the phone. "Sorry," he mouthed.

Smiling, she shrugged. *No hurry.*

Even though he was a few years older than Shelby, Xan's shaggy blond hair and freckles made him seem more like a teenager. He was obviously an athlete. A trendy T-shirt stretched tight across his chest and accentuated the muscles in his arms. Xan was a much better snowboarder than editor. But his enthusiasm, expertise, and the fact his father owned the magazine made up for any lack in that department.

After a few minutes, the call ended. "Feel like Thai?" he asked as he hung up.

"Thai would be great."

They walked through the office and stepped outside through the glass doors. A faint sun glowed through a screen of clouds in the sky over Denver. The air felt dirty and cold. Shelby and Xan strode down the sidewalk, avoiding patches of gray, frozen slush. She was glad she'd be back in the mountains tomorrow. Out of the city, the sun would be warm and the sky blue.

The restaurant was only half a block away on the same semi-deserted street as the *Wintersports* office. Realtor signs hung in the windows of many of the buildings, and the few shops or offices that were open didn't get much traffic. They stepped into the Isan Tai restaurant, and the aroma of foreign spices filled the warm air. They waved to the owner, Aroon, through the window to the kitchen. Xan helped Shelby off with her coat, and they slid onto the red vinyl benches of the booth.

Aroon, a small, impossibly thin man with a wispy black moustache, appeared, wiping his hands on his apron. "Ah, my favorite customers. I think you will like the *Pla nueng maneo* with coconut rice today. It is delicious."

Shelby lowered her head to hide her smile. She and Xan often joked about how Aroon didn't let customers order for themselves. But he was always right, and she knew the food would be wonderful.

"That sounds excellent," Xan said. "And can we get some drinks, too?"

"Yes, yes, two diet sodas. Aroon always remembers his favorite customers," he said, and then scurried away to start their order.

She and Xan shared a smile.

"Thank you, Aroon," Shelby said a few minutes later, when he set their glasses and straws on the table.

Xan took a long sip of his drink and looked at Shelby. "It's been a while since we've spent any time together, Shel."

Shelby squirmed under his gaze. Sometimes, she felt the way he studied her was too intimate, or too intense for a professional relationship. "What are you talking about? We ate here just last week." She smoothed out the thin paper placemat.

"Yeah, but I think that was the last time I saw you."

"You know, my boss is kind of a slave driver." She smirked and raised her brows, to let him know she was teasing. "But truthfully, I've been pretty busy."

Aroon delivered their food. One bowl was piled

27

high with coconut rice, and the other with noodles and fish. He made sure they had everything they needed and left them alone.

"How did it go, yesterday? Did you like Bear Creek?" Xan asked.

Shelby let herself relax, glad he'd brought the conversation back to work. "The resort was perfect. Fresh powder, blue skies, and not too crowded. You should've come."

"You know how places like that feel about snowboarders. And I also had that shareholders meeting my dad insisted I couldn't miss. Too bad you had to ski alone, though."

"Actually, I met someone up there, and he did some runs with me." Shelby leaned forward for a smell of the fish and lime dressing. Aroon was right. The food smelled delicious. Shelby scooped noodles onto her plate and reached for the fish. When she glanced up at Xan, she realized he was still staring.

"He?" Xan narrowed his eyes.

"Yeah, a really nice guy." Shelby took a bite of fish. "He's from the Middle East—Khali-dar. He was a fantastic skier and told me about the indoor slopes they have where he comes from. Have you ever heard of that? It's gotta be amazing, right?" When she realized she was rambling, she blushed. She pushed the rice around her plate with her chopsticks. *Why on earth am I uncomfortable speaking with Xan about Hakim?*

"Shel, you need to be careful. Are you blushing? Dudes like that totally prey on girls like you."

An expression she had never seen before flashed across Xan's face. Was it jealousy? She tipped her head to the side and lowered her eyelids to half mast. "Girls like me?"

"You're young and cute and from a small town. People aren't the same up here. You can't trust everyone you meet." Xan wound noodles around his chopsticks and stuffed the wad into his mouth.

Shelby couldn't believe what she just heard. She'd always thought of Xan as a good friend—kind of like a brother. But right now, he was acting like an over-protective parent. "Xan, I'm not completely naïve. I meet people on the slopes all the time. This guy was no different." She couldn't meet his gaze when she said this, but she kept speaking. "That's it. It was fun. Not a big deal." She glanced at him, and then back to her plate. "Why are you acting this way?"

"Shel, I'd never forgive myself if something bad happened. Don't get mad. I'm just looking out for you." His face reddened. "But, he was a tourist, so you won't have to worry about him anymore."

Shelby set down her chopsticks and looked Xan in the eye. Irritation tightened her muscles. "I invited him to come to Canyon Rim tomorrow."

Xan's eyebrows furrowed as he chewed. "I might come up to Canyon Rim tomorrow, too. If that's all right with you."

She studied his face but saw his expression was neutral. "What? Why? I mean, of course you're welcome, but are you coming just to keep an eye on me? I'm a big girl, you know. I can handle myself in a professional manner. I won't do anything to damage the reputation of the magazine, if that's what you're worried about."

"Shel, this has nothing to do with the magazine. You should have seen your face when you were talking about this guy. You just met him, and you're acting like the two of you are best friends." He leaned back in the booth and folded his arms. "I'll be there to keep things legit."

Xan was about the easiest going guy she knew. She couldn't believe he was blowing things so far out of proportion. Now, she wished she hadn't said anything at all.

They finished eating, and Xan used his company card to pay the bill. After saying goodbye to Aroon, the two stepped back out into the cold. An uncomfortable silence now cast a pall over the already dreary day as they hurried down the street toward the office.

Near the front doors, a white van with a flower shop logo pulled up on the street. A teenage girl in a red parka climbed out of the driver's seat carrying a clipboard. "Hey, do either of you know Shelby Jo Walker?"

"I'm Shelby." She glanced at the van and back at the girl, wondering what was going on.

"I'll need you to sign here, Miss."

Shelby signed the delivery slip. *Is this a mistake?*

The girl stepped off the slushy curb and walked back behind the van, only to re-appear seconds later carrying a crystal vase full of flowers. She was nearly invisible behind the grand arrangement.

Shelby held the door for the girl. Who could have sent these? Her dad? Brother? Not their style. Anyway, this over-the-top arrangement must have cost someone a small fortune. A little thread of hope wiggled its way into her mind, but she squelched it. *No way am I letting myself get swept away with crazy romantic ideas.* They must have been sent by a business she had done a story on. Not the typical thank you for a reporter, but still the only feasible option. *Just a coincidence.* She got swag from companies all the time.

"Where do you want me to put it?" the girl panted.

"Right here is fine." Shelby gestured toward her desk, avoiding Xan's gaze.

"I've delivered a lot of flowers, but I've never seen anything this nice. Someone must really like you," the red parka girl said over her shoulder. She pushed open the door and left.

Shelby gasped as she stared at the spectacular arrangement. It reminded her of something from the lobby of a fancy hotel. The cut crystal vase burst with roses, lilies, and other exotic flowers she couldn't name. She lifted the envelope inscribed with her name from the plastic card holder. *Shelby Jo Walker.* Her hands sweated, and she felt disgusted with herself. She wasn't the kind of girl to swoon over flowers. *Time to get a grip.* A small part of her wished for a little privacy, but her practical side knew she had nothing to hide from Xan.

He peered over her shoulder as she opened the card in a manner that she hoped seemed casual. The letter was written in loopy handwriting, which she assumed belonged to a woman at the flower shop.

Thank you for a delightful day of skiing. I am looking forward to another enjoyable outing tomorrow.

Your friend,
Hakim

Heat rushed to her face, and her heart pounded.

"I'll pick you up tomorrow morning—what time?" Xan's voice jolted her back into reality, and she noticed he'd started back toward his office. "Um, I'm leaving at eight."

"Eight, then." He closed the door behind him with a hard snap, the sound echoing through the quiet office.

Chapter Three

Shelby gazed out the window of Xan's SUV. Thursday morning had dawned crisp and bright, and the sun glistened on the snow. The hour-long drive up the canyon was quiet. She and Xan wore their usual winter work clothes—snow pants and boots. Their parkas were thrown across the back seat. They lapsed into a comfortable routine typical of two people who spent a lot of time together. In the center console, their drinks sat in the usual cup holders, and they'd shared a breakfast of champions—gas station donuts and cinnamon bears.

The tension between them had lifted, although she was still irritated at the way he treated her like a child at lunch the day before. Their conversation remained on neutral subjects like work, songs on the radio, and the weather. This morning, Shelby had taken more time than usual getting ready and had ignored the way Xan raised his eyebrows when he saw the shine of her lip gloss.

Xan slowed his SUV, searching for the turnoff to the Canyon Rim lodge. The sign on the small road was hidden behind a snow-saturated branch.

Thanks to Shelby's sharp eyes that they found it at all.

He stopped, flipping on his four-wheel drive before turning up the unplowed road. The only indication they were going the right way were the tire tracks packing down the snow into a slick, rutted trail.

Shelby was glad Xan was driving. Her car would never have made it in these conditions without getting stuck.

They bounced and slid along the road until they came to a rise, where the resort and parking lot came into view. The lodge was a large log cabin with a huge wrap-around porch. The cabin nestled on a gentle foothill of the mountain range, which rose behind and encircled the little valley to provide the isolated feeling people sought in the great outdoors. Snowmobile, snowshoe, and cross-country ski tracks wove across the snow behind the building in haphazard patterns, some disappearing off into the trees.

A sloping green roof hung over the balcony. Guests occupied the tables and chairs on the porch, sipping hot chocolate and coffee and taking advantage of the majestic view of the hills bathed in sunshine. The lodge had yet to emerge from the mountain's morning shadow.

Shelby saw a full-size, black SUV with the Bear Creek Hotel insignia parked near the front entrance. Her grin earned her a sharp look from Xan.

He pulled his car into a parking space, half cleared of snow, stopping on a crazy angle with one side of the vehicle a foot higher than the other. They were forced to reach across the seat to grab their coats and then struggle to climb out of the vehicle.

Shelby usually laughed at the games he played with his SUV, but this time, his fooling around just annoyed her. With careful steps, she started across the lot toward the lodge.

The driver of the black SUV stepped out and opened the back door of the vehicle.

Nasir unfolded his enormous bulk from the back seat and then stepped aside, allowing Hakim to climb out.

Now that Hakim wasn't wearing a hat, Shelby saw his hair was thick, dark, and short, combed forward in a Caesar-style. He wore the black designer ski coat, ski pants, and thick winter boots. Again, the image of him as a ski catalog model entered her mind.

Shelby felt her heartbeat quicken when she saw his white smile. As she approached, she returned his wave. "I'd like you to meet my boss, Xander Donovan. Xan, these are my friends, Hakim and Nasir."

"I am very pleased to meet you, Mr. Donovan. Thank you for allowing us to join you, today." Hakim extended his hand.

"Sure, no problem." Xan responded in a gruff voice as he shook Hakim's hand.

"And of course, I am pleased to see you again, Shelby Jo Walker." Hakim took her hand in both of his.

Xan pulled back and grimaced when Nasir offered his hand.

"Thank you so much for the flowers. They're beautiful." Shelby ignored Xan's discomfort and focused on Hakim.

"You are very welcome." Hakim continued to hold her hand in both of his.

She loved his elegant manners. She lifted her gaze to meet his dark eyes, and her stomach fluttered.

"You must be Shelby from *Wintersports*," a voice boomed from behind her.

Startled, Shelby whirled.

Jennifer Moore

A middle-aged man, wearing a dark blue parka with the Canyon Rim logo embroidered on his sleeve strode toward the group. Roy Barker looked almost exactly as she'd pictured him from his voice on the phone. He wore his hair in an army-style crew cut, and his nose and cheeks were a ruddy red from hours in the sun and cold.

"Hi, Roy. Nice to meet you in person." Shelby lifted her hand to indicate the other men. "These are my friends, Hakim and Nasir, and my boss, Xander Donovan." From Xan's stony expression, Shelby got the feeling he was annoyed she had referred to him again as her "boss" instead of her "friend."

"It's a real pleasure." Roy shook each of the men's hands. "I'm glad Shelby listened to my advice and brought along her friends. But enough of this chit-chat, I think you're all here to do some riding, right? So, come on inside, and let's getcha suited up!"

Shelby walked with the group up the stairs into the lodge, admiring the wide open space of the main room. A large stone fireplace with a pair of antique snowshoes hanging over the mantel dominated the main room. Comfortable couches and chairs were placed throughout. Huge picture windows took up the entire back wall, framing a view of the porch and the mountain beyond. A rustic wooden staircase led to the second story. Shelby assumed the doors upstairs belonged to the guest rooms.

Roy led them to a smaller meeting room. He indicated the upholstered chairs that faced a wooden table. On top of the table, he placed a duffle bag.

Shelby chose a seat next to Hakim.

Xan sat on the other side of her, draping his arm

across the back of her chair.

Ignoring him, Shelby scooted forward to the edge of her seat.

Nasir leaned back in his chair, causing it to creak beneath his weight.

Roy stood behind the table. "Company policy requires me to review safety procedures." He removed some equipment from the bag. "Okay, first off, we just need to go over your gear. Strapped on each vehicle is a pack identical to this. Inside's a shovel, a probe, a first aid kit, and water." As he spoke, he held up the items. "And each rider will need one of these." He counted out five long straps from a hook on the wall. A small, red box with a digital display hung from each strap. He passed them out, holding up the last one. "This is an avalanche transceiver. Any of you ever used a locator beacon?"

Seeing Shelby and Xan nod, Roy directed his explanation to Hakim and Nasir. "All right, when we set out, everybody sets their beacon to 'transmit.' If somebody were to get buried in the snow, the rest of us would flip our switches to 'receive' and we'd pick up the missing person's signal."

Hakim quietly translated for Nasir.

"Now, you fasten it around your waist and over one shoulder, like—" Roy snapped his head to the side. "Is something wrong?"

Nasir argued with Hakim. The larger man shook his head while Hakim reassured him, but Nasir was obviously upset by something.

"Is everything okay?" Shelby touched Hakim's shoulder.

"Yes, please excuse Nasir. He is only concerned

for my—I mean, *all* of our safety."

Roy held up a hand. "While avalanches are always a danger, we check out the trail every day and keep an eye on the snow pack. The area where we'll be riding has been cleared as safe. In my twenty-five years of leading snowmobile trips, I've never had to use any of the avalanche equipment. The worst things I've seen were a few broken bones or occasional dehydration."

Hakim spoke softly to Nasir.

Nasir eventually nodded, although his folded arms and frustrated expression told a different story.

Shelby leaned forward in her chair as she watched the interaction. Although she could not understand a word of what was being said, she saw them make some sort of a truce, though they didn't reach an understanding. She chewed on her lip, worried that either of her guests would feel uncomfortable.

Hakim did not look at Nasir. He stood, slipped his transceiver over his head, and put an arm through the strap, then reached behind his back, fumbling for the other end.

"You got it all twisted." Shelby took the buckle and reached her arms around his waist, straightening the belt to attach the two ends.

Hakim stood still. "Thank you."

She raised her gaze to respond, only then noticing how close they stood. When she saw his gaze locked onto hers, she sucked in a breath and her heart tripped. She realized she still held onto the belt around his waist and released it. "No problem." She quickly grabbed her own transceiver and fastened the strap.

When they were all suited up, the group followed Roy out of the meeting room, through the main area of the lodge, and out the door to the back porch.

Shelby walked down the stairs which were much shorter on the back side of the building to the group of snowmobiles Sunlight was spreading across the lodge and the meadow, causing the shadow of the mountain to shrink.

Hakim stepped outside and gazed at the stunning view.

Shelby watched, her throat growing tight as he scanned the splendor of nature. At the realization that he'd turned and she was now looking into his direct gaze, she jumped. Caught.

****

Hakim paid close attention to Roy's basic instructions: left hand brake, right hand gas.

"Before we head up the trail, we can practice out here in the field until you're comfortable with the vehicles." Roy pointed toward the line of machines parked in the shade of the lodge.

Hakim climbed onto a snowmobile and studied the machine, unsure of how to start it.

Shelby approached, smiling as she pointed to the key in the ignition. "Ready to try it out?"

Hakim thanked her. He turned the key, and the engine roared to life. It vibrated beneath him, and he experienced a moment of uncertainty, realizing he had no idea what to do.

Shelby climbed on behind him.

His heart leapt, and he tensed a bit. A woman had never touched him so casually before.

She leaned over his shoulder, pointing to the lever on the right handlebar. "There's the accelerator. Give it some gas."

Hakim squeezed the lever, and the machine shot forward.

Shelby wrapped her arms tightly around his waist.

They passed Nasir with Roy on the back of his machine, nearly standing in order to see over the larger man's shoulders.

Before long, Hakim grew comfortable driving the snowmobile. Figuring out every time he accelerated or turned sharply Shelby's arms tightened around his waist also didn't take him long. They had a jerky ride as he took advantage of this new-found fact. Hakim tried to concentrate on driving, instead of on the warmth of Shelby's body as she clung tight.

After twenty minutes of practice, Hakim followed Nasir and Roy to where Xan waited by the rest of the snowmobiles. Hakim was disappointed to feel the cool winter air on his back after Shelby dismounted. He missed her touch already. *Does Shelby feel the cold, too?*

Shelby and Roy climbed onto their own machines.

Roy checked everyone's transceivers one more time, making sure they were all set to 'transmit.' He indicated for them to put on their helmets, and the group set off.

The beautiful scenery in the back-country mountains amazed Hakim. Once he left the meadow behind the lodge, he saw the pristine snow was only blemished by the pressed snowmobile trail and lines of various animal tracks crossing between the scattered trees. The sun glittered on the snow, and he was glad his goggles protected his eyes from the glare.

Xan led the way, followed by Shelby, Hakim, and Nasir. Roy brought up the rear. Xan showed obvious skill as an experienced snowmobiler. Any time the trail opened up, he gunned his engine and circled back around in the powder.

A tinge of jealousy roiled in Hakim's stomach. *Do Xan's skills impress Shelby?*

After observing Xan a few times, Shelby signaled for Hakim to follow her off the trail. She flew through the powder.

With a cautious move, he turned his vehicle to join her. Too late, Hakim realized snowmobiling in powder required constant speed to stay on top of the light snow. By the time he figured it out, his snowmobile had already begun to sink. He pushed on the accelerator, but snow covered the runners.

Nasir followed, and when he stopped, his snowmobile immediately sank in the snow behind Hakim's.

Shelby circled back to the trail and onto the packed snow.

Hakim drummed his fingers against his legs. The snow was too deep to do anything but wait as Shelby hiked toward them with Xan and Roy to help dig out the two vehicles. Hakim and Nasir both dismounted, sinking in three feet of powder. Since he had no idea how to dig out their machines, Hakim watched as Xan and Roy pointed the snowmobiles in the right direction.

Then Nasir helped lift the backs of the runners to knock snow off the track.

Once they had enough traction, they powered the machines back to the others.

Nasir walked with Roy and Xan to the trail.

Hakim and Shelby waded back slowly, pushing through powder that rose past their knees. He followed her lead and removed his helmet, enjoying the cold air on his face.

"Having fun?" Shelby brushed away wavy strands of hair that escaped her ponytail. Her cheeks were flushed.

"Yes. However, I may need more practice before venturing into the deep snow. I apologize for sinking the vehicle." Hakim was captivated by her bright eyes.

"It's definitely not the last time we'll be digging out a machine. It's all part of the experience," Shelby said with a playful laugh. "That's why snowmobilers are so tired by the end of the day. It's a lot of work. You'll probably sleep like a baby all the way to Kentucky tomorrow."

At the reminder, Hakim's spirits fell. "I will be sorry to leave. This vacation has been quite an adventure. And I will especially be sorry to say goodbye to you, Shelby Jo Walker."

Shelby looked away.

He thought he could see the color on her face deepen as she chewed her bottom lip.

The two of them hiked through the thick powder, each lost in their own thoughts. A white rabbit scampered across the snow in front of them.

"Do you have rabbits in Khali-dar?" Shelby asked.

"Yes. Hares. Not small like this. My father and I see them often when we hunt."

"You sound like my brother, Chet. He sees any sort of wildlife and immediately thinks about hunting it down and slaughtering it." Shelby shook her head and smiled.

He studied her expression. Her face had softened as she spoke about her family. "And you are not a hunter?"

"I guess—I've gone out on the deer hunt with my dad and Chet, but I'm not much of a cold-blooded killer." Shelby paused. "Unless it comes to snowball fights."

An explosion of white powder hit his chest, causing Hakim to startle. He froze. *How dare she strike a prince!* He heard Shelby giggle and scurry away through the deep snow. His incensed attitude dissipated as a smile grew on his face.

Nasir immediately started toward him.

Hakim held up a hand to stop him, then picked up a small handful of snow and lobbed it in Shelby's direction. The ball missed. *Pathetic.* He grimaced.

"Is that all you've got?" she teased, her voice muffled by the tree she hid behind. She hit him with another shot.

Hakim crept to the other side of the tree and tugged on a heavily-laden branch, releasing its load of snow.

Powder showered down on her, and Shelby squealed. She pulled her ponytail from her hood and shook the snow out of her hair. "You're in serious trouble now, Mister."

Fighting to hold in his laughter, Hakim raised his eyebrows. "Oh yes? I think I have held my own quite admirably in my first snowball fight."

"I don't know if you've noticed or not, but I'm pretty competitive." She wagged her finger in his direction. "And now I've got revenge on my mind."

"Hel-lo? Are we riding today or playing in the snow?"

They looked toward the group waiting by the snowmobiles.

"I'd almost forgotten about those guys." Shelby rolled her eyes at Xan's exasperated tone and winked.

"I wish I could spend more time alone with you, Shelby Jo," Hakim replied in a low voice.

Shelby met his gaze and opened and closed her mouth. Then, she bit her lip again and walked back to the trail.

He followed, irritated with himself for making such a bold statement. He had only a few hours left with Shelby as "Regular-guy-Hakim" and he mustn't make their time together strained, or allow his inner struggles to cause either of them discomfort. Soon enough, he'd resume his responsibilities as Prince of Kahli-dar. If only the time would not end so soon.

****

Xan held up his fist as a signal to stop, pointing up the mountain to a group of pine trees.

Looking closer, Shelby saw a large bull-moose camouflaged in the shade. His early-spring antlers were only about half the size of what they'd be in a few months, but they were still impressive. She twisted in her seat to check if Hakim had spotted it and was rewarded with a "thumbs-up" and a heart-melting smile.

Shelby turned back and tried to concentrate on the trail. Did Hakim really mean what he said about wanting to spend more time with her? Why was she letting her feelings for him deepen when she knew he would be leaving tomorrow? *Come on, I need to just enjoy myself and stop with the day-dreaming already.* But no matter how she tried, she couldn't get the image of those dark eyes out of her head.

After a few more miles, Roy pulled ahead and

signaled for a stop. He switched off his engine and motioned for the others to do the same. They were on the edge of a huge bowl carved out of the mountainside. The rounded depression appeared as if it had been scooped out with a giant melon-baller. The far rim cast a shadow that bent with the curve of the mountain, splitting it vertically.

"Here's a good place to take a break and make sure you get some fluids," Roy instructed. "What do you all think so far?"

"You've got great equipment." Xan smacked his hand on one of the snowmobiles. "I'm loving these Arctic Tigers. You got 800 C.C.'s under the hood?"

"You better believe it. Just wait until we crest that hill. There's a huge meadow on the other side. Then you can really open these cats up and see what they're made of." Roy pushed his hand forward with his palm down to illustrate his point. "Cruising across all that open powder on one of these babies makes you feel like you're floating on air."

Shelby left Xan and Roy to their snowmobile talk. She removed her helmet and walked back to where Hakim and Nasir leaned against their machines, drinking from their water bottles. Stretching her legs and getting sensation back into her rear end felt good.

Hakim looked up and smiled. He joined her, and they strolled a little closer to the edge, admiring the spectacular scenery.

Nasir remained near the snowmobiles.

Shelby looked across the bowl. "It's an amazing view, isn't it?"

"Yes, it is," Hakim said, his gaze never leaving her face.

Shelby's breath caught, and her heartbeat sped. But any response she might have made was interrupted by Roy calling them all over.

"I need to give a little instruction." He held his helmet under his arm and used both hands as he talked. "Going across this bowl is the most dangerous part of our route. Fresh snow on top of packed snow is never great. Also, the shape of the mountain and the direction it faces causes the snow to melt and re-freeze more often, making it less stable than other places. To minimize the weight on the snow, our safest course is to cross one at a time." Roy turned toward Nasir while he spoke. "I'll tell you right now I've crossed this bowl hundreds of times with no incidents. But our policy is to be as safe as possible in the back country."

Again, Hakim translated for Nasir.

The big man looked as if he might argue but pursed his lips, resigned to the fact that the decision had been made. Shelby wondered if under his bulky, tough exterior, Nasir was a little bit of a scaredy-cat.

"I'll go first," Roy continued, "And then you guys follow one at a time. When I get to the other side, I'll wave to let you know it's your turn. No yelling across the bowl."He pulled on his helmet and rode along the track around the inside of the bowl.

Xan strode over and stood between Hakim and Shelby. "Nervous?" he teased her, turning his back to Hakim.

"Nope." Shelby walked to her snowmobile.

Roy broke out of the mountain's shade into the bright sun on the other side and signaled.

"Looks like I'm up." Xan jumped on his machine, revved the engine, and flew off in a spray of powder.

The three of them watched silently as he crossed.

Roy waved his arm over his head to indicate it was Shelby's turn.

She crammed her helmet on her head, twisted so she could flash a smile at Hakim, and then she started across. The path was about halfway up the mountain. It followed the most level part of the slope, but was by no means flat. Shelby loved flying across the snow with an endless expanse of white around her.

Just as she neared the line of shadow, she heard a loud *CRACK* resound across the small valley, followed by a deafening roar. In an instant, a wall of snow hurled down the mountain toward her. She had no time to brace herself or even to scream before the tidal wave slammed into her.

Instinctively, she pushed away from her snowmobile, praying it wouldn't crush her. Shelby's heart pounded, and she thrashed her arms and legs, fighting against the force of the snow as the force tossed her like a ragdoll. The violent impact ripped off her helmet and propelled her end over end. Black. White. Black. White. The avalanche tossed her in every direction at once, and her body writhed as she strained to regain control of her movements.

Shelby was completely disoriented, but after only a few seconds, her panic eased, and she remembered her emergency training. She tried to "swim" on top of the churning snow by going with the flow, instead of fighting against it. Wave after wave pounded her body from every direction. Snow packed into her ears, her nose and mouth, and even under her eyelids. When she opened her mouth to breathe, she choked, spitting out a cold snow plug. The stampede of the mountain pummeling over her was deafening as she was buffeted to and fro and her limbs yanked in all directions.

Something smashed into her head, causing sudden sharp pain to jolt through her. More pain exploded in her ankle. Exhaustion replaced adrenaline. Unable to fight the sheer force of the snow as it dragged her downward, Shelby put her hands over her face for protection and allowed herself to be swept in the current.

As suddenly as it began, the momentum plunging her down the hill stopped. More terrifying than the thundering roar was the abrupt silence that followed. In the darkness, the weight of the snow was crushing. It packed around her, freezing her body into an uncomfortable position. Shelby squirmed, trying to move in the small space. She fought against her fear to keep herself from falling to pieces. Luckily, her right arm was near her face. Pushing back the panic and ignoring the pain in her head, she used the last of her strength to punch the snow away from her mouth and nose, forming an air pocket before the snow hardened into concrete.

Shelby knew her air supply wouldn't last long, so she tried to breathe evenly, taking shallow breaths. Dark fear, unlike anything she had ever experienced gripped her heart. She knew moving was useless, but the terror thrusting through her veins screamed to do just that.

Her heart beat with such force against her ribs that it hurt. The pain in her head and ankle became more intense—throbbing fire that she could not ease by shifting her position. *Am I bleeding...?* Were her friends safe? Was Hakim? If only...Would he have…But her thoughts became muddled, and she gave in to the welcome relief of sleep.

Chapter Four

Hakim watched Shelby ride across the bowl. A warm bubble grew in his chest when he thought of their snowball fight and her playful smile when she'd teased him. She hadn't responded when he told her he wished they could spend more time together. *Does she feel the same?* Right now, he would do nearly anything to postpone his trip to Kentucky. However, he had promised his father. With the problems in his kingdom, Hakim wasn't sure how long he could stay away.

A thunderous crack shattered the silence, jolting him from his thoughts. His first impulse was to duck and protect his ears. The snow in the bowl split apart, breaking into chunks like jagged bits of pottery, then slid in a jumble down the mountain. The ground shook as giant clouds of snow billowed toward him.

Nasir immediately yanked Hakim off of his machine and shielded him behind a tree. The force of the avalanche pushed at their bodies, but Nasir anchored them both in place. The mountain shook and roared.

Hakim clung to the tree as the cold bursts of snow surged over them in a blinding cloud. The rumbling subsided with a quiet that left a ringing in his ears. A moment later, he could see again as the mountain resettled. He tried to discern how much snow had covered them. Their position on the rim had protected them from the majority of the danger. After a moment, they burrowed out from the thick snow drifts.

Hakim and Nasir brushed off the snow and waved across the bowl to Roy and Xan, assuring the other men of their safety. Through the years, he had visited and skied mountains on nearly every continent, but this was the first avalanche he'd experienced. He processed the situation in a daze, before a terrifying realization seized him. Shelby! Would they find her? Was she alive? Sickening panic welled up, churning his stomach as he scanned the altered terrain for any sign of Shelby or her snowmobile. Yelling her name, Hakim charged toward the bowl.

Nasir laid a strong hand on his arm, and held tight. "It will not help Miss Walker if we do not follow procedure," he said in his calm voice. He carried the emergency kit from the snowmobile. Piece by piece, he unpacked the bag and handed Hakim a shovel and a folded aluminum probe.

Hakim knew the ability to remain composed in an emergency was what made Nasir such a valuable soldier. As he observed Nasir's efficient movements, Hakim's panic decreased until he cleared his mind and focused on the job of finding Shelby.

Both men checked their transceivers, setting them to Receive, and pushed through the snow toward Roy and Xan.

Roy called for help on his satellite phone.

Pale faced, Xan pointed with a shaky hand toward the last place he had seen Shelby.

"That's where we'll start," Roy said. "She should hopefully be straight down from here."

The four men spread out, rushing down the

mountain to where the snowpack was thicker.

As the seconds slipped away, desperation surfaced. Hakim stared at the digital display on his receiver as he traveled down the hill. Could the snow have carried her this far? How long did they have? What would they do if they couldn't find her? Or if they found her, but discovered her too late? He shook his head to purge the negative thoughts.

After what seemed like an eternity, Roy yelled that he had a signal. The men ran to the area, unfolded their aluminum probes and jabbed them into the hillside.

"Here!" Xan unfolded his shovel and attacked the snow.

They joined him, and soon flying clumps of white surrounded the group. Before long, the snow began turning pink and then red as the hole got deeper and they got closer to Shelby.

The sick feeling of panic returned as Hakim tried to estimate the amount of blood she had lost.

Roy shook his satellite phone. "Reception's not great down here. I'll head up farther and update search and rescue."

Xan wrenched one of Shelby's frozen gloves out of the rock-hard snow. Almost a foot deeper, he unearthed her left hand.

Hakim's relief mixed with stomach-twisting dread at what condition they would find Shelby in. He wondered how long she had been buried. It had felt like hours. *Can anyone survive under the snow for so long?*

Shelby's hand was dark red—nearly purple. Snow packed into the sleeve of her parka.

Hakim pulled off his own gloves, the coldness of the snow shocked him and numbed the tips of his fingers as he worked to dig as much out of her sleeve as he could. He remembered hearing the danger of an avalanche was not only broken bones or suffocation, but even more, hypothermia.

Nasir and Xan continued to use their shovels—more gently, to pry up the hardened snow.

Finally, Nasir uncovered Shelby's face, revealing a deep gash in her forehead.

Hakim winced.

Shelby lay on her side, trapped by the snow in an awkward position.

"Dig," Nasir instructed the other men.

Xan moved toward Shelby's head.

Hakim grabbed the sleeve of his parka, stopping him. "Nasir is trained." He lifted his chin toward his bodyguard. "He will know how to help her."

Xan conceded with a shake of his head and continued lifting the chunks of snow off Shelby's body.

Nasir pressed his fingers against a pulse point in Shelby's neck. Bending close to her face, he listened for her breathing. Worry clouded his face and replaced Nasir's typical calm expression. He tipped her head back and breathed into her mouth. Periodically, he stopped and inclined his head to check for a response.

As he watched, Hakim felt his throat tighten and his breathing speed up. He was helpless to do anything.

Shelby coughed.

The tension around Nasir's eyes relaxed. He reached for the first aid kit, and then examined the wound on her head.

With slow blinks, Shelby opened her eyes and looked around. The men had moved as much snow as they could in order to lay her flat on her back.

"Nasir," she whispered through chattering teeth, "I'm so cold."

Using a hand under her neck, Nasir elevated her head and, with gauze, applied pressure to the wound on her forehead. In their shared language, he spoke to Hakim.

"Nasir said it is good for you to feel cold," Hakim translated Nasir's words in a low voice. "If you stop shivering, your body has dropped into severe hypothermia." He scooped more snow out of her hood and from under her chin, observing her reactions with tensed muscles.

Hakim and Nasir both took off their parkas, wrapping them around Shelby's upper body. Needing to touch her, Hakim kneaded her hands and rubbed her arms.

Xan continued to lift the hardened snow off of Shelby's still-buried legs. He reached under her right leg, and started to lift it.

Shelby gasped, and what little color she had drained from her pale face, turning her a startling ghostly white. "My foot hurts," she whimpered.

As he removed his hand, Xan frowned, creasing his forehead.

Following Nasir's instructions, Hakim moved to kneel behind Shelby and held the gauze on her injured forehead. He spoke words he hoped sounded comforting, trying to distract her from the cold and pain. "Do not be afraid. Everything will be all right."

Xan and Nasir carefully raised her leg, slipping off her boot.

Nasir peeled away her dark red sock, revealing her misshapen and swollen ankle. A jagged bone poked through a tear in her skin.

Xan gasped.

At the sight, Hakim's stomach rolled over. He turned away, taking deep breaths to keep from becoming ill.

"Search and Rescue's on the way. There's nowhere to land a helicopter here in the bowl, so they'll be another twenty minutes or so." Roy panted as he returned.

Nasir and Xan set Shelby's leg back into the snow. Nasir packed snow around her ankle to stabilize it and ease the swelling. He checked Shelby's pulse and breathing again, murmuring to Hakim.

"Nasir says Shelby is going into shock," Hakim translated for the other men. "Her pulse is weak, and she has lost much blood. We must keep her head elevated, her leg still, and maintain her body temperature until help arrives."

What was in reality twenty minutes seemed to Hakim like hours.

Xan's frustration at Nasir taking over Shelby's care was nearly tangible. He glared back and forth between Nasir and Hakim as he held Shelby's hand.

Roy stood a bit away from the group as he continued to give instructions into the phone.

Hakim watched, unable to help as Shelby's skin paled further, and she became disoriented and less responsive.

She repeated her requests for water, but Nasir insisted it would cause her to vomit. The most important thing was to keep her warm and control the bleeding.

The adrenaline that had fueled Hakim's rush to

save Shelby ebbed and exhaustion took its place. The silence between the men grew, and he supposed the others must feel the hopelessness of their despairing thoughts as heavily as he did.

The purr of snowmobiles sounded, and soon after, the Search and Rescue team came through the trees.

Two EMTs parked and hopped off their machines.

A technician knelt in the snow and inspected Shelby's injuries. He held her hand and leaned close to look at her eyes. "What's your name?" he asked. "Can you tell me your name?"

Shelby was unresponsive.

The technician looked at Hakim who still pressed the gauze to her forehead. "How long has she been like this?"

"Perhaps twenty minutes. She was speaking when we uncovered her, but has become increasingly confused and exhausted. Her name is Shelby." Hakim heard the despair in his own voice.

"Shelby, can you hear me?" The technician patted her cheek. "How long was she buried?"

"Around twenty to twenty-five minutes," Xan answered.

"The survival rate decreases significantly the longer a person is buried," the EMT told them, checking Shelby's eyes and pulse. "Someone uncovered within fifteen minutes has a ninety-two percent survival rate, but after thirty-five minutes, that rate drops to thirty percent."

Anguish twisted in Hakim's chest like a snake. It devastated him to see someone so full of life a half hour ago lying limp and pale in the snow. Especially when that someone was Shelby.

"She's in shock," the EMT told his partner, who unloaded their equipment. "We need to get her off the mountain, now."

The technicians used an inflatable splint to stabilize Shelby's leg, as they lifted her onto a toboggan attached behind one of the vehicles. They wrapped her in blankets, stretching straps across her body to hold her onto the sled.

"She's real lucky." The technician threaded an IV into her arm. "Most of the avalanche rescues I've been on have turned into recoveries."

"Are you giving her something for pain?" Hakim asked.

"Not with her head injury. We'll leave that up to the doctor. Just fluids for now. She's pretty dehydrated from loss of blood. You did the right thing by not giving her anything to drink. The digestive system is one of the first things to shut down as the body goes into shock. She would have been sick."

"Where are you guys taking her?" Xan asked.

"We're meeting the ambulance on the canyon road about two miles west. Follow us, and we'll find out what hospital they're going to."

With little effort, Xan and Roy plodded across the transformed bowl, retrieved their machines, and met Hakim and Nasir on the trail.

The trip out to the road was somber.

The rescue team rode through the trees, taking the smoothest route, followed by the four men. When they reached the ambulance, the technicians loaded Shelby inside and packed hot water bottles around her body.

Xan spoke to the driver and returned to tell the others they were taking her to Wilcox General.

Hakim rubbed his hand across the back of his neck. His chest was heavy as he watched the doors close, and the ambulance pull away.

****

Pushing through a fog of confusion, Shelby struggled to open her eyes. Where was she? What was that beeping sound?

"Shel, hey."

Xan's face came into focus. Suddenly, everything came rushing back—the darkness, the roaring of the mountain, the horror of being trapped under the snow. She tried to sit up, but the pain in her head made her stomach roll over.

"It's okay, Shel. Just relax."

She was grateful Xan kept his voice low, because her head felt like it would burst. "Xan," she managed to whisper. "The room is spinning."

"Close your eyes. I'm right here." He lifted her hand.

She squeezed his fingers gratefully and started to slip back into the fog until Xan spoke again.

"Just worried sick about you." He kept his voice low. "You've been in surgery for a while. I called your dad. He'll be here in a few hours."

Knowing her dad was coming eased some of her anxiety. "Thanks, Xan," she whispered as she drifted back to sleep.

****

"It's all right, I'm just checking your vitals," a stranger's voice said as Shelby opened her eyes.

A large African-American woman stood over her, viewing the dial of the blood pressure cuff around Shelby's arm. "Still pretty low, hon." She pulled out the

58

ear buds and wrapped her stethoscope around her neck, then noted something on a chart. "My name's Linda. You're in post-op recovery. Can I get you anything? Water?"

Shelby smiled at Linda's rubber ducky-decorated scrubs. "No, thanks. I'm okay." She looked around, but the effort caused the room to spin again. Instead, she focused on the ceiling tiles.

"How's your pain level?"

"Not too bad," Shelby lied. She did not want any more medicine muddling her thoughts until she knew what was happening.

"You've got a morphine drip here. Anytime your pain gets too strong, just push on this button for another dose. The beep means it's working." Linda bustled around the room as she talked. "You can't do it more than once every six minutes, but it will help. I'll wrap the button around the arm rail so you can find it. Anything else I can do?"

"Could you turn off the lights?"

"You got it, hon." Linda switched off the fluorescent lights.

The relief on Shelby's eyes was instantaneous. A soft nightlight glowed on the wall behind the bed, preventing the room from becoming completely dark. "Thanks, Linda." Shelby spoke slowly in order not to slur her words.

"Here's the call button if you need me." Linda draped the cord over the other arm rail. "Dr. Gardner should be checking on you in the next half hour or so. And your collection of handsome young gentlemen is waiting out in the hall. I've had to kick at least one of them out of here every hour in order to do my rounds.

You must be quite the heart-breaker." Linda's voice carried a note of laughter. "All right, then. I'll open the door and let the hottie-parade begin."

Shelby heard Linda speaking to someone in the hall, and a figure walked through the open door. In the dim light, Shelby couldn't make out his face. She rubbed her eyes to get rid of the dazed feeling in her head. Her skull felt like cotton was stuffed inside.

"Hey, Shel."

"Xan." Shelby hoped he couldn't hear the disappointment in her voice. She'd thought for a moment...

"How's the ankle?" Xan grasped her hand.

"Aches, but my head is killing."

"Yeah, you got a concussion. Your forehead is pretty bruised, and you've got some stitches. But it's your ankle they operated on."

Shelby had a vague memory of the ER. She remembered being wrapped in an air blanket that surrounded her with heat. X-rays, doctors, hot water bottles. The mention of surgery helped dispel any lingering mugginess, and she forced her mind to concentrate. "How bad is it?" Her heart sank. An injury would kill her entire ski season.

"Pretty bad, from how the break looked up on the mountain. The doctor didn't tell us much, since we're not family. You know, HIPAA or whatever."

She shifted and sucked in a breath through her teeth as pain shot through her head. "I can't remember very much. Must be the drugs."

Xan rubbed his thumb over the back of her hand. "You're lucky to be alive. We were freaked out for a while there."

"Thanks, Xan. Thanks for rescuing me."

"I helped, but really, the huge Arab was the one who saved you."

"Nasir?" Shelby asked.

"I guess he has some kind of commando training. He knew what to do to stop your bleeding and even did mouth-to-mouth. Who knew such a giant guy could be so gentle?"

Shocked, Shelby didn't know what to say. The thought of Nasir doing mouth-to-mouth made her stomach clench in embarrassment. "Is Nasir here?"

"Yeah, he and Hakim have been in the waiting room all day."

Her heart leapt. "Could you get them? I want to thank them."

"Uh…Yeah, sure," Xan said. "I'll see if I can find 'em."

She thought his voice sounded a little reluctant and squeezed his fingers to show her gratitude. "Thanks, Xan."

"I'll be back to check on you, okay?" He laid her hand down on the bed.

While Shelby waited, the hammering in her head grew worse. The pain in her ankle rose to a throbbing ache. She still hadn't seen a mirror and had no idea what her head injury looked like, and she couldn't lift her head to see her ankle. She needed to push the morphine button but wanted to act coherently when she saw Hakim again. *He is here!* Did this mean he wasn't going to Kentucky? Would he keep in touch? Maybe see her again?

A soft knock drew her gaze to the doorway. Although the room was semi-dark, she recognized

Hakim's silhouette as he came to stand next to the bed.

"Shelby Jo," he said in a quiet voice.

Her heart rate sped up and the monitor beeps followed suit. "You're still here. I thought you'd be in Kentucky by now."

"I could not leave until I was certain that you were all right."

"Where's Nasir? Xan told me what he did. I want to thank him."

"I will give your message to Nasir." Hakim gave a short nod. "His ways are very traditional. He would not wish to offend you, but he would feel uncomfortable coming into your room to speak with you."

Shelby realized what she had interpreted as rudeness—his unwillingness to make eye contact or to shake her hand—had really been a form of respect. She grimaced, feeling ashamed for judging him so harshly. "Oh, I understand. Please tell him how grateful I am."

"I will. I also owe Nasir a debt of gratitude for what he did. If not for his training…"

In the darkness, she felt his fingers brush her hair off her forehead, avoiding the wrappings over her stitches. She reached up and grasped his hand. Even though almost every part of her body pulsed with pain, what she felt from Hakim's touch caused her skin to tingle.

"Hakim…" Shelby said after a moment. "This is goodbye, isn't it?"

"Yes," he said. "Shelby Jo…"

"You have to go, I know." Tears pricked at the back of her eyes. She had only known this guy for a few days. *Why am I crying? It has to be the medication.*

"I have enjoyed the time we spent together, Shelby

Jo Walker." He paused. "There have been very few opportunities for me to make new acquaintances. Your friendship has been very special."

"Yeah, bruised, bloody, and doped-up on painkillers is how you'll remember me." Shelby wrinkled her nose and grimaced.

"I am confident there are enough pleasant memories of our time together to overshadow the sad ones. My first snowball fight, for example."

"That reminds me, I owe you some major payback for that little snow shower you gave me." She let go of his hand and tapped her fingertips together like an evil genius.

He laughed quietly and then took her hand again. "I wish I did not have to leave you like this. Your recovery will be a difficult one, and—"

"My dad will be here soon to take me home to Culver Springs." Shelby's words rushed out. "I'll manage."

"Goodbye, Shelby Jo Walker." He set down her hand and turned to go.

"Goodbye, Hakim." She barely managed to whisper the words before pushing the morphine drip button, hoping the drug could dull the ache in her heart.

Chapter Five

Shelby stretched across the back seat of her parents' full-size pickup. Her mom had covered her with blankets and propped her up with pillows, but Shelby still felt every bump and curve in the road on their five-hour drive.

The conversation with the surgeon had left her discouraged. He'd explained she had a trimalleolar fracture, which meant all three bones in her ankle were broken and held together with plates and screws. She couldn't put any weight on her foot for six weeks. Her dad pushed her to the car in a wheelchair and loaded her new crutches in the back of the pick-up with her luggage.

Shelby's parents, Burke and Debbie, stayed with her in the hospital overnight, although she asked them to at least sleep in the soft bed at her apartment. She hadn't been surprised when they insisted the chairs in her hospital room were just as comfortable.

They always meant well. They loved her and wanted to take care of her, but she knew the next few weeks would be hard. Her parents weren't the best at giving her the space she needed.

She sat up and rested her cheek against the cold window. Shelby always enjoyed the familiar drive to Culver Springs. Even in the dead of winter, she saw a beauty in the desert country that most people overlooked. The car twisted through another canyon, and she gazed across the barren terrain. A few straggly bushes and trees stood stoically, breaking up the harsh landscape. Here and there, fences marked cattle country. Most ranchers built their enclosures using odd-shaped, crooked branches strung together with barbed wire. Shelby thought this type of fence complemented the desert terrain better than the artificial-looking manufactured railings used by wealthy ranchers.

Frozen snow drifted in ribbons across the road, blown by the almost-constant wind. Cracks formed by water zig-zagged here and there in the hard, flat ground, invisible until a person practically fell into one. Some of the deeper cracks ran for miles, forcing animals and humans alike to find alternative routes around them. The land was unpredictable and exciting, and in winter, the weather was severe.

Shelby let out a frustrated sigh. After trying so hard to be independent, here she was, totally reliant on her parents. Not doing things for herself piqued her frustration, and she dreaded the "talk" her parents would have about where her life was going. She knew they would bring up her accident as another reason for her to move back home and settle down.

As the vehicle left the highway and drove into town, Shelby felt memories leap from every direction. Unlike most towns its size, Culver Springs had resisted modern super-stores. Instead, the majority of business took place in small, family-owned shops. The two-block expanse of Main Street functioned as the commercial hub for the town and surrounding ranches. Main Street ended at the high school, where the entire community turned out on Friday nights to support the football team, The Culver Crusaders. The oldest houses stood in the center of town, with newer constructions growing on the edges.

Her dad drove straight down Main and turned west on Center. They still had another ten miles to go, and Shelby braced herself for the bumpy ride as Center became a dirt road. As the pick-up bumped over the road, the sun went down. Burke turned onto the gravel drive and the truck's headlights illuminated the ranch house where Shelby had grown up.

The Walkers lived in a white, two-story Victorian with pointed gables and a wrap-around porch. During the day, a large oak tree shaded the porch. A wreath of painted wooden snowflakes hung on the front door. Shelby let out a slow breath. The familiar sight of her childhood home thickened her throat. Even though six years had passed since she'd moved to Denver, every time she visited, the happy memories of this place soothed her. She closed her eyes and allowed herself to enjoy feeling warm and comforted before the inevitable smothering by her mother began.

Burke parked the pick-up and carried Shelby across the porch and straight upstairs to her room.

Her mom rushed ahead to pull down the sheets while her dad settled Shelby on the bed and then left to check the animals.

Debbie tucked blankets around Shelby. "Do you need anything, dear?"

"No. Thanks, Mom. I'm fine."

"Honey, you are far from fine." Her mom fussed over the pillows.

Aside from a few streaks of gray, Debbie Walker's hair was the same strawberry-blonde as Shelby's, but her style was a bob, instead of long like her daughter's. They had the same bright blue eyes, but Shelby's infectious smile came from her dad. "I'm running downstairs and get a little broth and crackers. I'll put your cellphone on the night stand. Call me if you need anything."

Shelby sighed. Her mother was a natural care-giver. She always managed to find someone to nurture, ever since Shelby could remember. Debbie cooked dinner for new mothers and delivered fresh homemade bread to anybody who was sick. She volunteered at the hospital and served on the library board. Burke often said that half of Culver Springs depended on Debbie.

This had frequently been a source of contention between Shelby and her mom. Debbie wanted to take care of Shelby, almost to the point of running her life. Shelby had struggled to be independent. Maybe that was why she had been such a rebellious kid, always getting into mischief, just as a way of showing she was going to making her own choices.

****

Shelby woke to the familiar sights and smells of her childhood bedroom. The sun shone through the sheer lace curtains Debbie made when Shelby was a little girl. With slow moves, she sat upright. Her room had remained untouched while she was gone. Stuffed animals sat on a shelf above her bed. Posters of country western singers and high school dance pictures covered the walls. The dream catcher Lacey's mom made to keep away Shelby's nightmares still hung from the headboard. She fingered the faded flower bedspread she'd slept under since she was twelve and wrinkled her nose. *The décor could use a little updating.* Especially when she saw her old boyfriend, Jake, grinning from so many different photographs. She wanted to wipe that cocky smirk right off his face. Why had she thought that guy with his blond hair flopping into his eyes was so handsome?

"You awake, honey?" Debbie entered, bringing soft-boiled eggs with butter—her classic cure for all ailments. "There's someone here to see you."

"Hey, Shels!" Shelby's younger brother, Chet, bounded into the room. "Dude, can you believe you were totally in an avalanche? I mean, what the...? My own sister: Back Country Disaster Survivor. You know, you could get a reality show." He plopped down on the bed.

"Chet! Shelby is in no condition to be bounced around!"

"You think sitting on the bed bounces her more than an *avalanche*?" Chet turned toward his sister, tipping his head and widening his eyes.

Shelby recognized his look as a you-know-how-mom-is expression

He moved to her desk, lowering his lanky frame into the chair. He grinned, and dimples appeared in his round cheeks. "So, tell me all the deets, sis. What was it like?"

In spite of the bouncing and the jolts of pain in her leg and head, Shelby grinned. Chet's enthusiasm was contagious. "I'll tell you about it another time, Chet." Her gaze slid sideways toward their mom then back to his. Understanding registered in his face. They both knew how sensitive Debbie was, and hearing how her daughter nearly died was something she wouldn't handle very well.

"No prob, Shels. Great to have you home. Hurry and get better so you can come open the chutes while I practice my roping. Rodeo season is just a few months away. Catch ya later." Chet hurdled out of the room, riding the same wave of energy he had arrived on.

"See ya," Shelby called after him.

Shelby hated to admit her mother's care was just what she needed to heal.

Debbie carefully removed the wrappings from her head and clipped the hair around Shelby's forehead to give her bangs.

The stitches were close enough to her hairline that the new style hid the wound. Shelby contemplated the new look in her bedroom mirror. *Not bad.*

In the reflection, Shelby saw Debbie studying her high school pictures. Her mother turned toward her with an innocent expression that Shelby knew all too well.

"You know, I ran into Jake's mom at the grocery store a few days ago. She told me he really misses you. Maybe now that you're back, you could give him a call. He'd probably love to come over to watch a movie or something." Her mother lifted a hand, palm up, and tipped her head to the side.

Shelby pursed her lips in frustration. "Mom, I've told you. I don't want to call Jake."

A week later, Shelby started to use her crutches to make her way downstairs in the mornings and sit on the couch for most of the day, watching TV or folding laundry. After two weeks cooped up inside the house, she thought she would go insane and decided she felt well enough for a walk. She seriously needed fresh air. With her mom's help, she bundled up against the early spring cold, grabbed her crutches, and started down the lane toward the barn.

"I didn't mean to be nosy, but your cellphone was down on the coffee table, and I answered it last night without thinking." Debbie matched her steps to Shelby's slow pace.

Shelby took a calming breath. *Here we go.* She kept her voice light to hide her irritation. "Oh? Who was it? Lace?" Shelby's best friend, Lacey, and her husband lived just south of town.

"No, it was your friend, Xander." Debbie focused on Shelby's face.

"Did he say what he needed?" Shelby was careful to keep her expression neutral. She knew her mom was digging.

"No. He was just checking on you. What a nice young man he is. Your father and I are so grateful he called us when you had your accident. I was surprised the two of you were together up at the resort. Does he usually go along on assignments?" She tipped her head and smiled, blinking.

"Mom, are you asking if Xan and I are in a relationship?"

"I don't mean to pry, honey, but he seems to care a lot about you." Debbie shrugged and continued to smile.

"I think you're right, Mom, but the problem is I don't feel the same. He's a super friend, but since you asked—in your crazy roundabout way—there is someone else. Actually, I guess there *was* someone else." Shelby turned her gaze to the gravel road in front of her.

Debbie inhaled a breath.

Shelby braced herself for the volley of questions she knew would follow.

"Who is he? Someone you met at work? What happened between the two of you?"

"Mom, I don't really want to talk about it." Shelby knew her evasive answer frustrated Debbie, but would her mother ever give her space?

Debbie smiled and brushed the hair off Shelby's shoulder. "If you change your mind, honey…"

"I know." Shelby balanced on one foot while she rubbed her sore palms, before swinging around her crutches and tottering toward the house.

****

Three days later, Shelby leaned back, exhausted. She had just spent the last hour unloading the whole story to Lacey while the two sat on Shelby's bed sipping sodas.

Lacey hung on every word. The only interruption came when she said that this story was too juicy to listen to without chocolate. Then she rummaged through her perpetually stocked purse, until she found a small package of chocolates and ripped them open on the bed between them. "Okay, I'm ready now."

That had been twenty minutes ago.

"Wow, Shel," Lacey gushed as she swung her straight, chestnut brown hair over her shoulder with the back of her hand.

Shelby recognized the familiar gesture from the all the years the girls were inseparable. They still kept in touch, but Shelby thought nothing compared to actually being with your best friend.

"It's like you're living in a movie or something," Lacey continued. "A tall dark stranger rides into town, sweeps you off your feet, saves your life, and then leaves as mysteriously as he came." She held the back of her hand against her forehead in a dramatic pose, pretending to swoon.

"Oh, brother." Shelby sighed, and they both giggled.

"And the flowers," Lacey said, between breaths. "Xan's face when he saw the flowers. Priceless."

Again, they erupted in laughter.

"What in the holy heck's going on in here?" Chet stormed through the door and grabbed the chair from Shelby's desk. Swinging it around, he straddled it, resting his arms on the back. "What did I miss?"

"Oh, just a little girl talk." Lacey winked.

Chet pointed his finger into his mouth, pretending to gag as he grabbed a handful of chocolates. "So, Lace." He popped a few into his mouth. "Is that husband of yours coming tomorrow?"

"Dan wouldn't miss it," she replied. "Next to the deer hunt, branding is his favorite time of year."

"Excellent." Chet grinned, showing his dimples. "Maybe he'll bring Jake. You know Shels will be there."

Shelby curled her lip. Jake was the last person she wanted to see.

"That's just what she needs." Lacey raised and lowered her brows. "Another handsome guy thrown into the mix." She started to giggle again.

Chet's forehead wrinkled.

Shelby's insides clenched at the thought of running into her old boyfriend, although she told herself that she didn't care. Jake was Dan's best friend, and he and Shelby had dated steadily during high school. When

Shelby chose to go away to college six years earlier, and then stayed in the big city to be a journalist, she'd learned Jake claimed to be just as surprised as everyone else in town. Lacey and Dan got married right after graduation, and Jake's and Shelby's parents had expected they would do the same.

Shelby considered his response further evidence Jake had no idea what her actual goals were. He'd expected her to fit into a mold and live her life like a typical small-town girl.

"You sure you're okay to go branding, Shel?" Lacey asked. Her brows wrinkled as she pointed toward Shelby's cast.

If everyone doesn't stop treating me like I'm made of glass, they'll make me scream. "Yeah, I'm feeling better. I've been resting up for two and a half weeks. I'll be fine."

"Dad is under strict orders to keep her from over-doing it." Chet hopped up and gave a mock salute as he left the room. His boots clomped down the hall.

Shelby was starting to feel tired but would never admit it. Not when the entire world seemed determined to baby her. *Overdoing it? Seriously, doesn't anyone understand I'm an adult?*

"I'd better get going. Dan will need some help getting the kids to sleep." Lacey swung her long legs off the bed and grabbed a few more chocolates. "Are we still on for tomorrow night? I've got a babysitter lined up."

"Yep." Shelby grinned. "I can't wait to see your new house."

"And I can't wait to actually go *out* to dinner."

"I know my mom is disappointed I'm not taking

Jake. I wish she realized I'm not her."

"Shel, she knows. I think she only wants life to be easy for you. She knows you've outgrown Culver but isn't ready to accept it. She really just wants you to be happy." Lacey lingered with her hand on the door frame.

Shelby let out a breath. She knew her mom meant well, but could she just give her a little credit? "I know, but maybe she could try to understand what *makes* me happy."

Lacey sat again on the bed and squeezed Shelby's hand. "Moms have a funny way of showing love sometimes."

Shelby considered Lacey, and the realization hit her for the first time that Lacey was speaking as a mother. She understood Debbie's feelings because she had a daughter, too. Shelby felt the change in their relationship and realized things would never be the same between them. A lump grew in Shelby's throat

Lacey leaned across the bed wrapping Shelby in a hug, then drew back until their pinkies were linked and their foreheads touched.

The action was something they used to do as kids, and the backs of Shelby's eyes prickled.

"Don't worry, Shel. Things change and people grow in different directions. But no matter what, you and me, we will always be besties."

They both smiled and hugged again, and Lacey steered the conversation toward more light-hearted topics before she stood to go.

Shelby pulled her knees to her chest and wrapped her arms around them, resting her cheek on her knee and smiling. Lacey was tall and long-waisted, giving her a graceful walk. Although her baby was just a few months old, she still looked like a super-model. After all the time she'd spent sitting on this same bed, listening to Lacey's adventures in dating land, Shelby had to admit, she'd enjoyed being the one with the stories.

****

The next day, Shelby awoke to the sound of cattle lowing. She pulled on her clothes, fitting the slit in her jeans over her cast. Then she drew her hair into a ponytail and crammed on a cowboy hat. Today she felt no need to worry about her appearance. Arriving downstairs, she found her mom in the kitchen buttering toast slices.

"I'll come down to the field in a few hours with lunch," Debbie said. "And bandages," she added with a wink.

After a quick breakfast, Shelby followed her dad out to his pick-up and threw her crutches into the bed. They drove about a half mile down the lane that ran through the middle of the ranch. "The field" was what her dad called the area of his property where they kept the cattle.

Chet and some of his friends had worked since before dawn, separating the newborn calves from their mothers.

The cows, penned close by, were the source of the mournful noise—bellowing to have their calves returned.

"We've got a pretty good group this year." Burke ran his palm over his short hair and replaced his white cowboy hat. "Let's hurry and get these calves done and back to pasture."

The smells and sounds brought back waves of nostalgia. For as long as Shelby could remember, branding day was a big deal. As far as traditions went, the event rivaled Christmas. Even as a toddler, she'd watched her dad and the other men through the fence while they worked. As Shelby grew, her responsibilities increased. The last few years, she worked as hard as the men wrestling the calves. Shelby felt a bit disappointed that this year, thanks to her injury, her jobs would be much less physical.

She crammed her hat over her hair and leaned on her crutches, zipping up her coat against the cold. Taking a deep breath, she followed her dad across the melting snow and mud to the corral. Shelby smelled the smoke from the fire. The flames had burned down, and the brands already sat in the hottest coals.

Burke and Chet rolled a large barrel over to the fence and overturned it outside the corral by the fire for Shelby to use for her equipment.

Shelby hopped around on her crutches, getting her tools and other paraphernalia set out and ready on the barrel. She was in charge of the tags and vaccinations, which she'd pass over the fence to the men. She put more wood on top of the fire to keep the irons hot, and then propped her crutches against the corral fence to keep them out of the way.

State law required each calf to be branded and tagged through the ear. Females got one color tag and males another. Shelby used a marker to write the numbers on the ear tags and loaded them into the hand-tool that attached them. Then, she filled a syringe with the clear liquid containing vitamins, antibiotic, and vaccination for the animals.

"Shels," Chet yelled, "Look who's here!"

Shelby glanced up and saw Dan had arrived with Jake. The sight of her old boyfriend made her stomach turn. *Great.*

"If it isn't the fancy city girl getting her boots dirty." Dan walked over and swept her into a giant bear hug. He set her back on the ground carefully, helping her to balance against the barrel before releasing her.

"Hey, Dan." Shelby smiled at Lacey's husband, refraining from comment on his new mustache. "Hey, Jake."

"You're looking good, Shel." Jake gave her a quick, one-armed hug.

An awkward silence followed, and Shelby could have kissed Chet when he jogged over to thank Dan and Jake for coming.

"We got us some early winter calves this year. I think a few of 'em are big enough to give us a little rodeo." Chet patted the two of them on the back.

Shelby hopped back and forth on her good leg, handing the men in the two pens the equipment as fast as she could. The men always competed light-heartedly to get the most calves done, and she didn't want either group blaming her for losing because she was too slow.

Chapter Six

Hakim fought against the pounding of his heart, and his mouth went dry. He paused at the bottom of the steps, inhaled a deep breath, and rubbed his hand on the back of his neck. His gaze darted once toward the car. Stepping onto the wooden porch stairs, he hesitated a moment, deciding whether to knock or ring the bell. Squaring his shoulders, he made up his mind and pushed the doorbell.

While he waited, doubts flooded his mind. Had he made a mistake? He thought back to the conversation earlier that morning. Nasir had raised various concerns about their expedition—How would they find Shelby in this town? How could he ensure Hakim's safety in a place where they had no contacts and no information on the area? But, once Nasir understood Hakim's wishes, he stopped trying to sway the prince.

The flight to Culver Springs in Hakim's Gulf Stream had taken all night and most of the previous day. They had landed at the small airport twenty miles outside of town, rented a car, and found the ranch easily enough with the map and directions from the gas station attendant. Hakim found he had quite enjoyed the excitement of their unplanned adventure. He'd never done anything like it before.

When they arrived, Hakim had wanted to go alone to the ranch, but Nasir refused. Hakim almost laughed when Nasir surveyed Culver Springs with suspicion, complaining he couldn't do his job and keep the prince safe in this unpredictable environment.

Nasir pointed out most of the street signs were riddled with bullet holes. The roads twisted randomly, giving minimal visibility.

They reached the compromise that Nasir would drive him and remain close by in case of an emergency. To Nasir, this meant patrolling the perimeter of the property. Hakim worried the Walkers and their neighbors would feel uncomfortable with the large Arab driving around, but Nasir's training enabled him to be invisible and assess any situation. He had assured Hakim he could be discreet.

The sound of footsteps pulled Hakim back to the present. The knob turned. The woman who answered the door appeared so much like Shelby that he was speechless for a moment. Then he saw her nervous expression as she looked him over, taking in his entire appearance. He hadn't even considered people might be alarmed at finding a foreign stranger on their front porch. "Is this the Walker residence?"

"Yes." She glanced behind him and then returned her gaze to his. "I'm Debbie Walker. How can I help you?"

"I am looking for Shelby. My name is Hakim Khalid." When he saw hesitation on Mrs. Walker's face, he continued, "I was with Shelby when she had her accident. I wanted to make sure she is all right." He still sensed a little reservation in her manner.

Debbie smiled tightly. "I'm just headed out to the field with lunch. How about you ride along?" She squinted her eyes. "You'll have to change your shoes, though. Let me see what I can find in Chet's room. Go ahead and make yourself at home, I'll be right back."

Hakim turned and signaled to the car.

As he'd promised, Nasir waved and drove out of the driveway.

Hakim followed Debbie into the house, and once he was left alone, he studied the living room, fascinated. The first thing he noticed was the deer head hanging above the fireplace. The couches looked old, comfortable, and well-worn with a knitted afghan draped across the back of each. An old TV sat in the corner next to a bookshelf full of DVDs.

This was the first time he'd ever been in an American home. In fact, he couldn't remember ever coming to any house and ringing the doorbell for a visit. Nearly all of his appointments were planned, scheduled, and announced weeks, sometimes months, ahead. Most of his interactions with others took place only in formal meetings.

Walker family pictures in mismatched frames filled the mantel above the fireplace. Studying them, Hakim recognized a picture of Shelby as a little girl wearing cowboy boots and sitting on a tire swing holding a popsicle that dripped all over her hands and shirt. Her hair was pulled into two braids, and she grinned with a mouth full of missing teeth. How different her childhood had been from his. He tried to imagine growing up in this house. Hakim still held the picture when Debbie returned with a pair of boots and a jacket.

"Wasn't my little Shelby adorable?" she said. "She was quite a little spitfire. Never wanting to comb her hair or wear girl clothes. While her friends were dressing like princesses, she was running around outside with her pockets full of frogs."

Hakim smiled at the image and placed the frame back on the mantel.

"I rustled up some boots. I think you and Chet probably wear close to the same size." She held up a pair of worn leather boots. "Also, I grabbed you a jacket. It's my husband Burke's. You don't want to get your nice clothes all dirty."

Looking at Debbie, Hakim recognized Shelby's bright blue eyes. They were the same color and shape, but where the skin around Shelby's eyes was smooth, and they shined with life and energy, the fine lines around her mother's spoke of experience and compassion. "Thank you."

Debbie excused herself to give him a moment to change.

He slipped on Chet's boots and traded his leather jacket for Burke's denim one. He had never borrowed clothes before. Hakim was surprised to feel so comfortable with Debbie fussing over him. His throat constricted, and he felt the loss of his mother all over again. For a moment, he wondered how different his life would have been if she had lived to raise him. A succession of nannies and tutors had ensured his safety and education, but they had been paid to care about him. Shelby's mother's small act made him realize how much he missed a mother's attention.

"All set? Let's get going then." Debbie re-entered the room carrying a cooler. "Here you go. Can you put this in the back seat while I grab my keys?"

"Of course." Hakim held the door for Debbie, put the cooler in the car, and they rode the short way down the lane. He felt the nagging self-doubt that had accompanied him throughout the last few days. Was he doing the right thing? Would Shelby want to see him again?

Hakim watched out the window as Debbie drove down the dirt lane, passing corrals and outbuildings. They pulled in next to a group of pick-up trucks, and Hakim could see the black-and-white masses of cattle separated into various pens. He tried to discern what was taking place. People worked with the smaller animals, and as soon as Hakim got out of the car, he spotted Shelby. He raised a hand in greeting, his heart racing.

Shelby turned from handing something through the fence and froze with her brow wrinkled. "Hakim?"

"Shelby." He closed the gap between them with a few long strides and took her hand in both of his. Her confused expression was replaced by a wide grin, dispelling any question about whether he had made the right choice about coming.

"Hakim, what are you doing here?"

Hakim glanced over her shoulder at the unfamiliar people, uncomfortable with all the gazes scrutinizing him. "Shelby, I was unsure what to say when I arrived." He paused, rubbed the back of his neck, and then leaned closer. His heart felt light when he saw her smile. "I just knew I needed to see you again."

Shelby squeezed his hand. "I'm so glad you came."

"What's going on here?" A tall man in a cowboy hat tromped over to them. "Gosh, Shels, you could at least introduce us."

Shelby rolled her eyes. She let go of Hakim's hand and grabbed the handle of her crutches. "Hakim, this is my annoying little brother, Chet."

"Little, nothing," Chet held his hand toward him. "Hey, Hakim, how's it going? Cool beard."

"It is a pleasure to meet you, Chet," Hakim said. "Your mother loaned me your boots. Thank you." He stared at Chet's extended hand, unused to another person acting familiar enough to initiate a greeting.

"No big deal. You can borrow my ropers whenever." Chet grasped his hand and shook it, clapping his other on the back of Hakim's. "Looks like you got here right in time. We've still got some wrangling to do. You ever branded calves, Hakim?"

"I have not, but would be glad to assist you as much as I am able." *Branding...me?* Hakim hoped his uncertainty didn't show on his face.

"Good man." Chet grinned, smacking Hakim on the back and heading over to where Debbie was handing out sandwiches.

"Hakim, you don't have to do this. My family would understand if we got out of here." Shelby jerked her head to the side.

"I came to be with you, Shelby. If you are branding cattle, then that is where I wish to be. Besides, I have the boots." He smiled and held up a foot. "For me to miss my opportunity to be an American cowboy would be a shame."

"I don't think you know what you're getting yourself into." She shook her head. "You'd better come meet my dad. He's always grateful for extra help."

They walked to where the group was eating lunch. The men all sat or leaned wherever they could find a spot.

Debbie and a man whom Hakim assumed was Shelby's father sat in the cab of a pick-up. When

Shelby and Hakim approached, the older man opened the door and stepped out.

"Dad, I want you to meet my friend, Hakim Khalid." Shelby moved her hand back and forth between the men. "Hakim, this is my dad, Burke Walker."

Burke wiped off his hand on his jeans and extended it to Hakim.

"It is a pleasure to meet you, sir," Hakim said with a small bow.

"Howdy, Hakim." Burke nodded. "You were one of the friends with Shelby when she had her accident?"

"Yes, sir."

"Thank you," Burke said in his gruff voice. "Thanks for helping my little girl." He patted Hakim on the shoulder and cleared his throat. "You hungry, son? You'll need your energy if you're gonna wrangle with these boys."

Debbie hopped out of the truck and opened the cooler on the ground. "We've got sandwiches here. Most of them are ham." She paused, and her gaze moved to Hakim. "I hope I don't sound too ignorant. I mean, we don't get many foreigners around here. Do you eat ham, Hakim? If not, I think there are still turkey sandwiches on the bottom."

"Thank you for being sensitive to my culture. I am not forbidden by religion, but pork is not a very common food in my country. I would prefer the turkey."

Shelby rested her crutches against the truck and used her arms to push herself up onto the tail gate.

Hakim sat beside her while they ate their sandwiches.

"Hey, Shels. So's this your 'gentleman friend' Lace was talking about?" Another man with a dark mustache strode toward them.

Shelby gave him a playful shove on the arm, holding on to the side of the truck bed for balance. "Hakim, this is Dan Peterson. He's married to my best friend, Lacey."

"Nice to meet you, Dan." Hakim shook his hand

Another cowboy walked past without looking at the three of them and grunted.

Hakim raised his eyebrows, appalled by the floppy-haired man's lack of respect. Such a thing would never happen in his country without a penalty.

"And that idiot is Dan's friend, Jake," Shelby said. "Just ignore him."

After the meal was over, Burke handed Hakim a pair of gloves.

Chet walked with him to the corral. He swung a leg over the fence and jumped down into the pen. "Climb on over, Hakim." Chet continued, "Most people only see cows as animals grazing in a field. Then, they order a hamburger in a restaurant. There's a lot of stuff that comes between, and most of it ain't pretty. Branding is actually the most humane way to track these animals."

Shelby put her hand on Hakim's arm and looked into his face. "You really don't have to do this. Branding's not as fun as it sounds, and it's kind of dangerous if you don't know what you're doing," she said in a low voice.

Hearing this, Hakim was even more determined. He tightened his jaw and pressed his lips together. Shelby's smile was all the encouragement he needed to put on the gloves and even though he was uncertain of exactly how to do it, he followed Chet's example and swung a leg over the bars of the fence, dropping into the enclosure.

Chet strode to the pen separating the calves from the work area, swung open the gate, and shooed out one calf toward Hakim before closing it again. "So, what ya gotta do is grab him and flip him on his side. They may look small and fragile, but a calf is a hundred pounds of pure muscle. When ya get him down, sit on him. Watch out for his legs. They pack a punch. We gotta get hustling if we want to beat Dan and Jake." He motioned with his chin toward the other pen.

Hakim approached the calf, feigning confidence as he followed Chet's lead. He didn't want to disappoint Shelby by showing how anxious he felt. With Chet's help, he reached across the animal's back and heaved it onto its side. The strength of the young calf surprised him.

Chet showed Hakim how to hold the calf still and keep himself from being kicked by straddling the animal and putting his knee between its back legs. Chet held the calf's front legs, and Burke stepped close, and with efficient movements, immunized, tagged, and branded it.

Hakim hoped his horror did not show when he heard the click as the tag was pierced through the calf's ear, or when Burke held up the scruff on the back of its neck to inject the serum. A hot iron was pressed into the animal's hide, and the smell was overwhelming. Bile rose in Hakim's throat. The animal bellowed. Hakim took a deep breath.

"You ready, Hakim?" Chet asked. "On the count of three, we let him up. You gotta get out of the way of those back legs quick. One, two, NOW!"

Chet let go of the calf's front legs before Hakim—still a little light-headed—stood all the way up.

In one swift movement, the calf twisted into a standing position, sending Hakim flying onto the churned-up ground.

"You okay?" Shelby called from the other side of the fence.

Hakim stood and smiled weakly as he brushed at his jeans. "Yes. It is only a little mud."

Chet laughed. "That ain't mud, dude."

****

Shelby felt a fluttering in her chest as she watched Hakim work with her family. After a little practice, Chet and Hakim fell into a rhythm. The early spring sun combined with the physical labor left the two drenched in sweat. Hakim removed Burke's coat, revealing a tailored button-down shirt.

Shelby was distracted by the muscles in Hakim's back and arms when he strained and sweated under the weight of the calves. She hadn't realized he was in such good shape. She heard the sound of Dan's voice and dragged away her gaze. She realized she'd been staring, and her cheeks colored.

"Hey, Shel! You giving them the advantage by making us wait?"

"Sorry, I guess I'm getting tired."

With about a dozen calves left, Burke lifted his hat and wiped his forehead. "Hakim, you'd better get Shelby Jo home. We can finish up. Her mother will have my hide if I keep her out here all day."

Shelby knew her dad's concern was genuine, but he was also making sure the two of them had alone time. She flashed him a grateful smile.

"You get some rest." Burke nodded to Shelby before he put his hat back on.

Hakim stepped on the fence rail to climb back over the fence.

Burke patted him on the back. "Thanks for your help, son."

"Thank you." Hakim stepped down and shook Burke's hand. He recognized Shelby's bright smile on her father's face. "I enjoyed this experience very much." He climbed over the fence to join Shelby.

Burke handed Hakim the keys to the pick-up.

"See ya, guys." Shelby waved her fingers.

Hakim helped her into the cab, put the crutches in the back, and walked around to the driver's door. He turned the key, but the engine didn't start.

Shelby leaned back against the headrest. "You gotta step on the clutch." She rolled her head to the side to watch him.

Hakim looked down at the pedals on the floor and then back at Shelby with a wide-eyed expression.

"You don't know how to drive a stick shift?" Shelby sat up.

"I should be able to figure it out with a little instruction," he said.

"All right, push in the clutch and put it in neutral." She reached over and pulled the stick on the column into place. "Now turn it on." The engine started, and Shelby scooted closer, putting the truck in gear. "The trick is to let up on the clutch at the same time you push on the gas."

Hakim tried once, and the truck bounced and stalled. His face colored under his tan skin.

"It's okay. Try again." Shelby helped with the gear shift, and with a lot of jerking and grinding, they made it up the lane to the farm house. She braced herself with one arm on the dash and one on the seat since her right leg was useless.

"I am sorry. That drive must have been very uncomfortable."

"Don't be sorry. I'm a cowgirl, remember? Chet drives worse than that on purpose." Shelby looked around the yard and squinted as she realized something was missing. "Hey, where's your car? How'd ya get here?"

"Nasir drove me."

"Oh, so where is he?" she asked.

"I asked him to allow me time alone with you."

Shelby's heart tripped at his words.

He caught her gaze. "Do not worry. Nasir is not a social person. He will find ways to occupy his time."

Hakim got out of the truck, walked around the front, and opened Shelby's door. He pulled the crutches out of the truck bed and handed them to her as she slid down from the high seat.

Smiling her gratitude, she put them under her arms and pointed to the porch swing.

Moments later, they sat, stretching their legs in front of them.

"So, what did you think, cowboy?" She bumped his shoulder with hers, and winced at the mud and manure on Hakim's designer jeans.

"I think I need a shower." He grinned, lifted the brim of her cowboy hat, and brushed aside her hair, examining her healing scar.

"I love that you came here, Hakim." Heat spread

through her chest. "I know it's disgusting, wrestling cows in the mud, but I love that you did it to be with me."

He ran the back of his fingers along her cheek, leaving a path of heat. "I cannot think of any place I would rather be."

Chapter Seven

Later that evening, Hakim drove down the dirt road. He glanced in the rearview mirror at Nasir following in another sedan. He had spent a good part of the afternoon convincing Nasir to allow him to come alone. The second rental car was their compromise.

Nasir pulled over on the highway where the lane curved toward the Walker's ranch and parked the car to wait.

For the second time that day, Hakim stepped onto the wooden porch and rang the doorbell—this time his heart pounded in anticipation instead of anxiety.

Shelby's mother answered, the open door emitting a splash of light.

"Good evening, Mrs. Walker," he said.

"Come on in, Hakim. Please call me Debbie." She opened the door wide and called up the stairs. "Shelby! Hakim's here."

"Thank you for permitting me to borrow these boots and coat." Hakim handed Debbie the clothes Nasir had cleaned.

"You're so welcome. Burke and I appreciate any help we can get with those calves. He's not as young as he used to be, you know."

"It was my pleasure," Hakim answered with a small bow, but froze, distracted as Shelby made her way down the stairs and into the room. She wore a long floral blouse, belted at the waist over a T-shirt and black leggings. On her good foot was a red cowboy boot.

Hakim realized that aside from the hospital, he had not seen Shelby when she wasn't wrapped in a winter coat. He couldn't help but notice how the outfit emphasized her small waist and athletic curves. He schooled his expression, not wanting to stare. Her hair was longer than he'd expected, curling in silky copper waves over her shoulders. As usual, though, his gaze was drawn to her face. "Good evening, Shelby Jo. You look lovely."

"Thanks. You look pretty great yourself." She waved a hand at his designer jeans and charcoal sweater. "Ready to experience the excitement of the Culver Springs night life?" She pulled a coat from a hook on the wall.

"Of course." Hakim helped her with her coat. Her soft hair brushed across his hand when she shook it out over her collar. He slid his hands into his pockets, controlling the temptation to touch her hair again.

"See ya, Mom!"

"Good night, Debbie," Hakim said.

"You two have fun!"

He passed the car on the side of the road and glanced in the rearview mirror as Nasir pulled out to follow. While he drove them to Lacey and Dan's, Hakim listened as Shelby gave a brief tour of the town. He tried to imagine her life as a child.

They passed the high school and the Native American Cultural Museum. Sheby shared memories of stopping for ice cream after school and pointed out where she crashed her bike and broke her arm.

"Shelby, you seem so happy here. Why did you leave Culver Springs?" he asked.

Shelby bit her lip for a moment, before she answered. "Here's the thing. In a small town, everybody knows you. They know your parents, your grandparents, your high school boyfriend, what you wore to prom, what kind of grades you got—sounds pretty cozy, right?" She paused, her fingers drumming on the door handle. "Since they know you so well, they assume they know what's best for you, too. And your future is pretty much laid out for you. You're expected to live your life a certain way. Be who everyone thinks you are. I left to see who I could become in a place where nobody knew me or had preconceived ideas of who I was. I wanted to see if I could find my own way, to meet people and see if they like me for *me*. Map out my own path, you know?" She stopped speaking and glanced at him. "That probably makes no sense to you."

"No," he said in a quiet voice. She could not know how perfectly she had described his own feelings. "To me, this makes perfect sense."

Following Shelby's directions, Hakim pulled into the driveway of Dan and Lacey's brand-new house. He helped Shelby out of the car and grabbed her crutches from the back seat, glancing down the road to where Nasir parked on the street.

A dark-haired woman, who he assumed was Lacey, waved from the window and then opened the front door.

Shelby gave the woman a quick hug and introduced Hakim.

"Good to see you again, Hakim." Dan clasped Hakim's hand.

Shelby held Lacey's new baby, Cole, cradling him while she spoke with his four-year-old sister, Shay.

Shay's hair was the same striking dark brown as her mother's. It curled in bouncing ringlets. She wore a princess costume with a plastic tiara. Hakim couldn't help but smile at the sight.

"Shay, this is my friend, Hakim," Shelby said, waving a hand in his direction.

"I am four." Shay held up four chubby fingers to show him.

"It's nice to meet you, Shay." Hakim knelt down to Shay's height. "Shelby told me this is your new house." He glanced around the small entryway, feeling claustrophobic with the low ceilings. The décor seemed cluttered, and like Shelby's house the furniture was mismatched and the tables and shelves held keepsakes and pictures. *A home.* Not a showpiece of elegance like his palace.

"I have my own room," Shay said. "Wanna see it?"

Unsure of what was appropriate, he looked to Shelby, eyebrows raised.

"Hakim would love to see your new room, and so would I." Shelby reached for Shay's hand.

The child reached instead for Hakim's hand, grabbing it, and then she led them up the stairs.

Having little experience with children, he was touched and a bit bewildered by her gesture.

Shay stopped at a doorway and held her hands out in a grand gesture. "My own room."

Hakim followed her into what he supposed was a typical American little girl's room. A dresser and canopy bed were her only furniture, and a giant pink dollhouse filled the rest of the space.

Shay instructed Hakim to sit on the floor and began to hand him different toys, telling him each of their names.

Before long, he had a lap full of dolls. He had rarely spent time with a child and did not know how to act around a little girl.

"Which princess is the most beautiful?" Shay asked.

"Hmmm…" Hakim tapped his chin, pretending to consider her question. "I think Princess Shay is the most beautiful princess of all."

Shay giggled and clapped her hands together. "Then *you* can be the prince."

"Very well. What does the prince do?" Hakim lifted his shoulders. *If the child only knew.*

"He rides a horse, and rescues the princess, and dances with her," Shay explained.

"Then, I will indeed be the prince."

"We'd better save Hakim," Lacey said from where she stood in the doorway beside Shelby. "It's not often Shay has such a captive audience."

Shay held tightly to Hakim's hand as Dan and Lacey gave them the rest of the tour.

Five minutes later, the babysitter arrived, and Shay reluctantly said goodbye to Hakim, after he promised to try and return another day to play.

He was surprised when she hugged him, and when she planted a sloppy kiss on his cheek, an unfamiliar sensation stirred in his heart. He had never given much thought to having children of his own. Obviously, he was expected to produce an heir. He understood his duty, but he had never considered being a father would mean loving a child—and having a child love him.

Putting away the thought to ponder later, he closed Shelby's door and walked to the driver's side of the rental car.

Hakim drove them to what Shelby claimed was the best restaurant in town: "Italian Garden." He opened the door, and the smell of garlic and pasta sauce floated on the air. Shelby had informed him the restaurant hadn't changed as long as she could remember. Built-in glass cabinets hung on the walls, encasing a never-changing display of faded silk flowers. The booths were upholstered with light blue vinyl, and yellow-paned light fixtures hung low over the tables.

At the side of the booth, Hakim helped Shelby take off her coat, noticing she exchanged waves with nearly every person in the restaurant. He stood aside to allow her onto the cushioned seat, but she preferred to keep her injured leg on the outside, and so he slid in first, realizing he'd never sat on a vinyl bench in a restaurant booth. He hoped his expression didn't betray how completely out of his league the situation made him feel. They sat across the table from Dan and Lacey.

Dan draped his arm across the bench, and when Lacey scooted in close, he gave her an affectionate kiss on the cheek as she opened her menu.

Hakim wondered if he and Shelby would ever be that comfortable together.

Shelby laid her crutches on the floor next to the booth and slid next to him.

Hakim caught a whiff of her perfume. *Subtle, and feminine, but not too flowery, Just like Shelby*. He tilted his menu toward her. He could feel her heat where their thighs touched.

The waitress arrived at their table. "If it isn't

Shelby Walker and Lacey Barton." She put a hand on her hip.

"Shannon!" Shelby jumped up, balancing on one leg to hug the small blonde woman. "I didn't know you still worked here."

"Yep. Been almost ten years. I should own the place by now, right?" Shannon raised her eyebrows at Hakim. "So, who's this?"

"My friend, Hakim." Shelby slid back into the booth. "Hakim, this is Shannon Price."

"Pleased to meet you, Miss Price." Hakim reached over to shake Shannon's hand.

"Handsome *and* polite. Shelby, you sure know how to pick 'em. So, Hakim, have these girls told you about all the trouble we used to get into?"

"No, however I would be very interested to know what Shelby was like when she was younger." Hakim smiled at Shelby. Her smile in return caused the increasingly familiar warmth to spread in his chest.

"Wow. Where should I start?" Shannon asked.

"Of all the people in this town, I bet Shelby is the most famous for the scrapes she got into," Lacey said with a wave of her hand. "She's a local legend. We could be here all night telling you stories."

"Food first, childhood memories later," Dan complained. "I'm starving."

"Some things never change." Shannon winked. "What can I get you guys?"

"Does everyone want pizza?" Shelby asked, glancing around the table.

They all agreed and placed their orders.

Hakim leaned across the table toward Lacey, feeling Shelby's softness where his arm brushed hers.

"I would love to hear about Shelby Jo as a child."

"I've got a great one for you."

"Nothing embarrassing, Lace," Shelby pleaded.

"All right, all right." Lacey paused and spread her fingers on the table, taking a deep breath before she began her story. "So, we were about eight, and the rodeo was in town…"

"Lace," Shelby groaned.

The edges of Lacey's mouth rose, but she kept speaking. "The guys who bring the animals had this one really mean bull. I mean, this thing was huge. Things are different now, like more regulated, but back then, a rider would get extra points for riding one of these enormous bulls. So they all wanted to draw him. The bull was so dangerous he couldn't even stay penned up with the other rodeo animals, so Burke let them keep it out in his corral."

Hakim smiled at Shelby's mortified expression.

Shannon set the drinks and salad on the table. "Oh, my gosh! I'd totally forgotten this story. Your pizza's almost up. Don't finish 'til I get back!" She twirled and hurried toward the kitchen.

"Okay, after school, a bunch of us got off the bus at the Walkers' and went home with Shelby to check out the bull," Lacey continued. "We were too scared to even get close to the fence. The bull wasn't doing anything but standing in the corral chewing its cud. It didn't so much as look at us, but we were still terrified."

Hakim bent forward, not wanting to miss a word, and using the excuse to graze his arm against Shelby's.

Dan shook his head and laughed. "We yelled at the bull to get its attention. But nothing happened. We threw stuff at it, and finally, we all got to daring each other to go inside the pen and touch it."

"Shelby was the only one who would do it," Lacey broke in.

Shannon returned with their pizza.

After everyone was served, Dan continued with a laugh, "I can still remember how she looked. Little Shelby with her freckles and her hair in ponytails, scrunching up her face all determined to prove how brave she was."

"I thought you guys said it wouldn't be embarrassing," Shelby muttered.

Dan glanced at her and turned back to Hakim. "Shelby climbed over the fence and tip-toed across the pen. She touched the bull with one finger, and when it turned toward her, she ran like her hair was on fire. She got to the fence and instead of climbing back over, she wriggled under. The problem was, her jeans got snagged on this hank of barbed wire."

"Oh, yeah, I love this part." Shelby took a bite of pizza.

"She tugged and tugged, but those blue jeans were stuck tight," Dan said with a wide grin.

"I don't even remember the next few minutes," Shannon chimed in with a laugh. "We totally panicked!"

Lacey held up her hands, opening her fingers wide. "We all started screaming bloody murder. I'm pretty sure I was bawling. We all thought that bull was going to get Shelby."

Shelby rested her elbows on the table, hiding her face with her hands.

"Without missing a beat, Shel kicked off her boots

and wiggled out of her pants. Debbie came out to see what all the screaming was about, and there was Shelby, covered in mud, wearing her little purple panties."

Hakim chuckled, trying to imagine what his tutors would say if they'd discovered him playing in the mud. He found he couldn't do it.

Shelby grimaced, but when she saw Hakim laugh, she allowed a smile. "Yeah, that wasn't too humiliating. Thanks, guys."

The entire table burst into laughter.

"How do you like your pizza, Hakim?" asked Shannon.

"It is delicious. Thank you, Miss Price."

"I'd better get back to work. Thanks for the laugh. Great to see you, Shel." Shannon waved to the group.

Dan set down his pizza crust and leaned back, putting his arm around Lacey and brushing a finger over his mustache. "So, Hakim, what kind of work do you do?"

Hakim had anticipated this question and gave his rehearsed answer. "I work as a consultant for my father's business."

"I don't know much about the business world—just enough to get along, if you know what I mean," Dan said. "What do you do for fun?"

Hakim shifted in his seat. His leg brushed Shelby's again. He felt a little guilty, but he loved the feel of her and tried to think of any excuse to touch her. "I enjoy hunting. And skiing, of course." His gaze met Shelby's, and he smiled. "But my real passion is horses."

Dan nodded. "Now, that's something I can definitely relate to."

The two men continued talking about horses while they ate, and Dan told Hakim about his construction business.

Hakim was surprised by how much he enjoyed the conversation. He was interested in the details of this man's life and the way he worked hard to provide for his family.

After a little while, Lacey looked at her watch. "We'd better get going. I'm worried about the sitter trying to get Shay and Cole to sleep."

The four of them scooted out of the booth, and Hakim helped Shelby with her coat and crutches as she rested her hip against the table for balance.

"Should we head over to the drive-in for a shake?" Dan held up Lacey's coat.

"You know I can't eat that stuff—not with all this baby fat still hanging on." Lacey patted her tummy. "Anyway, I need to be getting back to the kids."

"You look great, honey." Dan lifted his wife's face with a crooked finger beneath her chin and winked. "Why don't we just grab it and eat it on the way home? We can share."

The group returned to Hakim's rental car, and he helped Shelby into the passenger seat and stowed her crutches in the trunk. He heard a car start and glanced to the far end of the parking lot where Nasir was parked.

Dan and Lacey climbed into the back seat.

As he drove, first to the Shake Shack and then back to their house, Hakim had to remind himself to stop staring in the rearview mirror. He was fascinated by the way Dan and Lacey treated each other. She finished his sentences, and he was constantly putting his arm around her or kissing her cheek. Surprised, Hakim realized he felt jealous. By his standards, their home was beyond small. Shabby, even. Their furniture and clothes were not expensive, and yet, they had everything he wanted.

After dropping off the Bartons, Hakim was quiet as he drove through town. He glanced at the lights in the rearview mirror and wondered if Shelby had noticed Nasir following them.

"What are you thinking?" Shelby asked.

"I have something to confess, Shelby." He tapped his fingers on the gear shift. "This is the first time I have ever been on a date."

"Are you serious?" Shelby lifted her brows and tilted her head, looking at him.

"Yes. It is not part of my culture to court in this way."

"So, what do you do instead?"

"Khali-dar is one of the more westernized countries in the Middle East, but there are still traditions which are generally adhered to. First of all, it would be highly inappropriate for us to be alone like this without a chaperone. In some countries, such a thing would be punishable by prison time, or worse. Many of the more traditional families still arrange marriages, although this practice is becoming rarer."

"Oh." Shelby rubbed her arm as she gazed out the window. "Has your family picked someone out for you?"

When he heard the anxiety in her voice, Hakim couldn't fight the jump in his pulse. "No, my father does not believe in arranged marriages. He was very much in love with my mother and would not want any less for me."

"That's good then, right?"

"Yes, it is good." Hakim stopped the car in front of the Walkers' house.

Although it was early, the windows were dark. The family had worked hard all day, and Shelby was the only one who'd taken a nap.

Shelby twisted in her seat to face him. "I'd better give you some advice to make up for your lack of dating experience."

"Thank you."

"Let's just say, a guy surprises a girl by coming to town and spending the day helping her family, then takes her to dinner, and doesn't run screaming out the door when her friends tell embarrassing stories about her. If that's the case, she'll probably expect him to kiss her."

"Shelby Jo, do you always say exactly what you are thinking?" His heart pounded on his ribs.

Shelby wrinkled her nose and grimaced. "I guess you're not used to women acting so bold."

"Well"—he scooted closer—"I have no reason to mistrust your counsel."

The porch light did little to illuminate the inside of the car. Hakim gently touched the sides of her face, enjoying the sensation of her softness. He trailed his hands down her neck, stopping at her shoulders. Her face tilted, and he bent his head until his lips brushed against hers. At first hesitantly and then, covering her mouth with his own, he inhaled her smell, noticing again how perfectly it fit her. He drew back, watching as she sighed and opened her eyes.

He held her face in his hands, the taste of her still on his lips. "Yes, you were right. Excellent advice."

****

Shelby let herself into the dark house, her lips still tingling from Hakim's kiss. In the living room, the TV flickered.

Chet was sprawled out asleep on the couch. He must have been waiting up.

She took the remote off of Chet's stomach and clicked off the TV. "Chet"—she shook his shoulder— "Hey, it's time to go to bed."

"Wha...? Oh, hey, Shels. How was your date?" Chet swung his legs onto the floor and rubbed his bleary eyes. He stretched out his back and winced.

"Nice." She fought to repress a grin. "Actually, more than nice. Hakim's pretty great, don't ya think?"

"Where'd ya go? Italian Garden?"

"Yeah. Come on." She tugged on his arm. "You need some sleep."

"Hang on a sec, Shels. I wanted to talk to ya."

Shelby sat on the love seat and propped her crutches against the wall. "What's up?"

"Listen, Shels, I don't want to be 'that guy'." He used his fingers to make quotes in the air. "But I'm your brother. I just want to know what's going on with you and this Hakim dude."

"What do you mean by that?" Shelby grabbed one of her mom's knitting needles from the side table.

Chet fidgeted. "Shels, You obviously like him, I know you well enough to tell that much. But where will something like this lead? I guarantee Hakim isn't planning on staying in Culver Springs. Is he just playing around with you?"

Shelby's chest felt tight. "I'm aware, we haven't known each other that long. I haven't even thought about that kind of thing." She shifted, crossing her arms and scratching her shoulder. The truth was, she *had* thought about it. A lot. She'd thought of little else since Hakim had arrived. What *were* his intentions? If he was hoping for a fling, would he have kissed her so chastely?

"That's bull, Shels, and you know it. Stop lying to yourself."

Shelby couldn't find words to respond. She stared at her brother with her jaw dropped. This was so unlike her easygoing, happy brother.

"Listen..." Chet scratched the back of his head. "You haven't had a ton of experience with guys. I mean, I know you've dated some, but you've never been serious with anyone besides Jake, right? You feel flattered since a hot, rich dude is paying you all this attention. You need to ask yourself why. You're awesome, Shels, and I know it, but I'm trying to figure out his motivation here."

"Really? Because it's so hard to believe someone like him could actually be interested in me?" Shelby choked on the words, fighting back her tears.

"Sorry, Shels, I'm just being honest. Guys don't think the same way chicks do. Most of us are total jerks."

"Hakim isn't a jerk, Chet. He flew halfway around the world and spent the day in cow crud, then hung out with my friends at a tacky small-town restaurant. Does that sound like a guy with ulterior motives?" Shelby crammed one of the needles inside her cast, scratching her leg fiercely.

"Yeah, you're right, I guess." Chet ran his fingernails over the leather stitching on his boots.

Shelby could tell this wasn't easy, but didn't cut him any slack. Chet was always the one on her side. *If I can't get my brother to see how great Hakim was, how can I ever hope to get my parents onboard?*

"Ya know," Chet said. "He could be totally on the up and up. But I want you to be careful." He leaned forward, dangling his hands between his knees. "Do you think you might just be liking his exotic-ness? I mean, you're always saying how you don't want to end up like everyone else in this town—you want to do great stuff, see the world. Then a guy comes along who's as different from Culver as turkeys are from turnips. Don't be blinded, Shels."

She rested back against the cushions, feeling exhausted. "You're right. I love it here, and I love you guys, but I don't want to end up here. I want to do something important, Chet—something nobody thinks I can do. Hakim has never questioned my desires to do something great. He wants me to be happy, and he would support me no matter what." Shelby wished she didn't sound so defensive, but what Chet said hit a little too close to home. She did worry about Hakim and his motives. What could someone like him see in her? And what sort of future could they ever have? Or was Chet right, and Hakim was just looking for a little fun?

"You know, Middle Eastern guys aren't exactly known for treating women really great, right?" Chet edged closer on the sofa. He took away the knitting needle, setting it on the coffee table before enveloping her in his lanky arms. "I'll support ya, Shels. I never said I wouldn't. It's just my job as your brother to worry."

"Hakim's been a real gentleman, Chet." She rested

106

her head on his shoulder, squeezing him back.

"He seems cool. Just be careful, Sis. I don't want to see you hurt. And I don't want to have to kick his—"

"I know, Chet. Thanks."

Chapter Eight

Hakim called Shelby the next morning, and they made plans to see the Anasazi Indian ruins which were about a half hour away by four-wheeler from the Walker farm. The weather was perfect—cold enough that the ground was still mostly frozen, but sunny so they would be warm. She had told him she'd pack a picnic lunch.

Half an hour later, Hakim rang the bell, and Debbie answered, as was becoming routine.

"Good morning, Hakim. Shelby's in the kitchen getting your lunch ready. Sounds like you two have a fun day planned."

"Good morning, Debbie. Thank you." Hakim followed the direction Debbie indicated and walked through the living room and into the kitchen.

"Morning, Cowboy. How'd ya sleep?" Shelby grinned.

"Very well, thank you."

Shelby grabbed water bottles from the refrigerator and shook sandwiches into small plastic bags before putting them into a backpack. She wiped the crumbs off the counter with a rag.

As he observed her doing what she most likely considered mundane chores, Hakim couldn't help being captivated. These actions that came so easily to her were completely unfamiliar. He moved his gaze to her face, and thinking about their kiss the night before, he glanced at her lips and wondered if he would have the chance again.

"So, should we get going?" Shelby asked. "Chet is letting us use his four-wheeler." She handed Hakim a blanket, slipped her arms through the backpack straps, and grabbed her crutches.

He followed her through the back door.

"Looks like Chet left me some bungee cords." She strapped her crutches onto the back of the ATV. "Do you wanna drive? It's pretty much the same as a snowmobile."

Hakim nodded.

She climbed on behind him and pointed out the accelerator and brake. After giving him a few instructions, she wrapped her arms around his waist. "Let's go!"

Shelby pressed close, her body warmed his back. They rode down the ranch road and out into a wilderness that Shelby told him belonged to the Bureau of Land Management, and was referred to as B.L.M. land. She showed him which trails to take, but was content to let him set the pace. When they ran out of road, she pointed out the easiest route.

Hakim drove slowly, worrying about how the jostling must hurt her injured leg as he navigated through the rocky landscape. He loved the way the cold contrasted with the desert—so different than his homeland.

After a little while, Shelby indicated where to stop. She unstrapped her crutches and pulled off her backpack.

Hakim took it and slid his arms through the straps.

She flashed him a wide smile. "There's a great picnic spot—just a short hike up that hill." She pointed.

Shelby didn't display any trouble walking up the trail with her crutches, but Hakim still maintained a slow pace, keeping an eye on her movements for any sign that the hike was too difficult.

A light breeze lifted her hair. "You'll love it up here," Shelby said.

He noticed her words sounded breathless. "This landscape is like a scene from a cowboy-western."

Shelby turned her face toward him and flashed a smile.

His stomach did a slow roll at her expression.

A hawk wheeled overhead. The few trees around them were twisted with rough bark on their thick branches.

As he neared the top of the hill, he saw the rocks got bigger and the trail got steeper. Shelby struggled to find flat places to set her crutches.

Hakim took the crutches and held them in one arm, sliding his other arm around her waist to support her weight.

She held onto his shoulder, hopping the last few yards to the top of the hill where the ground was flat. "Sorry," she panted. "I didn't think that out very well."

"Should we rest for a moment before going farther?" Hakim was becoming more concerned that she was pushing herself too hard.

"Sure. Can you spread out the blanket?"

He opened the checkered woolen blanket and spread it over a flat piece of ground, then sat, facing her with his legs stretched out in front of him. Hakim took the water bottle Shelby offered and rested back on his elbows, careful not to bump her cast with his thigh. "This would be a perfect time to learn all about you, Shelby Jo."

"Oh, really? You're more of a mystery than I am." Shelby used her hands to lift her injured leg to rest it on her other ankle.

"Ah, but you are much more compelling." He firmed his lips into a straight line. "I want to know everything about you."

"That's debatable." Shelby rolled her eyes. "I am definitely *not* more interesting. But it's a good idea. You ask me a question, and then I get to ask you one." She leaned back with her palms flat on the blanket, fanning out her fingers. "But we both have to be honest. You don't have to say *Wintersports* is your favorite magazine, and I don't have to say the beach of Khalidar is my dream vacation. Okay?"

"Very well." Hakim sat up, resting his arms on his bent knees. "Ladies first."

"What's your favorite movie?"

Hakim squinted, surprised by her question. "My favorite movie?"

She pulled up her shoulders. "I didn't want to start out with something too personal right out of the chute."

Hakim tapped his finger on his lips. "I am quite partial to Wild West movies—cowboys, horses, guns. Although, truthfully, I cannot say I have a favorite. Now it is my turn."

Shelby raised her eyebrows.

"What is your favorite childhood memory?"

"You mean besides losing my pants in the bullpen while all my friends were watching?" Shelby rolled her eyes, and the corners of her lips quirked.

He smiled and twirled his finger, indicating for her to continue.

Shelby was quiet for a moment before answering. "One year, my parents took us to California. I was ten and Chet was seven. We drove straight through, so the trip took about fourteen hours, and we slept in the car. My mom woke us up in the middle of the night to see the Las Vegas strip all lit up. When we got to California, we went to Disneyland and the beach. It was great. Besides my trip last year to Canada, that's the farthest from home I've ever been." Shelby shifted on the blanket to lean on one arm. "Have you been to California?"

Hakim nodded as he tried to imagine Shelby's family vacation. He had traveled extensively as long as he could remember. Her quaint story and the memory of the time spent with her family touched his heart. He opened his mouth to answer.

But Shelby held up her hand. "Wait, don't answer that. I don't want to waste my turn."

Hakim watched her as she chewed her lip with her brows drawn together.

"What are you thinking about right now?" Shelby asked.

"Is this your official question?"

She nodded, mimicking his finger twirl.

"I was thinking I have not been on a picnic since I was a very young boy. I remember my mother had obtained a large, Bedouin-type tent. We would go inside and play games or tell stories. One day, my father joined us. We had a picnic dinner, and the two of them told me stories until I fell asleep." As Hakim remembered, he softened his voice. "This is one of the few memories of both of my parents together with me. My father was very busy and seldom had time for play. My mother died when I was five years old."

"I'm so sorry, Hakim. I can't even imagine how hard that must have been."

"It was very difficult." He took a deep breath. "But pain lessens over time. Until I observed your family and the Bartons, I had almost forgotten how much I miss my mother. I must confess I feel envious."

"You still have your dad, right?" Shelby asked.

"Yes. And my father cares for me very much, but he is extremely busy."

"I'm sorry, Hakim." Shelby reached for his hand. "Sounds like you've been very lonely."

He rubbed his thumb on her palm, noticing how small and soft her hands were. "I do not feel lonely, now. I adore being with you, Shelby Jo." His heart skipped a beat when her gaze met his.

Shelby's cheeks turned pink. She squinted and tipped her head to the side. "Really?"

"Is it so difficult for you to believe?"

Lowering her gaze, she started picking at the hem on the blanket. "You're a distinguished businessman who's traveled around the world, and I'm a cowgirl from a small town. What about me could possibly be interesting to someone like you?"

She didn't give herself enough credit. Shelby fascinated him every moment since he'd met her. Hakim lifted her chin with his bent finger and tilted his head to catch her gaze. "I could ask you the same thing. I fear if you knew the real me, you would feel differently."

"As long as the real you isn't a better skier than

me. That would definitely change my feelings."

He could tell she was trying to lighten the mood.

"I'm sorry." Shelby lowered her gaze. "I didn't mean to go on a self-pity trip. Sometimes I just get kind of insecure when I'm in a new relationship."

Hakim smiled and gave her chin a gentle squeeze. "Is that what this is? A new relationship?"

"I'm not answering that. I lost track of whose turn it is, anyway." She tugged on his hand. "Come on. Help me up."

Hakim stood and pulled her to her feet, handing her the crutches and putting on the backpack.

"Let's just leave the blanket here. I want to show you something," she said.

They hiked another fifty yards until they came to the crest of a canyon.

Hakim couldn't believe the view. Inside the opposite wall was a network of caves. Ancient dwellings.

Shelby removed a small pair of binoculars from the backpack and offered them.

He peered through them and found he could see the living spaces in amazing detail. The canyon lip protected the small community from rain and invaders.

Shelby waved her hand toward the canyon floor. "The only access to the caves was with ladders which could be pulled up at night, or if danger arose. Pretty ingenious, right? And terrifying. I imagine the mothers must have kept a close eye on their children."

He nodded and tried to picture ancient people living in a canyon wall, so high above the ground. "No matter where in the world one lives, protection is a basic instinct." He thought of the high walls around the palace and the guards that insured his family's safety. *Especially now…*

They sat on a rock overlooking the ravine, and Shelby handed him a sandwich. "See those rocks?" She pointed to a hill off to their right. Large black boulders spotted the entire hillside. "Petroglyphs are up there. Should we go check them out?"

"Are you sure you are not getting too tired?" Hakim indicated her leg.

"It's not much farther, and then we can go back."

Closer to the rocks, Shelby pointed out the ones with the ancient pictures. "You have to climb a bit, but they're worth it. Some were carved eight hundred years ago." She sat on a rock to wait.

Hakim climbed up for a closer look. "It's fascinating," he said when he returned, impressed at the differences and similarities between the ancient American carvings and the primitive artwork in his country.

"I know. Chet and I love to explore up here. We've found really cool old carvings. And some that aren't so old. We even found where my great-great-grandpa carved his name in the 1800s," Shelby said. "Ready to head back?" She stood slowly and sucked in a sharp breath when she put weight on her leg.

"Shelby Jo, I think you have overdone it today."

"I'm just a little stiff. Once I get moving…"

Before her sentence was finished, Hakim had lifted her, crutches and all off the ground.

"Really, I can walk."

He ignored her protests and held her tighter.

She shifted so her crutches were both in the same hand, and her other arm circled around his neck.

Shelby was not heavy, and Hakim was in good shape, but one hundred yards over uneven rocks was a long way to carry anyone. He worried when he felt his arms tire, but when he felt Shelby's head drop onto his chest, his strength revived.

"I'm sorry, Hakim," Shelby said as he set her on the blanket. "That was a long way."

Instead of answering, Hakim sat next to Shelby and put his arm around her. Placing her head onto his shoulder, he lay back, pulling her down to lie next to him, resting his free hand behind his head. "Just rest for a few minutes, Shelby Jo."

She didn't argue and instead, rolled on her side, nestling closer.

He held her tighter, feeling the heat from her body where she pressed against him. Hakim listened to Shelby's breathing slow and deepen as she fell asleep. As he kissed the top of her head, he breathed in the fresh smell of her hair.

Hakim had never had this kind of closeness with a woman. He had never spoken with anyone about his mother or the pain he still felt over her loss. Soon after her death, he had tried to talk to his father, but it was not long before he learned men in his family were expected to cope with their feelings silently.

When he thought about leaving Shelby, he felt an emptiness in his heart. He knew their separation was unavoidable, but seeing her again made it so much harder to imagine being without her. Could the two of them ever have a future together? He didn't know how such an eventuality was possible, but he held on to the hope that he would figure out a way to keep from losing her. It would obviously mean telling her the truth, but he was sure he would find a way to do it, and she would forgive him for keeping his identity hidden.

Eventually, he would need to make some decisions, but for now, he was content to just hold Shelby and feel her soft body melt into his and hope that somehow their relationship would last.

Shelby woke and lifted her head. "Hakim." She turned to face him and blinked. "How long did I sleep?"

"Perhaps an hour. I did not keep track of the time."

"I am so sorry. How embarrassing. I…"

Hakim brushed his thumb across her lips. "Please do not apologize. I cannot remember ever spending an afternoon in a more pleasant manner." Rolling onto his side, he caressed her cheek with his fingers. He stroked her hair, studying her face before he pulled her closer, kissing her forehead, her nose, and finally her lips.

Shelby tickled the back of his neck, sending shivers down his spine. The kiss deepened, and Shelby's hand tightened on his back. Hakim kissed her cheek and felt her tremble when his lips touched her earlobe.

She laid her head back onto his arm, her hair splaying around her head.

"What are you thinking about right now?" he whispered, nuzzling her ear.

Her face reddened. "Do we still have to be honest?"

Hakim ran his fingers over her collarbone. His mind briefly acknowledged the lack of restrictions in America, and how welcome they were. He would never be permitted to take such liberties with a woman in his country. "Definitely."

Shelby licked her bottom lip. "I was thinking your lips are really soft, for a guy, and your whiskers are tickling my face." She traced the hair around his lips with her fingers.

Hakim chuckled as he bent to kiss her again, relishing the sensation of warmth that spread throughout his body.

The afternoon air grew cool. Hakim gave Shelby a piggy-back ride down to the ATV, and they drove back to the ranch. They approached the house and saw a black car parked in the driveway.

"That is Nasir." Hakim drew his brows together. "I wonder what…"

"Go ahead and talk to him, I'll take in this stuff." She indicated the backpack. "Nasir is welcome to stay for dinner." Shelby waved to Nasir, and turned to go into the house.

Hakim caught her arm and turned her toward him. He brushed a kiss on her lips and then strode toward the car.

Nasir stepped out of the driver's seat

Hakim's chest tightened. Nasir was not supposed to be here. His bodyguard would only have changed the plan and acted against the prince's wishes if something were wrong. Five minutes later, Hakim walked up the wooden steps of the front porch.

Nasir followed. "I must insist again that we depart immediately, Your Highness."

Hakim turned, holding onto the wooden railing with one hand. Anger and fear battled inside him, making his stomach quiver. "I will not leave Shelby without an explanation, and again, I wish to speak with her alone."

"I acknowledge your demand, Your Highness, but after what has happened, I will not allow you from my sight."

Hakim turned and ascended the last steps. He remembered how nervous he had been the first time he had stood at this door. That paled in comparison to the stomach-twisting fear he felt now. The front door stood slightly ajar, and Hakim knocked before pushing it open.

Debbie glanced up from where she sat on the couch, folding clothes. "Are you feeling okay, dear? You look a little pale."

"Yes, thank you. I am just a bit tired."

"I'm sure Shelby won't mind changing plans if you aren't feeling well."

"Hey, Hakim." Chet didn't look up from where he was sprawled next to his mom scrolling through the channels.

"Hello, Chet."

Nasir stepped into the doorway, moving behind Hakim.

Debbie widened her eyes.

"Debbie, this is my friend, Nasir." Hakim swept his hand toward the man behind him. He tapped his fingers against his jeans as he looked past her, wondering where Shelby had gone.

"Hello, Nasir." Debbie looked back to Chet. She edged away from the door and toward her son when she saw the large man in her house.

Seeing her nervous behavior, Hakim turned to Nasir and in Arabic asked him to wait outside.

Nasir folded his arms across his chest and shook his head.

Debbie widened her eyes and lifted a hand to the base of her neck as she heard the men arguing.

Hakim said as much to Nasir.

"It does not concern me, Your Highness. I am here to protect you, not the feelings of others."

Shelby entered the room from the kitchen.

Hakim felt a small relief at seeing her, but his anxiety returned when he thought of what he must do.

"Hi, Nasir. My dad's about ready to fire up the grill, then I thought we could check out his Western DVD collection." Shelby saw Hakim's expression and her smile faded. "You okay?"

"Yes," he said. "Shelby, I—" His cell phone rang, interrupting him. "Excuse me."

"Sure."

Hakim stepped back onto the porch. He spoke quickly into the phone, knowing Shelby and her family waited. He finished talking and walked back into the living room.

Nasir closed the door behind them and leaned against it.

Hakim noticed Burke was in the room now, pretending to watch TV with Chet and Debbie, but Hakim knew he was there for his wife and children's protection because of the two foreign strangers in the house. Hakim turned his head until his gaze found Shelby. She had come to rest her hip against the arm of the couch while he was on the phone. He took a few steps closer.

"Is everything okay?" She linked her fingers into his.

He squeezed her hand. "No, Shelby, there is something I need to speak with you about. Can we talk privately?"

The next moment, Chet shouted and pointed

toward the television.

Hakim jumped and whipped his gaze around to Nasir. He knew the big man was on edge, and he needed to stop him before he overzealously tried to protect Hakim from Chet.

But Nasir wasn't looking at Chet. He was frozen, staring at the television.

Chet turned up the volume, and they all watched as Hakim's picture flashed on the screen. The anchor was finishing the story, "...his only son and heir, Hakim Abdal-Salam bin Rashid Al Khalid, is expected to take his place as the ruling monarch. Again, authorities have not been able to identify the source of the explosion, though it's widely believed the *Nahl* group is behind the attack. Sheik Rashid's condition has been upgraded from critical to stable. We will keep you updated as details of this story become available."

An icy feeling filled Hakim's chest.

Chapter Nine

Shelby froze, her mind reeling in confusion. Thoughts flew through her head, and she didn't know which ones to grab onto.

"Shelby," Hakim squeezed her hand.

Chet clicked off the TV, and he and his parents turned to stare at Hakim across the back of the couch. Chet was, for once, completely speechless.

"Shelby," Hakim said again. "Can we talk?"

Nasir spoke in a clipped tone. He grabbed Hakim's arm, pulling him toward the door.

Shaking his head, Hakim said something in an angry voice.

Nasir dropped his hand and stood next to the door, glowering.

Shelby's family gaped through the entire interaction.

Unable to form a coherent thought, Shelby just stared at Hakim. She'd never heard an angry tone from him...and directed at Nasir? She started to understand the dynamic between the two. *Do I even know this man?*

He reached for her elbow.

Shelby's stomach was in a knot. She folded her arms and raised her eyebrows, waiting for an explanation.

"Good luck, dude," Chet muttered.

"Shelby"—Hakim's voice wavered—"I am so sorry. I—"

"So, it's true?" With a shaky hand, she pointed toward the TV. "That news story was really about you?"

Hakim dipped his chin. "Yes, I am the prince of Khali-dar. But I didn't want you to find out this way."

"How did you want me to find out?" She heard her voice had taken on an edge, but didn't care.

"Truthfully, Shelby Jo, I hoped to keep my title from you as long as possible. You were the first person I had ever met who did not know. I did not intend to mislead you. But the longer I knew you, the harder it became to tell you the truth." He glanced toward Shelby's family and frowned.

They watched across the back of the couch.

Shelby glanced toward them and pursed her lips together. Her family was acting like this was some kind of soap opera. *Good. Let him feel uncomfortable.*

"Shelby, you have no idea. Being a regular man meeting a regular woman, and not having her opinion of me biased because of my position was freeing." Hakim lifted her hand.

She jerked it away. "Everything you said about being honest…that apparently just applied to me, right?" Her emotions swung from confusion to anger.

Nasir folded his arms and spoke again.

Hakim silenced him with a glance. "I never lied to you, Shelby."

"So, this was just some kind of game? A little experiment?" Angry tears stung the back of her eyes. She looked away and saw her family still staring. *Maybe they'd like some popcorn.*

"No, truly, everything I said was sincere. I was not lying when I told you how I feel about you."

Shelby tried to sort out her feelings. *Is this for real?* Had she let herself develop feelings for someone who turned out not to be who he claimed? He'd seemed so genuine when he'd told her he cared. He had flown halfway across the world just to see her. Why would he do that if she was just a joke? There had to be plenty of women in Khali-dar, if he was looking for some fun. For all she knew, he had a whole harem. Then why was he here? Why *her*?

"Shelby Jo, please say something."

She studied him for a long time and finally asked, "Is your dad okay? Is he in the hospital?"

Hakim blinked and paused for a moment before he answered. "That was the reason for the phone call. He is safe and recovering."

She nodded, but her anger didn't dissipate.

"Please tell me how you are feeling. What are you thinking?" He reached for her hand again, but rubbed his palm on the back of his neck instead.

"Does it matter?"

"Of course, it matters."

"Hakim, I'm not stupid. Nasir—what is he, your bodyguard or something?" *Duh, how did I not see that?* She flicked her gaze to the larger man. "He's waiting to take you home, and you aren't coming back." Shelby could feel waves of 'I told you so' floating through the air from the direction of her family. "Deep down, I knew this relationship wouldn't end well, but I kept talking myself into believing it could." The tears flowed now, and Shelby swiped them away with her fingers. "I really thought you would never hurt me."

"Shelby Jo, I…"

"Just go, Hakim." She grabbed her crutches and moved to walk away.

Hakim caught her elbow and pivoted around to face her.

Both Burke and Chet stood, frowning.

Nasir moved to stand between them and Hakim.

Hakim lifted up her chin and held her gaze. "I promise, Shelby Jo, I would never intentionally hurt you. Whether you believe it or not, everything I said to you was true. I care about you more than I would have believed possible." He brushed a kiss on her cheek and left with Nasir following him.

Shelby walked through the living room in a daze. Her family still stared between her and the closed door, apparently stunned into silence.

"Too bad he left," Chet said. "I was just thinking of all the fun we could have with his diplomatic immunity."

She could tell her brother's attempted humor was forced.

"Hush-up, Chet." Debbie swatted at his knee and turned to Shelby. "Are you okay, dear?"

Even though her mother's expression was filled with compassion, Shelby only wanted to be left alone. She shook her head and kept going, climbing the stairs to her room. She closed the door and got into her bed without taking off her shoe. Pulling the quilt over her head, for the first time in twenty years, she cried herself to sleep.

****

"I can't believe it, Shel. A real prince. No wonder he acted so classy, and did you notice his posture? And how delicious he smelled? He even had great table manners eating pizza. He used his napkin and somehow managed to look sophisticated drinking out of a straw. That had to be a first for Italian Garden."

"Lace, did you hear what I've been telling you for the last twenty minutes?" Shelby set the mug of hot chocolate on Lacey's kitchen table. "*Who* he is isn't the issue. He misled me."

"Yeah, but Shel, you can see why he did it, right? Can you imagine how he must feel to have people always tip-toeing around all the time because he's royalty?" She wrinkled her nose and smiled to soften what could have been a reprimand. "He knew you liked him for real because you didn't know the truth. I can see why he wouldn't want to tell you."

"Are you seriously taking his side?" Shelby thought if anyone would understand it would be Lace.

"I'm not taking any sides—I just want you to see he's not the creep you're making him out to be." Lacey lifted her hair over her shoulder. "The guy is totally crazy about you. He gazed at you like you were the most precious thing on the earth. He hung on every word you said. He spent the day branding calves to impress you. Knowing who he is now makes everything he did even more meaningful, right?"

"Lace, I rushed over here first thing this morning to get some support." She leaned her forearms on the table. "Or at least some sympathy."

Lacey reached across the table and squeezed Shelby's arm. "I always support you. You can just see the big picture easier when you're not the one in it. Know what I mean?"

"I don't think it matters now, anyway. He's gone,

and after the way I treated him, I'm sure I won't be seeing him again." A lump grew in her throat, and Shelby swallowed hard.

"So, what's your plan? When do you have to head back to your jet-setting life in the big city?"

Shelby smiled at her friend's belief that her life was glamorous. "I called Xan this morning on my way over here and told him I'd take the bus back to Denver tomorrow. But he wants to pick me up. Maybe I'll see if Chet can drive me and meet him halfway."

They drank their hot chocolate in silence for a few minutes, listening to the music coming from the TV in the other room, where Shay watched a movie.

Lacey giggled. "You know what you need, Shel?"

Shelby shot her a questioning look. "I don't think I want to know."

"A fairy godmother. Or maybe a bunch of mice to make you a dress." Lacey couldn't hold her laughter in any longer.

"Oh, brother," Shelby complained, but she allowed a small smile to slip out.

****

Chet pulled his pickup into the small town gas station off the highway, parking it next to Xan's SUV, and grabbed Shelby's duffle bag out of the truck bed.

Xan stepped out of the gas station loaded down with snacks for the road. He balanced drinks and nachos on top of the vehicle and helped Shelby out of the cab before enveloping her in an enormous hug. "I missed you." Xan brushed the hair off her forehead "Wow," he said. "That's a serious battle wound."

"Looks a lot better now," Shelby told him, smiling at his exaggeration.

"How do you feel? How's the foot?" Xan took a step back to inspect her cast.

"Not too bad. This thing comes off in a few weeks, and then I'll start physical therapy." She leaned a hand on the vehicle to balance. "I'll be a hundred percent recovered before the spring ski season is over. I'm excited to get back to work."

Xan turned to Chet. "Thanks for bringing her up."

"Sure." Chet put his arm around Shelby's shoulders and gave her a squeeze. "Take care of her, Xan. She's had a rough time."

Xan raised his eyebrows.

"Headaches," Chet clarified. He gave Shelby a wink, hopped into his truck, and waved his hand out the window as he peeled out on the parking lot gravel.

Shelby smiled and waved back as her brother drove away in his beat-up old pickup with a giant elk decal on the back window and country western music blaring from the speakers. Her family's love enveloped her like a blanket. Sure, they drove her crazy, but she could always count on them when it mattered, which was more than she could say about some people.

Xan put Shelby's duffle bag into the back seat with her crutches and helped her into the car, handing her a fountain drink and fussing over her leg before closing the passenger door.

Shelby thought the extra attention seemed a bit strange, but she couldn't help noticing how good being back with Xan felt. She told him about Lacey's kids and house, her family, branding, but left out Hakim's short visit.

Xan filled her in on what had happened at the office while she was gone and some assignments he had lined up.

"An Olympic speed skater interview? A feature story on a new ski goggle technology?" Shelby protested. "You don't have to baby me, Xan."

"I want to baby you, Shel." He lowered his voice, "I wish you'd let me."

They chatted about mundane things for the remainder of the two-hour drive until Xan parked in front of Shelby's apartment complex.

"Thanks for the ride." Shelby reached for the door handle.

"Hang on, Shel. I want to talk to you for a sec."

"Gosh, don't sound so serious. Are you firing me?" She flipped her hair over her shoulder to show that she was teasing and turned to face him.

"No, I'm not firing you. Just hear me out. We've worked together for two years now, and we've always gotten along really good, right?"

Shelby nodded for him to continue.

"We're great together. We have tons in common. I'm saying I want us to be together. I'm crazy about you." He gripped the steering wheel. "I have been ever since you came to the magazine as an intern. Seeing you laying there in the snow covered in blood...I couldn't wait any longer to tell you."

A heavy pit grew in Shelby's stomach. *Why is he doing this?* "Xan—"

"Shel, I'll do anything for you. I can give you the life you want. Home, family, career, travel."

But not love. Could she ever bring herself to love Xan? The image of Hakim's face swam in front of her eyes, and she knew the answer was no. "Xan," Shelby said, keeping her voice even. "I don't feel that way about you. You're one of my best friends, and I love you."

His gaze was intense as he leaned toward her.

She pulled back and raised her hand between them. "But not romantically."

"I know we belong together. We're perfect for each other."

"I'm sorry, Xan." Shelby pushed open the vehicle door.

Xan gripped her shoulder, turning her toward him. He pressed his lips on hers.

The kiss was warm and nice, and Shelby knew it came straight from his heart. She wished she could return the feelings, but she couldn't. Fire had spread throughout her entire being when she kissed Hakim. Xan's kiss was nothing like that.

She pulled away. "I am so sorry, Xan." Tears filled Shelby's eyes. "You're right, we would be great together. But you're too awesome of a guy to be with someone who isn't crazy about you. You deserve someone who's in love with you."

Xan's expression hardened. "Is this because of your stupid Arab boyfriend?" He spat out the words.

Shelby realized she'd never seen Xan angry before. Her stomach felt like ice.

"I know who he is, Shel. It's all over the news. He lied to you. He didn't care about you. He was playing a game with your feelings." He planted his hand on his chest for emphasis. "I would never do something like that."

Shelby said nothing and got out of the car, a mixture of hurt and anger welling up inside.

With jerky movements, Xan followed, pulling her

duffle bag and crutches out of the back seat.

Shelby reached to take the bag away.

But he started up the steps without saying anything.

She followed him and unlocked her front door, not knowing what to say to make things between them right again.

Xan set her duffle bag on the landing. "I hope you can grow up and realize there's a difference between school-girl infatuation and what we could've had together, Shel."

Shelby didn't say anything as he walked down the stairs to his car and drove away. She realized she'd lost a friend. Swallowing against the lump in her throat, she wiped her cheeks with her sleeve. Her stomach felt heavy, not only because of the tension between them, but how would this affect her job?

Despite it all, when she closed the door, she experienced a sense of release. As she inhaled the familiar scent of her little apartment, she realized something was off. Following the offending smell into the kitchen, she saw the vase full of flowers on her kitchen table. The flowers had died, and the water in the vase smelled rotten. The ache she had pushed away all day returned and infuriated her. Grabbing the vase, she crammed the entire arrangement into the trash can and closed the lid. Her dramatic action didn't really make her feel any better, but at least it helped with the smell.

Chapter Ten

Weeks later, Shelby stepped out into the cold night, closing the door to the bookstore behind her. She zipped her coat and started to walk the few blocks to her apartment.

"Hey, Shel. Wait up."

She turned and inhaled a quick breath when she saw Xan. She wasn't surprised he was there. They had both been excited to attend the X-Games skier's book signing. Shelby was surprised Xan was talking to her. He had scarcely said a word since their little 'incident.'

"What's up?" she asked when he reached her.

"Want a ride?"

"No, my place is close. And the doctor told me I need to keep working my ankle to strengthen it."

"Yeah, okay. I wanted to tell you, I got a weird call today. Some guy with an accent asking a bunch of questions about you."

"What kind of questions?" Shelby shivered in her coat.

"Where you live—he didn't sound like he knew you were local. How to get a hold of you. Stuff like that." He shrugged.

"What did you tell him?" The idea that someone was asking about her made her nervous, but she couldn't quite pinpoint why.

"I told him we don't give out that kind of

information." Xan zipped up his own coat. "Weird, right?"

The tightness around Xan's eyes was at odds with his casual words. He must not think this was a meaningless incident. Shelby didn't answer. Her skin prickled. Something about the exchange felt off.

"I wouldn't worry too much. You're a celebrity now, with the news coverage about your accident, the newspaper interview. Not to mention, the firsthand avalanche survivor article you wrote for *Wintersports* that totally skyrocketed the magazine's sales," he said, with dramatic flair. "Weirdoes are everywhere. I just wanted you to know."

"Thanks." Something still nagged at Shelby, like a thought she couldn't quite grasp, or a rock in her shoe.

"Sure you don't want a ride?" Xan asked.

"Yeah, I'm good." And she was. Aside from a little soreness from time to time, especially during cold weather, she was happy her foot seemed nearly as good as new. Stretching out her ankle as she walked felt great. She was glad she'd worn boots, since snow had started to fall, and the temperature was dropping fast. The weather was typical for spring in the Rocky Mountains—warm for a few days, then with no warning, snow and freezing conditions. Shelby hiked her laptop bag higher on her shoulder, picking up her pace.

Six weeks ago, she had returned to Denver. She hadn't heard from Hakim, but that didn't mean she thought of him any less. She'd even looked him up on the internet. All she'd found were a few news stories, the stock picture of Hakim she had seen on the news, and a grainy picture of him and his father. She enlarged the image to see him more clearly, but the photo had been taken from a distance, and the Sheik's face was partly hidden.

Her heart ached with regret. She wished she could go back and change how she had reacted when he told her his secret. Now she didn't even have the option of apologizing. It's not like his phone number was online anywhere. Shelby tried putting herself in his shoes. How would she have felt? She didn't blame him for not calling her.

Mulling over these thoughts, she climbed the outside steps of her apartment building and reached into her bag for the keys. She spotted her door was ajar and stopped. Her mouth went dry, and she unsnapped the strap on the mace canister hanging from her keychain and reached around the doorframe. She ran her hand over the wall until her fingers touched the switch. Taking a deep breath and holding her mace ready, she flipped on the light.

A hand clamped down on hers, twisted her around, wrenched the mace from her grasp, and pinned her arms behind her back—all in one quick movement.

But her legs still worked, and she wore thick winter boots. She kicked at her attacker's knees as hard as she could and was rewarded with a grunt and felt the grip on her arms loosening. Swinging her elbow, she made contact and spun as fast as she could back toward the door.

The door slammed shut, shattering her hope of escape.

She hadn't seen the other man in the shadow of the hallway. Shelby's heart raced and she darted her gaze back and forth between the two men. Her muscles tensed as she weighed her chances of escape.

"Please come in, Miss Walker," a woman's voice said from the living room. "We've been waiting for you."

The smaller man moved aside, holding his a hand to his ribs.

Shelby saw a woman sitting on her couch and gritted her teeth "Who are you?" She narrowed her eyes and stormed toward the woman.

"Miss Walker, Prince Hakim sent us. He believes you to be in danger." The woman regarded Shelby with a cool gaze.

At the mention of Hakim's name, Shelby's knees weakened. She pressed a hand against the back of the couch to steady herself. "What's going on?"

The woman stood. "As I said, we were sent by Prince Hakim."

Shelby regarded the two men, her breathing returning to normal. The smaller one still rubbed his ribs, and the other pushed his lips together as if attempting not to laugh. All three had the same thick, dark hair and caramel-colored skin as Hakim. The men were dressed in casual clothing, but the woman's pant suit gave her the appearance of someone who would be more comfortable in a board room than sitting on a yard-sale couch in a one-bedroom apartment.

"My associates and I would like you to accompany us somewhere safe where we can talk," the woman said.

Shelby folded her arms across her chest, raising her chin and hoping she projected a confidence that she did not feel. "I'm not going anywhere until you tell me what's happening."

The woman sighed, lowering her eyelids partway and tipping her head forward before taking out her phone. Her manicured nails clicked on the screen. She spoke in another language, before handing it to Shelby with a scowl.

Shelby lifted the phone to her ear. "Hello?"

"Shelby. Are you all right?"

The worried voice was achingly familiar. Shelby sucked in a breath. "Hakim?" Relief washed over her, followed by uncertainty, anger, fear, and a thousand other emotions. "Hakim, what's going on?"

"We must get you somewhere safe. Please. You can trust Shanayze. She will explain everything."

"Shanayze?" Shelby looked at the woman.

Shanayze glanced back and nodded, but continued her quiet conversation with the men.

Shelby guessed Shanayze was in her forties. She seemed irritated to be there and gazed around Shelby's apartment with obvious distaste. Who was she? One of Hakim's friends? "She will explain what?"

"I promise everything will be all right. I will talk to you soon, Shelby Jo."

"Wait, I haven't heard from you in over a month, and you're hanging up without telling me anything?" Panic wriggled inside her stomach.

"Please trust me," he said.

She could hear the strain in his quiet voice before he hung up. "He told me to listen to you." Shelby handed back the phone, trying to read Shanayze's expression, but finding her expression impossible to decipher.

"We will escort you to a secure location. Then we will explain everything, Miss Walker." Shanayze tucked the phone into a pocket of her pantsuit.

"Why can't we talk here? And why did you break into my apartment? Ever hear of calling first?"

Shanayze huffed out a sigh. "Miss Walker, we have no way of knowing if your location is compromised. We believe only a short time remains before people wishing to do you harm will find your address—in fact, they may have it already. I know you have many questions—please, accompany us, and they will be answered."

Shanayze and her friends were apparently not ones for small talk. Shelby followed them to a car, and they rode in silence for the next fifteen minutes, before pulling up in front of the nicest hotel in town. Not exactly keeping a low profile.

The valet opened the doors to let the four out of the vehicle, and Shanayze handed him what Shelby assumed was a tip.

Then the group walked through the large rotating glass doors. A huge chandelier gleamed in the front lobby. Ornate rugs decorated the floor. Carved mahogany furniture, upholstered with beautiful fabrics, was spread throughout the waiting areas. Mirrors and fine art hung on the walls. Shelby would have normally stopped to admire the surroundings, spellbound by the stunning beauty of the place, but under the circumstances, she could only glance around, following Shanayze to the elevators.

The two men stuck close behind.

The vigilant way they scrutinized their surroundings reminded Shelby of the way Nasir had scoped out the snack shop at Bear Creek.

Inside the elevator, Shanayze slid a keycard into a

slot and pushed the button for the penthouse.

After the doors opened, they entered a room with a large seating area. A colorful rug stretched over the floor beneath beautiful tapestry couches. A grand piano stood on one side of the room, and on the other, a glass dining table held a vase full of flowers. To the side was a hall with doors leading to other rooms in the suite. The windows looked out onto what Shelby imagined would be an impressive view of the city, once snow stopped falling.

The group moved to the couches and sat.

Shelby was ready to get some answers and immediately leaned forward in her seat.

Shanayze raised a hand. "Please, Miss Walker. Allow me to explain the situation in which we find ourselves, before you begin to ask questions."

Shelby sat back against the cushions, folded her arms, and waited.

"First of all," she said, "I will begin with introductions. My name, as you know, is Shanayze. These are my associates, Jahmal and Mujir."

Mujir was the larger man. He removed his coat, revealing a bulky and undoubtedly well-muscled physique. His eyes bore heavy lids, giving him a sleepy look. The man who had grabbed her, Jahmal, was much smaller, with a pointy nose and goatee. His dark gaze darted around, alert, watching her.

The men tipped their heads forward in a bow.

"Ahlan wa sahlan," Shelby returned their bow.

Shanayze raised her eyebrows. "As I said before, the three of us have been sent by Prince Hakim. We are under orders to ensure your safety by whatever means we deem necessary."

Shelby opened her mouth but snapped it shut when Shanayze kept speaking.

"I do not know if you are aware, but at the present time, there is unrest in Khali-dar. A radical group, calling themselves *Nahl,* is threatening to overthrow the government. As of now, *Nahl* does not have many followers—however, their methods are quite violent. In English, they would be called terrorists. *Nahl* is the Arabic word for 'bees' because the group refers to their attacks as 'stings.' *Nahl* is unhappy with the Khali-dar government, because they believe Prince Hakim and his father, Sheik Rashid, have become too westernized and are leading the people away from traditional ways."

Shanayze's tone was matter-of-fact, as if she were reciting from a textbook. Shelby struggled to swallow. Was Hakim in danger? She studied Shanayze's expression, wondering about her personal feelings concerning the prince or the state of her country. Shanayze's expression and tone gave nothing away.

"Our intelligence has been unable to locate the leader of *Nahl,* or to locate their headquarters. We have, however intercepted various communications. One communication mentioned Prince Hakim had spent time with a woman in the United States." Shanayze raised a brow and straightened her glasses. "We believe the recent interview you gave to the newspaper about your accident, naming your friends, 'Hakim and Nasir' may lead to the discovery of your identity. Prince Hakim and his personal guard, Nasir, fear your life would be in danger, should *Nahl* find you."

With a sinking feeling in her stomach, Shelby remembered what Xan had said about the phone call. Were they searching for her? "But, why would they want me?" Shelby asked. "That possibility seems ridiculous. I have no influence over Khali-dar's government."

Shanayze lowered her chin and held Shelby's gaze.

Shelby tried not to squirm under the intensity in the woman's scrutiny.

"No, Miss Walker, you do not. But Prince Hakim and his father, the Sheik, are inaccessible. Security has been increased since the attack on the Sheik, and it would be nearly impossible to hurt one of them. *Nahl* understands this, and they also know the best way to force the hand of the prince would be to threaten someone he cares about."

Shelby inhaled a quick breath as her heart pounded, and her stomach churned.

"There have been very similar situations in countries near Khali-dar. One instance in particular had an especially horrific outcome. The heir's betrothed was killed, as was her entire family."

If Shelby hadn't been sitting, she was sure she would've fainted. She put her head in her hands. Her family? If this group found out her identity, it wouldn't take much for them to find her family. "What can I do?" she whispered.

"As of now, we are reasonably sure *Nahl* has been unsuccessful in their attempts to locate you. If they had, we wouldn't be having this conversation. Prince Hakim and Nasir feel the only way to prevent your discovery would be for you to return with us to Khali-dar."

"What?" Shelby's head jerked up and her pulse beat faster. "Leave the country? Didn't you just say Khali-dar was in a state of unrest? What about the police? I'm sure there's some sort of government agency that handles stuff like this, right?"

"Consider what would happen if you went to the police with your concerns. Would they take you seriously? Could they protect you? Do you think you would be safe if you returned to Culver Springs? You'd not only be in danger, but you'd be putting your family in danger, as well."

Scenarios ran through Shelby's mind. Every word this woman spoke took away another one of her options. What could she do? Where could she go? Fleeing the country was not only an outrageous solution, but out of the question. Gathering her thoughts, she said, "There has to be another way. I have a job and a home and a library book that's due in a few days. What about my passport? I don't have any money or clothes." She stood. "I need time to think and figure out what's going on."

Shanayze also stood. "I suggest you sleep on it and make a decision in the morning. I'll show you to a room. Please, make a list of things you need from your apartment. Jahmal and Mujir will return and gather the items. You will be safe here tonight."

"Isn't it dangerous to go back to my place?" She jerked a hand toward the door. "What if *Nahl* has already found out where my apartment is?"

"There is obvious danger, but Jahmal and Mujir have been trained for this type of operation. They will be much more effective without having to worry about protecting a civilian."

So now sending someone to pick up my jammies is an "operation?" The adrenaline pumping through her body had worn off, and she realized how tired she was. "Thanks, Shanayze. You're right. Once I've had a good night's sleep, I'll think more clearly and figure out what to do."

Shelby followed Shanayze back past the elevators and to a hallway. She knew she needed clean clothes, but felt uncomfortable telling strangers where to find her underwear. When she remembered the fresh basket of laundry she had folded and left on her bed, she smiled in relief. They could just grab the whole basket. She also explained to Shanayze, who translated for the men, the whereabouts of her passport, cowboy boots, and library book—she would insist they take her to return it tomorrow.

Shanayze opened one of the hallway doors, revealing a luxurious room with a thick down comforter and pillows piled on the bed. Another door led to an enormous bathroom. "Please, make yourself comfortable. I will bring your things when the men return." She exited the room, closing the door behind her.

Shelby turned on the faucet and filled the deep tub then experimented with some of the bath salts and sank beneath the steaming water. *At last, a chance to think*! She considered her situation as logically as she could. The danger was obviously real. Shanayze was right, she couldn't go home until she was sure her apartment was safe.

Returning home to Culver Springs was also out of the question. Shelby knew if she called and told her parents about her situation, her father would insist she come home, and she wouldn't even consider putting her family in danger.

That left the option of going to the police. Would they help her? Shelby doubted it. They might listen, have her fill out some papers, and then tell her a patrol car would drive by her place a few times a night.

What about the FBI? Or the Department of Homeland Security? Wasn't this the type of thing they dealt with? What would they do? Put her in the Witness Protection Program? Send her to a safe house?

Then she considered Shanayze's suggestion she go to Khali-dar. The idea was terrifying. She had only been out of the country once—to do a story on some Canadian ski resorts. But, the Middle-East? How would she even get there? She had no idea if the money in her checking account would cover something like that. Also, what would she do once she was there? Would she be able to leave?

Hearing Hakim's voice today brought back all the feelings she'd buried since he left. Shelby didn't want the fact that she was dying to see him influence her decision, but who was she kidding? Maybe this was a chance to see how their relationship would play out. Could she forgive him? Her heart beat faster when she remembered the desperation in his voice on the phone. He was worried and he cared about her. Chet's words tickled the back of her mind.

Can I trust Hakim?

She felt like a teenager worrying about seeing her boyfriend at school the next day. Seriously, how could that scare her more than leaving the only world she had ever known behind and fleeing for her life?

Shelby wrapped herself in the thick hotel bathrobe and walked into the bedroom. The basket of her clothes sat on the floor next to her bed. She changed into her pajamas and curled into a soft chair, staring through the window at the falling snow.

What would seeing Hakim again be like? Did he really want her to come to Khali-dar? Or did he feel obligated to take care of her? Did she dare travel to Khali-dar? Could she trust Hakim with her life? Her heart?

Chapter Eleven

Shelby woke and looked at her surroundings, her stomach turning over as she remembered where she was. It hadn't been a dream. The revelations of the night before sank back onto her awareness. She quickly dressed. When she stepped into the main room of the penthouse, she saw Jahmal, Mujir, and Shanayze were already awake.

The three sat at the dining table, which was set with fruit and bagels.

"Good morning," Shelby said.

Both men nodded.

Shanayze motioned to the table. "Please help yourself, Miss Walker."

Shelby spooned fruit into a bowl and sat at the table facing the windows. She had been right about the view. New snow glistened in the early morning light. The storm had cleaned all the pollution from the atmosphere, and the landscape spread out before her, covered in a thick layer of powder. She loved this city.

Shanayze stirred her coffee. "So, Miss Walker, have you reached a decision?"

Shelby swallowed a bite of cantaloupe before answering. "Yes...No. I need to talk to Hakim before I make up my mind about anything."

Shanayze inhaled a quick breath.

Jahmal and Mujir scowled.

145

Shelby realized her mistake. "I mean, *Prince* Hakim. Sorry, I'm not used to using his title. Could you please help me call him?"

"Very well, Miss Walker," Shanayze spoke in a cool voice. "Please give me a moment to see if His Highness is available." She exited the room, leaving Shelby alone with the two men.

The tension in the room was palpable. Shelby grimaced. She would have to remember to be more careful with what she said.

Shanayze returned and handed Shelby a cellphone. She motioned to the two men, and they left the room to give Shelby privacy.

"Hello, Hakim?"

"Shelby Jo. I am so sorry to have put you in this situation."

A wave of relief washed over her at the sound of his voice, followed by a tightening in her chest as her frustration surfaced. "Hakim, this is ridiculous. I don't know what to do. I needed to talk to you."

"I cannot imagine this is easy, but I promise you will be safe in Khali-dar."

His voice was calm, but she heard an undertone of worry. "Shanayze told me about the problems over there. I just don't understand. How could I be safe there? How could traveling to Khali-dar keep my *family* safe?"

"This *Nahl* group, they hope to intimidate me by threatening the people I care about. If you are here, they will be unable to have access to cause you any harm. Once it is known you are in Khali-dar, your family will also be safe. Nasir is certain they have still been unable to find you, and once an announcement is made you are gone, they will stop searching in Colorado."

"So, I just leave behind my life and become a refugee in a foreign land indefinitely? That can't be the only feasible option. It's insane." She paced in front of the window. "What about my family? My apartment? My job?"

"I promise this situation will not be forever. We are getting close to eradicating this threat completely. The last thing I want is for you to be unhappy. Please. Trust me. To me, your safety is the most important thing. And you will love it here." He paused. "Shelby Jo, I must admit I also have selfish reasons for wanting you to come."

Hearing the softness in his voice, Shelby felt her anxiety calm. She sat on the couch and rested her forehead in her palm. She breathed for a moment before speaking, and when she did, she whispered. "I'm scared. Not just about this *Nahl* group or traveling halfway around the world." Shelby was unsure of how to continue. "The way we left things, I…I was so angry and hurt. I don't know if I'm ready to handle being with you again."

"Please, can we try? Let me protect you."

"I don't know." Shelby ended the call and leaned back her head onto the cushions, her mind a blur. Who could she talk to? After a few minutes, she stood, set Shanayze's phone on the table, and walked back into her room. Shelby had left her phone charging on the nightstand. She turned it over in her hands while she was thinking.

She couldn't call Xan. *Why did he have to go and ruin a perfectly good friendship?*

Lacey? This was too much for her to handle. She

had a family to think about. Even knowing about this might put her in danger.

Finally, Shelby made up her mind and called home. "Hey, Mom." Shelby swallowed her anxiety, trying to sound excited. "I actually called to tell you some news. Hakim invited me to go visit him in Khali-dar...and I accepted."

****

After hanging up the phone, Shelby took a few minutes to get a grip on her emotions. She entered the main room and found Shanayze at the table, working on her laptop.

"Well, Miss Walker? Have you reached a decision?"

"I don't really have any choice, do I?"

Shanayze nodded once. "His Highness will be pleased to hear you are coming."

Shelby studied the other woman's face, but it revealed nothing. "What do I need to do?"

"There are some security measures we need to have in place. However, I think we should be ready to leave in a few hours."

"Today?" A fluttering started in Shelby's belly. "Don't we need to figure out flights and things like that?"

"Miss Walker, I assure you, everything will be taken care of."

Two hours later, Shelby was riding in a limousine with Shanayze and the two men. She had left her library book with the concierge, who promised to make sure it was returned.

Mujir brought her basket of clothes, which the driver loaded into the trunk.

Shelby kept her laptop bag. She packed her wallet, cellphone, camera, and passport inside, planning to guard them vigilantly on what would probably be a crowded flight.

Nearing the airport, Shelby noticed the driver took an unfamiliar exit. She had only been to the airport a few times and assumed he knew a different route. The limo, however, pulled up in front of a building Shelby didn't recognize. She looked out the window at the large non-descript brick warehouse and read the sign: "Billion-Air."

The driver steered toward a gate leading to the runway.

But Shanayze leaned forward and pointed through the windshield toward the front doors. "Please drive to the front of the building. Thank you."

When the driver stopped, Jahmal and Mujir went inside, leaving the women in the car.

"Aren't we going to the airport?" Shelby asked Shanayze as she gazed around at the unfamiliar place.

"This is the FBO where we will board our flight."

"FBO?"

"I believe it stands for Fixed Base Operator. A private airport."

Jahmal and Mujir returned, nodding to Shanayze. They held the doors while she and Shelby got out of the limo and entered the building.

Inside, Shelby saw lounges with TVs, work stations, and a bar serving drinks and snacks. Conference rooms, desks for various limousine and car rental services, and a small gift shop branched off of the main room.

Shanayze led them to a desk where a woman with

curly red hair and glasses waved her over.

The woman maneuvered around the reception desk. "The G-650 is fueled and equipped for flight. The plane has remained under guard, per your request, in the hangar. Your pilots are making their final inspection, now. Follow me, please."

"Thank you," Shanayze said.

The group walked through the lobby through a set of double doors leading into the main hangar. They continued past various private and charter jets.

Shelby didn't know much about planes, but she could tell these must have been top of the line. Mechanics serviced some of the planes, while catering companies loaded others. Some planes were even being meticulously cleaned and detailed.

The red-haired woman led them straight to the area with the largest planes. When one of the pilots saw them approaching, he opened the door, lowering the boarding stairs. Mujir climbed the steps first, carrying Shelby's laundry basket which he stored in a closet near the front of the plane.

When Shelby stepped into the Gulfstream, she gasped. Instead of the hundreds of uncomfortable seats she expected to see, the plane was filled with leather couches and plush recliners. She walked through the small kitchen area. Bowls of fruit sat in depressions cut out of the granite counter next to a sink. Crystal goblets hung above the bar, held in place with a latch to prevent them from falling during the flight. A long console running up the side of the plane held a large flat-screen TV, flanked by vases of fresh flowers. Stepping on the thick carpet, Shelby brushed her hand along one of the ornate mahogany tables in between the leather chairs and couches. The plane's interior was like something straight from a movie. Instead of setting her at ease, the luxury made her realize just how out of her element she was.

The pilot stepped into the plane behind them, speaking to Shanayze in Arabic.

"We are cleared to take off immediately," Shanayze told Shelby. "If you'd like, the attendant can put your coat and bag in the closet. Please, make yourself comfortable."

The flight attendant wore a professional-looking black uniform, complete with a small hat. Sheer fabric hung from one side and wrapped around her neck like a scarf. The headpiece reminded Shelby of a genie. The flight attendant took her coat, but Shelby held on to her laptop bag.

Jahmal and Mujir sat in chairs near the back of the plane.

Shelby chose a recliner across from Shanayze. A table separated them. Her seat faced the back of the plane. Through the window, she saw people scrambling around inside the hangar, preparing for the plane to take off. She reclined back in her chair. "How long does it take to get to Khali-dar?"

"We should arrive in approximately sixteen hours."

After take-off, Shelby made herself comfortable. She and Shanayze both set their laptops on the table. Shelby found she could connect to the internet, so she spent a long time composing a letter to Xan. She struggled over what to say. How do you tell your boss your boyfriend's kingdom is in danger, and you must flee from evil terrorists to protect your family? She finally told him Hakim had invited her to come for a visit, and she wasn't sure when she'd be back. Xan would obviously be angry. When she returned, she didn't entertain any hope of having a job. During the flight, she finished up a few articles and sent them off.

Being Saturday, Xan was most likely snowboarding and wouldn't check his e-mail until Monday morning.

By then, she hoped to understand her situation better. Shutting her laptop, Shelby reclined in the soft cushion of the chair. She noticed Shanayze had also finished working. "Shanayze, what should I expect when I arrive in Khali-dar?"

"You will need to be more specific."

"What will people think of me being there? Is there anything I should know? How should I act?"

Shanayze considered her for a minute before answering. "It is obvious you are very important to the prince. That being said, we still live in a very traditional culture. Don't be offended if Prince Hakim does not show any type of affection in public."

Shelby nodded. "Okay, what else?"

"In the palace, there is a women's section. That is where you will sleep. For the prince to come to your quarters would be inappropriate, or for you to visit him in his. You will meet in the common areas."

The way Shanayze watched her after she spoke seemed as if she expected her words to come as a surprise. But Shelby remembered this sort of thing from her Middle Eastern Studies class.

"The rules are not as strict as they once were," Shanayze continued. "I do not believe you will be required to have a chaperone, especially at the palace, although Prince Hakim's bodyguard will always remain near."

Shelby felt a tinge of nervousness at the idea of seeing Nasir again. She schooled her expression. The last thing she wanted was for Shanayze to see anything less than confidence. "I'm sorry, I never asked you what your job is."

"I am Prince Hakim's personal assistant," Shanayze answered, squaring her shoulders.

He sent his secretary *to rescue me?*

"Do many people work at the palace?" Shelby asked.

"Many are required to keep the palace and the government running smoothly. Several servants live at the palace full time, and others return to their own homes at night." Shanayze slid her laptop into the bag next to her chair. "But aside from the servants and the occasional guest, the only people living in the palace are Sheik Rashid and Prince Hakim."

"What's the Sheik like?"

Shanayze's expression did not change, but she raised her chin as she spoke. "He is a great ruler. He has foresight and is leading our country toward modernization. While remaining respectful of the old traditions, he is open to new ideas. The Sheik is quite beloved by his people. Until these recent problems arose with *Nahl*, he was known to drive himself through the city with only his bodyguard. He is very much in touch with his subjects."

"I meant, what's he like as a person? Will he be upset that I'm there?"

"I believe he will respect the wishes of his only son. Other than that, I cannot assume to know what His Majesty's feelings will be."

Shelby got the impression Shanayze wasn't telling her the whole story. She didn't seem to want to share opinions or any unnecessary information. Was Shanayze just being careful? Or would Shelby be in the palace against the wishes of the Sheik? The twinge of unease was growing. "Thanks."

Shanayze dipped her head slightly.

Shelby took the gesture to mean that the conversation was over. She was glad. Everything Shanayze said about the palace just seemed to increase Shelby's tension.

The flight was peaceful and uneventful, but extremely long. They landed in Miami for half an hour to re-fuel.

The flight attendant, Hadara, offered her a platter set with a different arrangement of food every few hours. She dimmed the lights.

Curled up in a plush, furry blanket, Shelby sampled a few bites but had no appetite. She watched a few movies, but found herself barely able to concentrate on the screen as she worried about her unknown future. After hearing Shanayze's warnings, she felt even more nervous about seeing Hakim. How would he act? How should she act? She didn't want to embarrass him by saying or doing the wrong thing. What would staying in a palace where everything was so different be like?

Chapter Twelve

Hours later, Shelby cracked her eyes open when someone shook her shoulder.

"We're landing," Shanayze said.

A jolt of anxiety shot through Shelby.

Shelby gazed out the plane window and admired the city built along the ocean. Filled with skyscrapers, it looked like any modern city in the U.S. Boats and ships of all sizes floated off the coast. The city was bordered on one side by water and surrounded on the others by endless sand.

"Over there are the palace grounds." Shanayze pointed to the largest green area in sight.

Perfect location, close to, but away from the city. Roads lined by green trees connected the various buildings which dotted the grounds. Near the largest building, which Shelby assumed was the palace, was a sizeable body of water. A small pond or a huge swimming pool? How could there be so much water in the middle of the desert? She smiled as she remembered Hakim saying, "Khali-dar is an amazing place."

The plane landed smoothly, and Shelby said goodbye to the pilots and Hadara. Stepping out of the door, she choked on the heat radiating from the runway below. The sweater and jeans she wore caused her to start sweating instantly. As she followed her down the stairs to a waiting limousine, Shelby looked enviously at Shanayze's button-down silk blouse and flowing skirt.

Security guards with machine guns stood near the hangar and next to the limo. Shanayze spoke to them for a moment. Shelby, Shanayze, Mujir, and Jahmal climbed into the vehicle, the driver closed the door and then drove them through the city. Shelby was disappointed that nobody asked to see her passport, and she made a mental note to ask Hakim about getting it stamped.

All these thoughts flew out of her head as Shelby stared out the window, awestruck. The city was a blend of old and new. Huge, modern skyscrapers loomed over mosques with prayer towers and market stalls overhung with woven canopies.

Men wearing traditional white *dishdashas*, long shirt-dresses, with their heads wrapped in checkered cloth *keffiyehs*, mingled among people wearing business suits and casual clothes, who appeared as though they belonged in any city in the world. Many women wore head scarves, and Shelby even saw women wearing *burqas* over their entire bodies, their eyes peeking through a crocheted screen. She glanced at Shanayze. "I hope it is not offensive. I have just never understood why women must dress like this."

"In Khali-dar, women are not forced to wear a *burqa*. Many Salifi Muslims believe a woman's face is *awrah*," Shanayze explained. "*Awrah* means the parts of the body which should not be shown in public. This is an expression of their *hijab* or modest behavior."

"So, some women choose to cover their faces?" Shelby squinted her eyes in confusion. She thought they looked like ghosts.

"Yes. They see it as a symbol of devotion, not oppression. Women in Khali-dar are treated better than in many countries. They are allowed to drive and to have jobs and can even attend a university if they can afford it. The unfortunate thing is there is no women's university nearby. Sending away daughters for an education is expensive, and the cost is too much for most families."

"I'm surprised they can't just go to the same school as the men."

"While Khali-dar continues to move toward western ways, there are still traditions that remain unchanged. That is one."

"Oh." Shelby still felt baffled and turned her gaze back through the window. The city glittered, beautiful and clean with fascinating architecture. Plain buildings were not allowed, it seemed. Stone lattice work covered many of the windows in small, traditional-looking houses. But the tall, modern structures interspersed between them provided a unique contrast.

"We are approaching the palace now." Shanayze pointed toward the windshield.

The limousine drove toward a giant marble arch forming the entrance to the Sheik's compound. On top, statues of horses were sculptured in various poses. Inside the arch, between two guard towers, a pair of iron gates swung open. Forbidding stone walls stretched along either side, surrounding the property. As they passed through the gates, Shelby saw armed soldiers standing guard. The sight sent a chill over her skin. The limousine drove down a road lined with palm trees and immaculately trimmed hedges.

"Miss Walker, I would like to remind you about

the importance the royal family places on maintaining its image. Please exercise restraint, and respect the customs of our people. Proper etiquette would forbid any type of public display of affection."

Shelby narrowed her eyes. *Exercise restraint? Does Shanayze think all Americans are depraved cretins, unable to control themselves?* She bit the inside of her cheek to keep quiet. Possibly because they had been in close proximity for the better part of two days or the fact that she was exhausted, but Shelby was pretty sure she wouldn't be able to "exercise restraint" over what she said the next time Shanayze hinted she didn't know how to behave in a civilized manner.

The road widened, revealing the Sheik's palace. The vehicle stopped in a large curved driveway.

Shelby gasped, unable to believe the sight before her.

The driver opened the limo door, and Shelby stepped out, her neck craning as she took it all in.

Water sprayed in elegant arches from hidden fountains. Peacocks and other exotic birds strolled the lawns. Pillars, topped with large pots overflowing with greenery and flowers, lined a wide walkway the width of a city street which led to an enormous, elegantly arched entrance. Beautiful, hedge-lined gardens filled the grounds.

The view of the palace held Shelby spellbound. The white stone of the building was a canvas displaying balcony railings, carved with intricate geometric designs. The same arch, curved with a point at the top, surrounded all the windows. Shelby could barely see the roof of the palace where three gold domes—the largest in the center—crowned the elegant structure.

She stood still, completely dumbfounded. When it came to the size, she had no point of reference. A hospital? Airport? Casino? She had simply never seen any place as imposing.

Captivated by her surroundings, she took a moment to realize Hakim strode down the walkway, dressed in khaki slacks and a light blue tailored shirt. Shelby became painfully aware that she wore an old pair of jeans and a sweater she'd slept in. She couldn't even imagine how her hair looked. On the plane, she had attempted to pull it back into a ponytail, but she knew the humidity had not done her curls any favors. Her appearance wasn't helped because she couldn't stop sweating, either. Shelby waved shyly at Hakim, unsure of how to approach him.

He rushed toward her, relief evident in his face, taking her hand in both of his.

His touch made her skin tingle. Shelby glanced toward Shanayze, who raised her eyebrows in what was quickly becoming one of Shelby's least favorite expressions, but said nothing.

"Shelby Jo, I am so pleased that you came." He took a step back and glanced at her leg. "And your ankle has healed."

Torn between wanting to throw her arms around him and throttling him, but remembering what Shanayze said, Shelby settled on a simple smile.

Hakim maintained his hold on Shelby's hand and turned his attention to the people around him, speaking in Arabic.

Shelby watched the way they all bowed and scurried off to whatever task he had assigned. The way Hakim spoke softly and still commanded respect from people impressed her. In a moment, only Shanayze remained.

Hakim had obviously not heard the lecture about public affection from Shanayze since he continued to hold Shelby's hand. His touch was comforting, but she hoped nobody would think less of him for not behaving in accordance with the country's traditions. They strolled along the patterned bricks of the walkway. She noticed how quiet the palace was. Even this close to the city, the noise was unable to penetrate the walls and foliage. They climbed the wide stairs, stepping through the arched entrance.

Shelby's mouth dropped. Beneath the large, domed roof, the entrance hall soared at least ten stories high. An elaborate mosaic decorated the inside curve of the ceiling. She craned her neck, trying to see it all. Large pillars and potted palm trees surrounded the room which was easily bigger than her high school gymnasium. A colorful, thick rug stretched across the white marble floor, nearly reaching the pillars. Shelby couldn't help but wonder how long vacuuming a carpet that size took.

Hakim led her through a pair of pillars to where a grand staircase curved upward. The stairs were made of the same white marble as the floor. On the other side of the entrance hall, an identical staircase mirrored it.

Shanayze had disappeared, giving the pair privacy.

Hakim wrapped his arms around her. With a sigh, he drew her close and kissed the top of her head.

Shelby noticed the dark circles under his eyes. She breathed in his smell and rested her head against his chest. She wondered about all he had dealt with over the last few weeks with his father's health and terrorists threatening the safety of his people and himself. The simple embrace soothed away some of her worry. But she still felt shy and unsure of how to act *here*, and with *him*.

Taking a step back, he curled a finger under her chin to lift her face. "You have not said a word since your arrival, Shelby. Is everything all right?"

Heat from his touch spread over her skin. "I'm just overwhelmed. I mean, you *live* here?"

Hakim smiled. "I have missed you, Shelby Jo Walker." He rubbed her cheek with his thumb. "I am so relieved to have you safely in Khali-dar." He glanced behind her, and without releasing his embrace, said, "I am sure you are tired and anxious to wash up after your flight. Shanayze will show you to your room. I was hoping you would join me for dinner in an hour. I would love to give you a tour of the palace."

Shelby bid him farewell and followed Shanayze up the massive staircase, marveling at the grandeur of the palace. It was unlike any place she had seen before, and she felt as if she shouldn't touch anything. The railing was carved with delicate gold-leafed patterns. As Shelby ran her hand over it, she wondered what a childhood would be like, growing up in a place that was more like a museum than a home.

They didn't stop on the first landing but climbed all the way to the third floor. The staircase ended at a wide hall with a tall ceiling. A number of doors led off of it. Sitting areas complete with couches, elegant tables, and potted plants occupied the space between the doors.

Shanayze opened one of the doors and stood aside to allow Shelby to enter the room.

Arched windows stretched from the floor to the

ceiling, taking up an entire wall. A marvelous view of the grounds was revealed between sheer curtains that were pulled back from the windows. Stepping closer, Shelby realized the windows were all sets of sliding doors leading to a private balcony with lounge chairs and an outdoor dining set. She stepped outside. Potted palm trees and lovely plants Shelby didn't recognize softened the edges of the stone patio. On the table, beautiful flowers spilled over the lip of a large vase.

Walking back through the doors, Shelby paused again, drinking in every detail of the incredible bedroom. This one room was larger than the entire main floor of her parents' house. She couldn't believe all of this space was intended for just her. Intricate wood carvings separated the walls into sections. Between them hung various pictures, and one panel contained a large flat-screen TV.

Shelby spent a minute admiring the artwork. One painting depicted a beautiful woman sitting beneath a tree, her head tilting demurely. Her graceful fingers held a guitar-shaped instrument. Shelby guessed she was a queen because of her gold headdress. Another picture which caught her eye showed a lion with his front paws on a tree, reaching toward a bird that wore a necklace. Shelby wondered if the lion was trying to get the necklace or eat the bird.

A sitting area with soft couches and ornate chairs sat on a plush rug near the door to the hall. An alcove held a dark wooden desk.

"Prince Hakim wanted me to check with you before a computer was ordered. Do you have a preference?" Shanayze asked.

"Oh, I have my laptop here." Shelby opened her

bag and set her computer on the desk.

"Of course." Shanayze rested her gaze on Shelby's old model laptop with ski resort and University of Colorado stickers on the case. "I will make sure to get a voltage adapter."

Shelby knew she should feel more grateful for Shanayze seeing to her needs, but the woman's cold manner made her feel as though she was more of a burden. She got the impression Shanayze did not approve of the situation, "Thanks."

"You will be set up with an untraceable internet connection. The prince has given instructions that you should have the freedom to keep in contact with your family and friends. However, I would like to remind you to be careful. Do not give out any details of life in the palace which might jeopardize security. Do not mention the prince or his father by name, or discuss threats to the country, or any other political matters."

The reminder of the danger that had sent her cast a pall over the enchantment she felt at her surroundings. Shelby wasn't here on a luxury vacation and the realization made the warm, sunny room feel cold. "Got it." Shelby nodded. She turned away from Shanayze, hoping her expression did not show her apprehension, and continued to walk around the room

Aside from the desk, other tables and chairs and furniture were spread tastefully around, flower arrangements occupied nearly every flat space. The focal point of the room, however, was the magnificent bed. Carved wooden posts rose from each corner and attached with arches, forming a high canopy. Sheer curtains fell from the cross-bars, gathered and tied with golden tasseled rope. The bedding and pillows were made of a crimson and gold brocade pattern, and bordered by a soft fringe. Shelby ran her fingers over the bedspread. She noticed a digital clock on the nightstand next to the bed. The time was nearly three o'clock.

"In here is your bathroom." Shanayze opened a door. "And through here is the closet. Per Prince Hakim's instructions, a wardrobe has been ordered."

Shelby raised an eyebrow. The delight at what Hakim might have chosen for her mixed with unease. She was not used to being spoiled and didn't like the feeling of not having any control over her situation.

"I believe the prince was unsure if you would know what type of climate you would be dressing for." Shanayze flipped on the light switch, illuminating the large walk-in closet.

Shelby stepped past her. The closet was big enough to park her car in. The racks were filled with hanging clothes. Shoes, belts, scarves, jewelry, and other accessories filled the shelves and hung from hooks. Touching one of the soft summer dresses, she felt a thrill of excitement at all the beautiful light clothing. She was flattered and grateful Hakim had gone to all of this trouble, but she also felt an emptiness grow in the pit of her stomach.

How long does he think I'll be here? How could I ever reciprocate something like this? What does he expect? Her laundry basket sat on a plush bench in the middle of the closet. Behind the clothes, the closet walls were lined with mirrors, making the space appear even bigger. And among all of this opulence, Shelby felt even smaller.

She walked into the bathroom and admired the

jetted tub and marble counter with two gold sinks and an elaborately framed mirror stretching across the entire wall. Above her, a window, detailed with delicate ironwork and set with frosted glass, took the place of the ceiling. A soft light shone through it, setting the entire bathroom aglow. When Shelby reentered the bedroom, she saw a young woman standing by Shanayze.

"Miss Walker, this is Aaliya. She will be your personal attendant. Please feel free to ask her for anything."

Aaliya bent forward in a small bow.

"I will leave you to get ready and return in forty-five minutes to escort you to dinner," Shanayze said, looking down at her watch.

"Thank you, Shanayze," Shelby said, and she meant it. Even though Shanayze was not a warm person, and obviously not thrilled about her assignment, she had made Shelby's transition easier.

Shanayze bowed and left Shelby alone with Aaliya.

Aaliya was young and very beautiful. She moved gracefully with amazing posture. Her heart-shaped face held large dark brown eyes. She had flawless mocha-colored skin, a straight, thin nose, and long hair, braided into a rope down her back.

Aaliya walked toward the bathroom. "You will want to wash after your journey. May I draw you a bath?" The young woman's voice was soft and rose and fell in melodic tones.

"No thanks. I can do it myself."

Aaliya inclined her head and smiled. "I will give you privacy, then." She stepped out of the bedroom.

Shelby indulged in a long shower, trying to wash

away the aches and tiredness of travel. She tested out some of the fancy salon products on her hair, and instead of pulling it back into a ponytail, left it down, preferring to let it curl naturally, instead of fighting it in the humidity. Choosing a summer dress and strappy sandals, wishing they hid her scars better, she dressed and then studied herself in the mirror. Even wearing beautiful clothes, she still felt like a country girl—out of place in these stunning surroundings.

Aaliya knocked softly, and then entered the room carrying a plug adapter which she set upon the desk next to Shelby's laptop. She bowed her head. "Is there anything I can do for you, Miss Walker?"

Shelby shook her head. "Thanks, Aaliya. I think I'm ready."

Aaliya stepped next to Shelby and studied her in the mirror. "You look very beautiful."

"Thanks." Shelby chewed on her lip. She wondered if it was part of a personal attendant's job description to say stuff like that. Standing next to Aaliya, she felt big, awkward, pale, and freckled.

"I'd better send my parents an e-mail before I forget." Shelby turned toward the table. "They'll be wondering if I made it."

With Aaliya's help, she set up her computer, followed the onscreen instructions to make the wi-fi connection, and typed a quick e-mail to her mom. She hit send and a pang of homesickness stung her throat. She closed her laptop, hoping everything was all right back home.

Aaliya sat, waiting. When the computer lid clicked, Aaliya stood. "Is there anything else I can do to make you comfortable?"

Shelby took a breath to calm her voice. She swallowed the lump in her throat and smiled. "No, everything is great, Thank you."

"What type of drink would you like when you retire?" Aaliya asked.

Shelby was not certain how to answer. "Um…how about hot chocolate?"

Aaliya raised her eyebrows.

"What? Did I say something wrong?" Shelby asked, cringing. Had she already offended Aaliya?

"Miss Walker, Khali-dar and the entire Middle East are famous for its fragrant, delicious coffee," Aaliya said.

"Oh, sorry. I didn't mean to offend you. Hot chocolate just reminds me of home."

"Then, serving hot chocolate will be my pleasure, Miss Walker." Aaliya bowed.

****

Shanayze returned right on time and held open the door.

Shelby followed her down the staircase, through the grand entrance hall, and out to the garden.

Hakim stood as she approached.

The sight of him made her heart trip. *How can something as simple as a necktie make a man so handsome?* Shelby was glad she had put on a dress.

He smiled and motioned for her to sit across from him. "Thank you, Shanayze."

Shanayze inclined her head and left.

A man dressed in black slacks and a collarless shirt beneath an embroidered vest stepped forward to push in her chair when Shelby sat. He unfolded a napkin and draped it over her lap.

Shelby was reminded of an expensive restaurant on the top story of a hotel in downtown Denver where her parents had taken her after college graduation. Hakim had the same service in his back yard. What must he have thought of her home and their date at Italian Garden? She thanked the server.

The man bowed, averting his gaze.

Her first thought was that he must be uncomfortable, but then she thought he may act this way out of respect like Nasir.

The location was amazing. The table sat under a wrought-iron trellis hung with lanterns. Although the evening was not dark, the lanterns glowed with a golden light. A pond with large koi and goldfish surrounded them on three sides. The water cooled the air, making the temperature nearly perfect. A white tablecloth draped over the round table, adorned in the center with more fresh flowers. Shelby wondered where all of these flowers came from. *Aren't we in the middle of a desert?*

She inhaled deeply and tried to enjoy the setting, but so many thoughts pressed on her mind. Being so far from home, having to flee the country, people who weren't supposed to talk to her, places she wasn't allowed to go, the ambiguity about her role here, a culture she was trying to understand, and the superfluous luxury surrounding her. Topping it off was her uncertainty about her relationship with Hakim and, of course, jetlag. That was enough to make anyone a little edgy.

****

Hakim gazed across the table, utterly entranced by Shelby's beauty. His collar felt too tight. He could not

168

believe she truly sat before him. The lantern lights made her hair glow and her eyes shine. Her remarkable eyes were a deep blue with golden flames surrounding her pupils. An old Arabian proverb declared eyes to be 'the windows to the soul.' Shelby's eyes definitely fit the criteria. They sparkled with joy when she laughed, smoldered when he kissed her, and the last time he had seen her, they'd flashed, fueled by anger and hurt. Hakim had struggled, nearly unable to think of anything else for the past few weeks, and now she sat across the table from him, here, at his home.

What will her eyes reveal about her soul today? "I hope you found everything suitable in your room."

She smoothed her hand over the tablecloth and glanced at him. "Everything is wonderful. Thank you. I don't know how I can ever repay you."

"Shelby, you are under no obligation to me or anyone here. Hospitality in Khali-dar is an important part of our culture. We believe guests are blessings from Allah."

"Well, thank you anyway. Along with everything else you have going on, getting things ready for company must have been a lot of extra work."

When Shelby smiled, he noticed the expression didn't quite reach her eyes. They were dull. *Is she preoccupied? Tired? Angry? Disappointed?* "How was your flight?"

"Nice. I've never flown in a private jet before."

The server returned to fill their drinks and set a platter with sliced cucumbers and pita bread cut into triangles on the table. Small bowls on the platter contained hummus.

Hakim watched Shelby anxiously as she followed

his lead and spread hummus on her bread and bit into it.

Her eyes lit up in surprise.

"I hope you like hummus," he said.

"It's delicious." Shelby spread more onto her bread. "I've heard of it but haven't ever tried it. I always thought it resembled a blob of brown mush, but it definitely tastes better than it looks."

Her honesty made him chuckle. "I am glad you like it. It is a very common Arabian dish."

Shelby grew silent again and kept her gaze on her plate.

Hakim searched for the words to help him figure out why. "Have you heard from your family?"

"No." Shelby's face darkened. "I sent my mom an e-mail a little while ago."

"I am so sorry you and your family have become involved in my problems, Shelby Jo." He reached across the table to take her hand.

Shelby recoiled. "Hakim, do you have any idea what I've been through over the last forty-eight hours?" She jerked her hand away. "I came home to an apartment full of strangers who told me a terrorist group is threatening me and my family. I had to leave my home behind, and I don't know when I can return. You say that I'm your guest, but I am locked inside high walls with guards and security. There are places I am not allowed to go and things I can't tell my family. You're acting like nothing has happened, like I just dropped by for a visit, and we're out here on a date."

The anguished expression on her face made his lungs tight. He had no idea she was hurting like this. "Shelby…"

"Why are we pretending there's no eminent threat

to you or your father or your country or me? In two days, my life has been turned upside down. What will happen when I miss my rent or my car payment?" Shelby's voice rose as she blinked back tears. Her breath came in rapid gasps.

"Shel—"

Her hands were clenched on the tabletop and her cheeks were flushed. "And why didn't you call me? You left almost two months ago, and I didn't hear a word from you."

Hakim stood and walked around the table. He put his hands on her shoulders. "Shelby Jo, listen to me." He knelt so that he was looking into her eyes. "I was trying to protect you," he said in a soft voice. "I knew if *Nahl* discovered you, you would be in danger."

Shelby still breathed quickly then she opened her mouth to speak.

He swallowed hard against his dry throat and pressed his finger against her lips. "For the last month, I have spent every second thinking and worrying about you. I have wanted to call you or to come and find you so many times that I cannot count them. Not knowing if you were safe was torture. I read the articles you wrote for *Wintersports,* hoping as long as you were still working, you were all right." He brushed his fingers over her cheek. "When I heard about the newspaper interview and your television appearance, I knew *Nahl* might possibly link your name to mine. I sent a team to bring you to safety.

"The last time I saw you, you stated you did not wish to see me again. You have no idea how that haunted me. I wish I had acted differently when we first met" Shaking his head, he pushed out a deep breath. "I admit the circumstances that have brought you here are not ideal. But Shelby Jo, please, never believe I did not contact you because I do not care." As Hakim spoke, he could feel the tension leaving Shelby's body as he saw her shoulders relax.

"But what about the terrorists?" she asked. "I'm just so scared."

Her voice had softened and instead of angry, she sounded weary. "You are safe now. Your family is safe." He lifted her hands from her lap and held them in his. "You are not a prisoner. All of the security measures are in place to protect you. Not confine you. Trust me, Shelby Jo. Please?"

Hakim stood, pulling her up. His arms slid around her, holding her against him. She rested her head on his chest. She was so soft and fragile. He was determined to do everything possible to protect her.

Chapter Thirteen

Shelby had never enjoyed a lovelier meal. Delicious food, fantastic setting, and after her meltdown, she appreciated Hakim's efforts to steer the conversation toward neutral, pleasant topics. The sun had started to set, bathing them in twilight. The setting seemed perfect. Once Hakim had convinced her the threat to her family was obsolete, she relaxed and her worry lessened.

After they ate, Hakim stood and pulled back her chair. "Would you like to see the palace?" He lifted her hand to his mouth and brushed his lips over her knuckles.

His whiskers tickled her fingers and the kiss sent goose bumps down her arms despite the warm weather. "I'd love to."

Hakim led her through the gardens, down a different path than the one she had taken with Shanayze. Birds called from the trees above them. As the night grew darker, the garden glowed with beautiful soft lights that added to the ambiance.

"Everything here seems magical," Shelby said as they crossed a small bridge.

They strolled through the gardens, enjoying the quiet of the evening. In the distance, Shelby could see various buildings through gaps in the foliage. She followed Hakim through another entrance back inside, gaping at the amazing detail carved and painted onto every inch of the palace.

Hakim pointed. "Down this corridor are state offices, meeting rooms, and the press release area."

"So, is that where you work?" She took a step down the hall.

"Yes, my office is in this hallway. But let us not waste our time visiting an ordinary office when there are far more interesting things to see."

He led her through another long hall and they turned down another high-arched hallway toward a different wing. "Here is the area of the palace used for entertaining guests."

They walked through a dining room with a table that could easily seat a hundred people. He showed her a theater with both a stage and movie screen. A music room contained every instrument she could imagine and quite a few she had never seen before.

Shelby could feel Hakim's gaze upon her, studying her reaction to everything. He rubbed the back of his neck in a nervous gesture and seemed almost desperate for her approval. She squeezed his hand and smiled to reassure him. *How could he worry about impressing me?*

Another archway led to a hall containing a library that rivaled many museums. Beside the immense number of books, the treasures and history of Khali-dar were displayed. Hakim pointed out especially valuable and significant artifacts and told her the collection contained books in nearly every language.

Shelby made a note to come back when she could spend more time examining everything.

As they admired room after room, Hakim told her

of the history of the palace—what the various areas were used for, when different sections were built, and pointed out pictures and statues, explaining their meanings and origins.

Shelby was overwhelmed with the scope of the history within these walls. He must have considered Culver Springs to be quaint and insignificant since his world was so much wider. Her cheeks tingled in embarrassment at the way she'd given him the tour, bragging about her home town. Her mind buzzed and her muscles ached. "Is it all right if we sit for a minute?" She pointed toward a small couch nestled between pillars and potted palms.

"Of course." Hakim sat beside her on the couch. His eyebrows drew together. "Are you pleased with the palace?"

"I've never seen any place so extraordinary. Every time I look around, the splendor takes my breath away."

Hakim's face relaxed. "Shelby Jo, to me, your opinion is very important. I am so glad you approve of my home."

Shelby studied his expression, wondering how he could feel inadequate. And why was her approval so important? "I love it, Hakim." She smiled, but couldn't hold back a yawn.

Hakim stood and reached for her hand. "I did not realize how late it is. You must be exhausted. We can see more of the palace tomorrow."

Shelby put her hand over her mouth to stifle another yawn. They strolled through the entrance hall toward the stairway where Aaliya waited.

"Goodnight, Shelby Jo." Hakim cupped her cheek in his hand and ran his thumb along her cheekbone.

She closed her eyes, leaning against his palm. The feeling of comfort from his touch pushed away any lingering unease at the strange situation, reassuring her things would be all right. "Goodnight, Hakim."

****

Hakim stood at the bottom of the staircase long after Shelby had gone. He considered the evening with Shelby and its implications. She had placed an enormous amount of trust in him, and he did not take the responsibility lightly.

"Did you have a nice dinner?" a familiar voice asked.

"Good evening, Father." Hakim turned and took his father's arm. "The doctors said you should rest until your injuries are fully healed."

The Sheik waved his hand, shaking off the suggestion. "She is quite pretty, this American girl."

"Yes, Shelby Walker is a lovely woman." Hakim attempted to keep the defensiveness out of his tone. He hated these word games his father played. He braced himself for the lecture he knew was coming.

"It is natural for a man to be charmed by beauty. I assure you the novelty will soon wear off."

Hakim bristled at the condescension in his father's voice. "I know you do not trust American women, but Shelby is different."

"My son, we both know this infatuation you have is nothing more than a passing fancy. I have no doubt you will do the right thing as far as she is concerned."

"Father, you say we must move forward as a nation, that for Khali-dar to modernize and adopt some Western ideals is important. But I am expected to 'form a fortunate alliance within the country's elite inner circle.'" Hakim could feel his voice trembling with rage, but he fought to control it.

"I will not be dragged into this conversation again. I have promised never to force you into a relationship." The Sheik placed his hand on his son's shoulder. "Hakim, you are the only family I have." His voice softened. "Your happiness is important to me. But you also have a duty to your country. As much as we are leaning toward the Western ways of life, we must realize it will be a slow change. Our culture and traditions are very much a part of Khali-dar. It is a balancing act. We, as the leaders of this country, must not lean too far either way. Do you understand?"

"Yes, Father."

"And once the threat to Miss Walker and her family is neutralized, she will be sent back to America?"

Hakim swallowed, feeling the lump growing in his throat, and whispered, "Yes, Father."

****

Shelby followed Aaliya up the staircase with aching muscles. She hadn't realized how tired she was as she dragged her feet and had a hard time keeping her eyes open. The last few days had been physically and emotionally draining, and combined with jet-lag, Shelby felt like a zombie.

When she reached her room, she saw the bed was turned down and lights glowed on the walls. A golden tea set adorned the small table. Steam rose from the spout of the teapot next to a plate of butter cookies. The smell of rich chocolate floated in the air. She thought fondly of her old chipped FFA mug on her draining board at home, rinsed and waiting for a packet of instant cocoa.

"You seem quite tired, Miss Walker. If I am no longer needed, I will leave you now," Aaliya said.

"Thanks, Aaliya. Goodnight."

Left alone, Shelby changed into her pajamas and poured hot chocolate into a delicate tea cup before sitting at the desk to check her e-mail. Her family was safe, Lacey was going crazy for details, and no word from Xan.

Shelby was exhausted, but she couldn't sleep. Even though she sank into a pile of feather soft pillows on smooth satin sheets, she was unable to turn off the churning in her mind. She wanted to blame her inability to relax on the time change, but she knew it was the uncertainty about her situation. At dinner, she'd been calmed by Hakim's words and presence, but now that Shelby was alone, all of the doubts that had overwhelmed her returned full force. What had she gotten herself into? Would she ever be able to return to her normal life in Colorado? Did she want to?

****

Finding herself wide awake in a dark room, Shelby took a moment to remember where she was. A soft breeze blew through the open windows, billowing the curtains around her bed. She stretched luxuriously on the silky sheets and looked at the bedside clock. Two-thirty? Knowing falling back to sleep would be impossible, she wrapped herself in a robe and stepped out onto the balcony. Strategically placed lights dotted the grounds. Shelby wondered if their purpose was aesthetic or security. *Probably both.*

She chewed on her lip as she contemplated leaving her room. She opened the door, peering down the darkened hallway.

"Can I assist you, Miss Walker?"

"Oh, Aaliya. You scared me. Do you just wait out here all night?"

Aaliya laughed. "No, my room is next to yours. I heard you open the door. Is there something I can help you with?"

"Could you show me the way back to the library? I'd like to find a book to read." This was the first time she had asked anyone in the Sheik's household for anything, and doing so made her feel uncomfortable.

"Yes, Miss Walker. As you wish."

As they stepped through the silent arched halls and down the grand stairs, Shelby studied Aaliya. Again, she was impressed by her grace. Aaliya walked with her head held high, her beautiful hair swinging like a rope back and forth across her back.

The hallway finally started to look familiar, and Shelby recognized they were close to the library.

A few yards from the room, Shelby spotted two men, probably guards, step out of the large double doors and speak to Aaliya.

She answered them and when she turned to talk to Shelby, Aaliya was interrupted by a man's voice calling from inside the library.

The guards stood aside.

Shelby followed Aaliya into the room and glanced around to see where the voice had come from.

An older man sat in one of the leather armchairs near a corner of the room. His face was partly lit by lamplight.

Shelby felt sure if he hadn't spoken, she may not have noticed him.

Aaliya bowed and began to speak.

The man held up his hand, stopping her words. He spoke to Aaliya.

Shelby realized he must be the reason for security. He must be important. Who was he? The Sheik? He didn't exactly give off the royal vibe Hakim did. She looked closer, and decided he couldn't be the man from the grainy photograph she had seen on the internet. Maybe he was a librarian. But why had Aaliya bowed? Should Shelby bow to the librarian? Come to think of it, she hadn't asked the rules about who bowed to whom.

"I will return shortly to accompany you back to your room, Miss Walker." Aaliya bowed again to the man, and departed, leaving Shelby alone with the stranger.

The man's cheeks were sunken, giving him the appearance of someone who battled a lingering illness. His beard had started to gray, except for the area above and on the sides of his mouth where it remained very dark. *Kind of a black handlebar moustache.* She found herself unable to determine his age. He sat straight, like a younger man, and his eyes were intelligent and piercing. But his skin was a sickly color, and a cane rested against the wall next to him.

The man observed Shelby for a moment before he spoke. "You are the prince's friend from America."

"Hi. I'm Shelby Walker." She shifted her feet, wondering if she should shake his hand and decided against it. "I'm sorry to disturb you, but I couldn't sleep and came to find something to read."

"I suffer from the same difficulty. Reading seems to be the only cure for my insomnia, as well." He wore a robe and slippers and watched Shelby with narrowed eyes.

She searched for something to say, feeling the need to fill the uncomfortable silence. His staring made her insides squirm. "Do you work here in the palace?"

"Yes." He paused. "Much of my time is spent advising the prince."

She wondered what Hakim thought of his advisor watching him with the same calculating gaze. "The library is wonderful." She waved her hand to indicate the carved shelves which held thousands of books. She noticed ancient manuscripts and parchment illustrations encased in glass. Also, statues, instruments, weapons, and artwork adorned the walls and tables—each containing a unique story. Comfortable-looking leather chairs and sofas were set on thick Persian rugs, begging for Shelby to curl up and lose herself in a book.

The man nodded. "Are you searching for anything in particular?"

"I was hoping to find some kind of history of Khali-dar book. In English. And maybe an Arabic-English dictionary."

"I believe you should find what you are looking for on the shelf below the tapestry. All of the books in that section are written in English." He pointed.

"Thanks." Shelby found the shelf and selected a few books. Standing, she examined the elaborate tapestry. She couldn't believe so much intricate detail could be achieved with pieces of thread. The piece was fascinating. She recognized several elements of the picture: a bird with a jeweled necklace and a lion. "There is a picture like this in my room," she said. "What does it mean?"

He looked at the picture and then at Shelby. "It is a very famous story in our country told to every young child. You would call it a 'fairytale' or a 'fable' in English. Come, sit, and I will tell you the story the way my mother told it." He indicated the chair across from him.

Shelby set the books in a pile on a low table and then slid into the chair.

He inhaled a deep breath and lowered his eyelids before he began. "Long ago, before the time of the great waters, while genii roamed the earth and magic still thrived, there lived a songbird. The songbird had one possession, a ruby which she treasured above anything under the heavens. The songbird wore her ruby on a small golden chain around her neck. She soared through the sky to watch how the sun shone on her cherished possession.

"The songbird was happy. And as songbirds will do, her joy was expressed in melody. Throughout the land, she was known for her exceptionally beautiful voice.

"One day, while traveling through that part of the country, a lion heard her and became enchanted. He searched until he found the bird who sang the loveliest song. From the moment they laid eyes on each other, the songbird and the lion were in love."

Shelby leaned to the side pulling her feet onto the chair beneath her.

"Desiring his beloved for a wife, the lion resolved to live as a bird to be with her. He climbed into her tree and tried to survive on locusts and berries, but he was a lion and could no more live as a bird than he could fly.

"The lion invited the songbird to live with him. She

came into the cave where the lions slept and tried to live as a lion. But she found her wings would get stepped on by the other lions, and she couldn't survive on jackal meat. She was a songbird and could no more live as a lion than she could hunt."

Shelby was entranced by the story. She couldn't remember the last time she'd sat and listened to another person telling her a bedtime story. Surely not in the last twenty years. But under the circumstances it seemed completely natural. Perhaps it was a middle-eastern tradition.

"Determined to be with her true love, the songbird flew into the deepest canyon, farther down into the darkest cave where she finally found a genii and begged him to grant her wish.

"The genii regarded her for a long time with his evil blue eyes and said, 'Anything in this world worth having requires sacrifice.'" He pointed a long, bony finger at the ruby glowing in the light of his magic as it hung around her neck.

"She knew the only way to be with her true love was to give up her cherished treasure. The songbird felt her heart sink but surrendered her ruby to the genii.

"A short time later, a golden lioness ran from the darkest cave and climbed out of the deepest canyon. She ran as fast as she could to find her beloved. As she approached the den, she became afraid—worried the lion would no longer love her now that she had changed. Instead of going into the den, she returned to sit in the shade of her tree. The lioness sang a sad song. She had lost her precious ruby, and now she was sure she would lose her true love."

Shelby knew it was just a story, but her heart was

183

heavy. She credited the strange librarian's storytelling ability.

"Hearing her song, the lion ran to find her. When he saw a beautiful lioness singing with the voice of his songbird, he stopped. At once, he knew what she had done and loved her the more for it. For she was the same songbird. Her ruby was not her only treasure. She had her beautiful voice. And though her appearance had changed, she was still his true love. They were married, and Allah blessed them with happiness and peace."

Shelby straightened. "What a beautiful story."

"In Khali-dar, we believe sacrifice is always necessary. Often we must give up something we want now for something which will eventually be worth more."

"It's hard to know what's worth sacrificing for."

"We can find the answer in the principles governing our lives: duty, honor, bravery, honesty…"

"Love." Shelby spoke in a wishful tone.

He studied her, tipping his head and squinting his eyes.

Had she said something wrong? "Like in the story."

"Yes. There is also Love," he answered. "However, Love is a principle which must sometimes be sacrificed for another."

Shelby nodded, confused. Was he telling her something? Weren't they just talking about a fairytale? The conversation was turning into something else. Who was this guy? And why was he speaking so cryptically? Maybe old librarians just liked to kick around philosophical ideas when they got the chance.

"It's a wonderful story, and the tapestry is

stunning. Do you know who made it?"

He glanced at the tapestry and then held Shelby's gaze for a moment, squinting his eyes before he answered. "One of the wives of Sheik Hussein. It was woven during his reign in the early 1700s. You will read more about him in the book you have chosen." He pointed to the stack of books she held.

Shelby gazed at the books and then back toward the wall before looking again at the older man. "What was his wife's name? Does it say anything about her?"

"This is not America, Miss Walker." He wrinkled his brows into a scowl as he spoke. "Women here do not seek the same status or recognition as Western women. The women of Khali-dar are content to be wives and mothers and leave more worldly pursuits to the men."

Shelby bit her lip to keep from speaking in anger. She knew the Middle East was not the same as America, but the way the man acted made her grit her teeth. Who did he think he was? Is this how all men in Khali-dar felt? Like women were only good for sitting at home making tapestries and having babies? How could he have any idea what the women of Khali-dar thought or how they felt? Her heart reached out to this wife of Sheik Hussein who would only be remembered by her handiwork.

"I see I have upset you," he said. His expression was unreadable. Triumph? Guilt?

"I should be getting back to bed." She stood and glanced toward the doorway for Aaliya. Hugging the books to her chest, she felt completely confused by this entire encounter. "Thank you for the story. And for helping me find these books."

"You are welcome, Shelby Walker. I am glad we had the chance to meet."

"Goodnight." Shelby glanced back once before she followed Aaliya through the dimly lit halls, lost in thought. *Who was the creepy librarian and what did he have against her?*

Chapter Fourteen

Shelby opened her eyes to see the sun already shining through her windows. After following Aaliya back to her room, she had read for a few hours. Rolling over, she saw the clock display read eleven!

She showered and put on a robe she found hanging in the bathroom. When she stepped back into her room, she noticed the bed had been made, and a tray of fruit and bread sat on the small table next to a carafe of juice and a glass. Shelby sat and picked up a note that was lying on the tray.

Shelby,

> *Good morning. I hope you slept well.*
> *After you have eaten breakfast, please join me at the stables. Shanayze will show you the way.*

> *Hakim*

Shelby's heart leapt as she read the note. The idea of seeing Hakim again made her heart beat quicker. She ate quickly and ran a comb through her hair, and then threw on her jeans, boots, and a blouse from the closet. After opening her door, she found Shanayze waiting.

"Good morning, Miss Walker. Are you ready to see the stables?" Her gaze moved over Shelby's clothes.

"Yes. Thank you, Shanayze."

They walked outside, but instead of crossing the

bridge toward the garden, Shanayze led her down a tree-lined road winding in the opposite direction. Large lawns surrounded them as they neared a picturesque building. The structure was all one level with enormous arched doors. Different colors of stone created beautiful designs between the doors and around the high windows. A zigzagging roof line crowned the top.

"Are these offices?" Shelby asked.

"No. These are the stables."

Shelby looked at the sprawling building and thought of the beat-up old barn at her dad's ranch. She couldn't believe this grand structure was used for the same purpose. When they approached the far side of the stables, Shelby saw men tending to the horses.

Some led animals by their reins, while others rode around a track. All of the men working with the horses wore a uniform of black pants and collar-less black button-down shirts.

Shelby spotted Hakim right away. He wore tall riding boots over his white riding pants and a dark blue shirt, and she thought he appeared ready for a polo match. *He's got to be one of the only people who can pull off that outfit and still look amazing.*

He stood with a group of men admiring a beautiful white Arabian mare.

The horse's reins were held by a man wearing a white *dishdasha* and, on his head, a red-and-white-checked *keffiyeh.*

As they got closer, Shelby could see the man's clothes were worn and stained unlike the brighter off-white of the men she had seen in the city. When she realized that the man standing next to Hakim, leaning on a cane was the advisor from the library, she felt her stomach wriggle.

Hakim stroked the horse's neck as he and the advisor listened to the other man. He looked up and saw Shelby and Shanayze approaching then patted the horse and spoke to a man in a black uniform, who took the reins to lead the horse into the stable. Hakim and the other two men strode toward Shelby and Shanayze.

When the men got close, Shanayze bowed and spoke in Arabic.

Both Hakim and his advisor acknowledged her with a nod.

The other man, however, turned away his gaze from the women.

Hakim grasped Shelby's hand. "There is someone I want you to meet." He led her to his advisor who still spoke with Shanayze.

"Oh, we've already met. Hello, again," Shelby waved at the advisor. When she saw both Hakim and Shanayze turn and stare, Shelby was surprised. "I couldn't sleep last night, so I went to the library to find something to read. Your advisor was there, and we talked for a while." She turned to the man. "Actually, I don't think you ever told me your name."

The advisor gave a brief smile.

Shanayze kept staring at Shelby, and the man in the red-and-white *keffiyeh* continued to gaze into the distance.

Hakim cleared his throat. "Shelby, this is my father, Sheik Rashid."

Shelby's face burned, and her stomach hardened. *After all that coaching she'd given on how to act around Hakim, why hadn't Shanayze said anything about meeting the Sheik?* "Oh, sir...Your Majesty, I mean. I am so sorry…I, um—"

"Shelby Walker, I am glad we had the chance to meet." The Sheik held her gaze, but his expression did not change. "I do not think we would have had the same conversation if you had known the truth of my identity. Am I right?"

"Yes," Shelby managed to say. Her mind raced to remember everything she'd said last night. The conversation started to make more sense than she wanted. What was all that about duty versus love? Was he talking about Hakim?

"I was interested to find out for myself what was so special about this girl who my son had to fly halfway around the world to see." This last sentence was directed at Hakim. The Sheik spoke with a smile, but his eyes were cold.

Shelby was sick with humiliation. And also a little irritated. Was it a pattern for the men in the Khalid family to deceive people in order to learn more about them?

Hakim continued to stare at his father. His jaw was clenched and his eyes narrowed.

Shelby could feel tension flowing off him. She wasn't sure whether Hakim was more worried about her or his father saying something else embarrassing.

After an uncomfortable moment, Hakim turned his gaze to her. "Shelby Jo, we have a special visitor to the palace today. May I please introduce Usman bin Abd al Fattah Al Nuaim? He is an emissary from the largest Bedouin tribe in the region, *Al Nuaim*. He has brought a gift."

Hakim spoke to Usman.

Hearing her name, Shelby figured she was being

introduced.

Usman put his hands together, bowing in Shelby's direction. *"Ahlan wa sahlan."*

She noticed as he spoke one side of his face hung limply. She wondered if he turned away because he was embarrassed by this deformity, or if he displayed the same mode of respect Nasir had shown. Shelby bowed and repeated the greeting.

Usman spoke again to the Sheik and Hakim. The three men bowed their farewell, and then he strode to where similarly dressed men waited. The small group walked around the side of the stables to a parking area.

Trucks and horse trailers were parked in the small lot Shelby hadn't noticed before. They were all shiny, expensive trucks, and even though they were across the yard, she could tell the trailers were nothing like the ones her father and Chet pulled. These were clean, tastefully painted, and she saw padding on the walls through the window.

The Bedouin men piled into the one truck that was attached to an old rusty trailer, which looked like it belonged in Culver Springs, and drove away.

The Sheik spoke again. "Please excuse me. I must return to the palace. I see you wore the right boots for riding, Shelby Walker. I hope you enjoy the horses."

Shelby imitated Hakim and Shanayze as they put their hands together and bowed.

He acknowledged them with a nod before making his way back toward the palace, leaning heavily on his cane, accompanied by two guards and Shanayze.

When she noted they were out of earshot, Shelby turned, her stomach burning. "Hakim, I am so sorry I embarrassed you. I had no idea he was your father. I thought he was the librarian or something. I guess I thought the Sheik would be wearing some kind of a crown, not a bathrobe and slippers."

"You do not need to apologize." Hakim led her toward the large stable doors. He darted a look at her. "What did the two of you talk about?"

She could tell he attempted to sound casual, but his voice was strained. "Let's see. He helped me find some books. That's why I thought he was the librarian."

Hakim smiled and nodded for her to continue.

"Then I asked him about a tapestry on the wall, and he told me the fable about the songbird and the ruby. He's a really great storyteller."

Hakim's mouth tightened. "Yes, that is very true. And he loves to use stories to teach a lesson. What was the lesson?"

"Um…well, he implied there are things that should be sacrificed for the greater good. You know, like for duty or whatever." The burning she'd felt earlier eased, but didn't completely dissipate. She hated that Hakim was upset. She saw the muscle in his jaw jump. "Then we discussed women's roles in the Middle-East. Just your basic controversial topics." She looked at Hakim, hoping for a smile. "I'm so sorry. If I had known who he was, I would have handled it differently."

"He loves to play these games with people. Not telling you who he is…it is just like him to try and catch you off guard."

"Yeah, who would do something like that?" Shelby bumped her arm against his to show she was teasing. "Come on. I don't want you to be upset. Will you show me your horses?" Shelby saw Hakim struggling to shake off his annoyance with his father as he led her on a tour of the track.

They arrived at the stable entrance and Hakim held the door, motioning for her to precede him.

Entering the building, Shelby thanked him, then froze mid stride.

Hakim stopped speaking and watched her take it all in.

The stables were unbelievable. The floor was tiled. A four-foot-high white stone wall ran down each side of the room about fifteen feet from the outside wall, dipping to meet the shorter gates leading to the various enclosures. Each animal occupied its own large pen. Although to call them pens seemed wrong to Shelby. They were more like guest rooms. The thing that was so amazing, besides the size and beauty, was how bright and clean the area was. The corners were free from hay or other messes that came with keeping animals.

And the horses. Shelby followed Hakim around the room admiring each of the magnificent animals.

"Some of the horses are for breeding," Hakim explained, "while others are for racing." He grinned as they walked up the wide walkway between the stalls toward the largest pens at the end. "Here are our racers. These two will compete in the Triple Crown this year."

The Thoroughbreds were undoubtedly athletes, tall and slim with long legs made for running. Knowing the rules of the Triple Crown, Shelby knew the two must be three years old. Looking at their muscles, Shelby could tell they were bred and trained to be sprinters. She stroked the muzzle and neck of the black horse nearest her. He had a white star on his forehead that swirled around with the grain of his coat. "How do the horses get to Kentucky?"

"In a special plane. A 747 jumbo jet. They will be leaving soon to become accustomed to the climate and track before they race." Hakim stood behind her and ran his hand down the horse's neck.

"Are you going to the races?" she asked, resisting the urge to lean back against his chest.

"Of course," Hakim tipped his head and leaned forward to look down at her. "And I hope very much you will accompany me."

"To Churchill Downs? Are you serious?" Shelby turned quickly, causing the horse to lift his head, annoyed at being startled. Excitement bubbled up inside her as she realized how soon the derby was. The first weekend in May. That was only a few weeks away.

"I am serious."

"How can you leave when there are these problems with *Nahl*?" She patted the horse to calm him. "Aren't you worried about your safety?" Her excitement ebbed when she remembered the real danger to Hakim, and to her.

"Yes, it is definitely a concern I do not take lightly." Hakim nodded. "However, we must continue to live our lives and not cower in fear, or the terrorists will have won. That is their goal, to spread terror. Safety will be a factor as it always is when my father or I travel. We have very diligent security agents who will do all in their power to ensure our protection."

"Was it a factor when you came to Culver Springs?" She reached to pet a different horse, a dark chocolate one this time.

"Yes, although Nasir would have wished for me to take my personal safety more seriously. He found it difficult to try to protect me when I wanted to spend time with you and your family undisturbed."

Shelby hadn't thought about the danger Hakim had been in when he was in Colorado. "And undercover." Hakim's smile meant her words had their desired result. She was glad they were at a point where they could joke about it.

"Now, Shelby Jo, if you will please follow me, I have one more surprise."

"Better than a date to the Kentucky Derby?" She hoped she sounded excited instead of nervous at the thought of leaving the safety of the palace.

"You must judge for yourself."

They walked back outside to another door in the other side of the building.

"This is where our riding horses are kept."

A young boy, no older than twelve, approached and bowed. Hakim spoke a few words.

The boy hurried into the stable. He returned leading the beautiful white mare Shelby had seen earlier.

She was a stunning Arabian, evidenced by her concave profile, arched neck, and the proud way she carried her tail. From the moment she looked into the mare's large brown eyes, Shelby was in love. She reached out, and the mare nuzzled her hand.

Hakim brushed his hand on the horse's neck. "This mare is named *Al-qamar.* When she was a foal, the Bedouin tribe who owned her claimed she brought them good luck. A mare such as this cannot be bought or sold. She may only be given as a gift. Usman brought her today from his tribe as a show of support for our kingdom."

"She is gorgeous." Shelby stroked the mare's

velvety nose.

"She is for you."

Shelby gasped and jerked her head around to face him. "What? Hakim, you can't just give someone a horse."

"I believe I just did."

"But I can't accept a gift like this." The unease she'd felt the day before returned full force and heat flamed in her face.

He raised his shoulders and squinted his eyes. "I do not understand. Why?"

"Because, I could never repay you." Shelby stared at her hands.

"I do not give you this gift to obligate you." Hakim curled his finger beneath her chin, lifting her gaze to his.

His closeness stole her breath. "I know. I worry that you've done so much for me, and I have no way to do anything remotely as nice in return."

"Shelby, you coming to Khali-dar was the most wonderful gift you could have given me." He dropped his arm to hold her hand. "However, we are wasting time which would be much better spent riding, do you not agree?"

She answered him with a small smile she hoped he understood to mean the conversation was not over.

Hakim spoke to the boy who waited nearby.

He hurried off and returned, carrying an ornate saddle.

"I hope this is suitable. I thought you would prefer a western saddle to an English one." Hakim waved a hand toward the saddle.

"Do you ride those little English saddles?" Shelby

winced. "You better hope Chet doesn't see you on one of those." She sighed and rolled her eyes. "I guess I have my work cut out if I'm to make a cowboy out of you."

Hakim laughed. "Given the chance, I could probably convert Chet to a smaller, sleeker saddle."

The boy laid a colorful, tassel-lined blanket over *Al-qamar's* back and bent to pick up the saddle.

Shelby placed her hand on his arm to stop him.

The boy looked up, his eyes wide in question.

"*Maa 'ismuka?*" Shelby asked his name.

"Kadir."

"*Al-salaam alaykum*, Kadir."

"*Wa alaykum e-salaam.*" He bowed.

"Hakim, would you please tell Kadir thank you, but I can saddle *Al-qamar* myself?"

Hakim spoke to the boy.

Kadir bowed again and stepped aside.

Shelby swung the saddle onto *Al-qamar's* back. She reached underneath the mare and grabbed the girth straps, pushing her knee into the horse's side, to force out the air and tightening the cinch. She took the bridle Kadir offered, and she took a minute to figure out the elaborate gold piece that fit across *Al-qamar's* forehead and the tassels hanging down the sides. After Shelby pushed the bit into the horse's mouth, she fastened the buckle and tightened the leather straps on the side of the mare's head.

Once she was finished, Shelby admired the saddle. The leather work was beautiful and intricate. Sparkling silver and gold metal decorated the area under the seat and glittered its way down toward the stirrups. She had never seen anything like it. She'd always used Chet's old saddle. And even that had been purchased secondhand. Shelby murmured to the animal just like her father always did as she led *Al-qamar* away from the shade of the stables into the bright sunlight where a stable worker waited, holding the reins to a black stallion.

When it saw Hakim, the stallion nickered.

The prince stroked his neck. "This is *Khafif.*" He stepped into the stirrup and, in one quick move, was atop the horse.

Shelby adjusted the stirrup straps and mounted *Al-qamar* in a smooth motion. From her new vantage point, she glanced around, noticing the Sheik and his guards. She tightened her hands on the reins.

He sat under an awning on the far side of the stables.

Hadn't he said he was going back to the palace? Was he keeping an eye on her? She wondered if Hakim had seen him, but decided not to mention it.

They rode around the track a few times in order for Shelby and *Al-qamar* to get used to each other. The horse was well-trained and eager to please, and Shelby was a good rider.

"This is my favorite trail," Hakim told her. The horses ambled side by side up a slight incline until they reached the top of the hill.

Shelby admired the view. Behind them, she could see the palace, and in the distance, the skyscrapers of the city. In front of them, the path followed the lawn and then wound through trees until it disappeared from sight. Although she knew they were inside high walls, she couldn't see them. She felt exposed, nervous that the terrorists might see them in such an open space.

"How big is this property?"

"Nearly five miles across," Hakim said. "This is the edge of the tended gardens. Ahead is a sort of wilderness, though it has been somewhat tamed. The gardeners water the trees and keep the paths clear."

"Are wild animals in there?" Shelby asked.

"Yes, but nothing larger than a hare. My father and I often bring birds here to hunt."

"Let's check it out then." Shelby urged her horse down the path, breaking into a gallop.

Hakim chuckled as he followed her down the hill, passing her easily. When they reached the trees, the horses slowed and Hakim led the way. "Was that another race?" He turned in his saddle to show an exaggerated innocent expression. "Because I think this time I was definitely the winner."

The teasing in his voice made Shelby's heart feel light. She loved seeing him happy instead of worried. "It wouldn't be good manners for me to beat you on your home turf." She shrugged.

They rode beneath the trees. The horses' footsteps were muted as they walked through the forest.

After the heat of the desert sun, Shelby was grateful for the coolness of the shade, and she imagined the animals must enjoy it too.

"Shelby, there is something I wish to ask you." He halted his horse.

"Go ahead." Shelby reined in next to him.

"Tomorrow, my father is holding a reception for some…people. Guests of the kingdom. I would be very happy if you would accompany me."

"What kind of people?" Shelby tried to keep the nervousness out of her tone.

"Various heads of state and ambassadors of countries who have pledged their support to our government."

"Okay, so it's like a meeting?"

"The meetings will be in the day. The reception is in the evening. That is when the leaders bring their spouses or companions to the palace for dinner and entertainment. The event will also be an opportunity for you to meet some of Khali-dar's influential families."

Shelby felt her stomach tighten. Heads of State? Dinner? Reception? The last thing she wanted was to say or do something that would embarrass herself or Hakim again. And she couldn't imagine the Sheik would be pleased to have her at an event so important.

He watched her with his head tipped to the side.

She ran the reins through her fingers. "Does your father know you're asking me?"

Hakim gazed over her shoulder and took a deep breath. "He knows."

"But he doesn't want me to come, right?"

"I will bring a companion of my choice tomorrow." He locked his gaze onto Shelby's and leaned toward her. "*You* are my choice. Will you please come?"

The Sheik apparently doesn't buy into the whole "guests are gifts from Allah" idea. "Of course, I would love to come." She smiled but knew it didn't appear convincing. She hated feeling like she was the source of their discord.

"You are nervous. Please do not feel uncomfortable."

"I'm worried I'll say or do something stupid." She winced. "I'm not exactly a refined debutante who knows how to act in formal situations. I don't want to embarrass you, Hakim."

"I do not want you to be a refined debutante. I have spent enough time with those people to know they are not what I want." Hakim maneuvered his horse until he faced Shelby and their legs were nearly touching. He leaned closer, his gaze earnest. "What I want is you, Shelby Jo." He cupped her cheek in his hand.

Shelby felt her heart flutter and her nerve endings tingle as she lost herself in the deep brown pools of his eyes.

His thumb stroked her skin, leaving a trail of heat in its wake. He slid his hand into her hair and drew her closer, his lips covering hers.

When she drew away, Shelby inhaled deeply and grinned. "Hearing you put it that way, how could I possibly refuse?"

Chapter Fifteen

Early the next morning, Shelby hurried out to the stables. This was the first time she'd left her room without anyone stopping her to see if they could help. She guessed the household was busy preparing for the big event that evening. Either that, or they figured she knew her way around by now. Choosing how she'd spend her day without advice or a companion by her side was a relief. She saw guards outside the stables and worried they might stop her.

But they remained on the racehorse side and gave her no trouble.

She walked toward the section where the riding horses were kept. As soon as she opened the door, she saw Kadir. "*Al-salaam alaykum*, Kadir," she said in greeting.

"*Wa alaykum e-salaam.*" Kadir bowed.

"I came to see *Al-qamar*."

Kadir indicated she should follow him back into the building to the white mare's stall. He hurried to the wall and picked up the saddle.

Shelby shook her head. "Nope, I just came to visit this morning." She spoke in a low voice to the horse, stroking her velvety nose and neck. She found a halter hanging on the wall and led *Al-qamar* out into the sunshine. The horse bobbed her head and pranced. She obviously loved being outside and obediently followed

Shelby around the track.

Shelby loved being with the mare. In the world where she still didn't know how to fit in, being with the horse was one place she felt completely comfortable. Working with the animal made her feel like she had a purpose. When Shelby returned from their walk, she motioned to Kadir that she wanted to comb *Al-qamar*'s mane.

Understanding dawned in his eyes, and he ran to fetch a small box with various sizes of brushes and combs. "*Shukran*," Shelby thanked him.

Kadir bowed his head and went about doing his regular jobs.

Shelby spent the next half hour combing, brushing, feeding, watering, and talking to the mare. She had never spent much time around an Arabian and was amazed by how much *Al-qamar* liked people. The familiarity of the tasks was comforting and lessened her homesickness. She smiled as she noticed Kadir continued his duties, but he stayed close enough to be available if Shelby should need him. She was reminded of her ranch chores as she watched him feed and water the animals and heard his voice while he spoke to them.

After Shelby put away the tools, she let herself out of the low stall door and into the main area of the stable.

Kadir swept the walkway near the entrance. "Cowboy?" He pointed to her red boots.

Shelby pulled up the leg of her jeans a little. "Yep, they're cowboy boots."

The boy grinned.

"*'Ilaa al-ghad*, Kadir." She made a mental note to bring the boy a treat.

"*'Ilaa al-ghad*, Miss Walker." He bowed again.

Shelby felt lighter than she had since she arrived. Tending to *Al-qamar* made her feel like herself again. She returned to her room smelling like horses.

Shanayze was waiting.

"Miss Walker, there is much to do to prepare you for the reception this evening." Shanayze folded her arms across her chest and nodded her head once. "But first, you should eat some breakfast." She gestured to a tray on the table behind her.

"Thank you." If Shanayze wondered where Shelby had been, she hid it well. Shelby helped herself to a slice of sweet bread and butter. The food tasted delicious, and she hadn't realized how hungry she was. "What do I need to do?"

"First of all, there is the matter of your dress. You must choose a gown as soon as possible in order to give the seamstress time for alteration. Then, you will need your hair styled, and your nails polished."

Shelby thought Shanayze always spoke as if she held a clipboard in her hand. "What time's the reception?"

"You must be at Prince Hakim's side to greet the guests at seven o'clock."

Greet the guests? Shelby felt her stomach flop. She'd assumed she could find a chair in a corner somewhere and blend in while Hakim did all of the mingling. She set down the bread, no longer hungry. "Is it okay if I take a shower before trying on dresses?"

"Of course. I will have Aaliya bring up the gowns. We will be ready when you are done."

Shelby showered. She pulled back her wet hair into a ponytail, put on clean underwear and a robe, and opened the bathroom door. A large three-paned mirror surrounding a round, carpeted stair stood in the middle of her room. Two rolling racks full of gowns were on either side of the mirror with boxes of shoes, hosiery, jewelry, and hair accessories taking up another side of the room. Shelby's eyes widened, and she breathed in quickly.

Aaliya, apparently aware of the rise in Shelby's stress level, led her to a chair. "Miss Walker, before you try on any gowns, we will establish which colors and styles you like and dislike. That will make our task much easier."

Shanayze and Aaliya alternated pulling gowns off the racks to show Shelby. She discovered the two women had very different tastes. Shanayze preferred dark colors and high necklines, while Aaliya chose bright, airy fabrics and styles Shelby found much more exciting. In about a half-hour, they had narrowed their selection to around ten, and Shelby began to try them on.

She and Aaliya finally decided on a deep turquoise silk gown. It reminded Shelby of something glamorous from the Audrey Hepburn era. The gown had a sweetheart neckline and a fitted bodice which Aaliya thought flattered Shelby's figure splendidly, while still adhering to the Arabian culture's tradition of modesty. The hem touched the floor, and Shelby was glad the skirt hung long enough to cover the scars on her leg.

Aaliya helped her pick out stylish gold stilettos.

The seamstress took away the dress, and then Shanayze left.

Shelby put her robe back on and helped Aaliya clean up the rest of the gowns.

Jennifer Moore

"Aaliya"—Shelby shook out a gown and hung it on a hanger—"Did you pick out all of these dresses?"

Aaliya lifted her gaze to Shelby's. "Yes." She took the dress Shelby was holding and hung it on the rack.

Shelby picked up another from the back of a chair. "All of this work must have taken you forever."

"No. It did not take long. I know where the best stores are." Aaliya shrugged.

Shelby ran her hand over the hanging dresses, making the skirts swish, "Which is your favorite?"

Aaliya's eyes sparkled as she pulled out the skirt of a soft green dress.

Shelby took it from the rack. "So, what are you waiting for? Put it on!"

"No, Miss Walker." Aaliya shook her head and spread her fingers on her collarbone. "That would be very improper."

"I just spent at least two hours trying on dresses you picked out, and you don't get to try on any? Come on, Aaliya, please?" Shelby extended the dress.

"Miss Walker, I am your assistant. It is not my place."

Shelby saw the hesitation in Aaliya's face. "Aaliya, I think it would be beneficial to see that dress on you. Would you please *assist* me and put it on?" She winked.

Aaliya took the offered gown and stepped into the bathroom. Then she emerged, wearing it.

Shelby took her hand and led her onto the stair in front of the mirrors. "Now, twirl around."

She spun and admired herself in the mirror. Aaliya's dark skin shone in the light dress. The sheer fabric hung in layers making her look as if she were

206

floating.

"Aaliya, you are so beautiful," Shelby said. "You should be going to this party instead of me."

"I am not the one the prince has chosen, Miss Walker."

"Will you do me a favor? Can you call me Shelby? I know you have to be proper and everything, but I could really use a friend here."

"Of course, Shelby. Although I am not sure if Shanayze would entirely approve."

Both women burst out laughing at this. And for the first time since she arrived in Khali-dar, Shelby didn't feel alone.

****

Waxing, filing, polishing, and tweezing occupied the rest of the day. The beautician spent nearly an hour styling and straightening Shelby's thick hair. After the styling was through, Shelby couldn't believe how soft it felt. Two gold combs worn low behind her ears held her hair away from her face. A makeup artist made Shelby's freckles and the scar on her forehead disappear.

Aaliya helped Shelby into all of the undergarments, nylons, and her gown. She stepped into her shoes and put on a tasteful gold necklace and sparkling bracelet. Staring into the mirror, Shelby couldn't believe the transformation. An elegant, beautiful woman with sleek auburn hair gazed back. *What happened to the cowgirl with the red curls and freckles?*

"You look lovely." Aaliya clasped her hands under her chin. "The prince will be proud to have you by his side tonight."

Shanayze appeared in the doorway to take Shelby

to the reception.

Shelby stepped down from the podium between the mirrors. She grabbed her camera from where it sat on the desk and handed it to Shanayze. "Here goes nothing." Shelby followed Shanayze down the grand staircase, concentrating on walking down the steps in her heels, and at first didn't notice Hakim standing at the bottom. When she saw him, Shelby felt her butterflies return. This was the first time she had seen Hakim dressed as a prince.

He wore a black tuxedo with a white tie and a striped sash in the colors of Khali-dar's flag crossing his chest from shoulder to waist. He stood straight and tall. As he watched her descend, Hakim opened his mouth slightly, and he took a small step back. "You are beautiful," he said in a quiet voice, regaining his composure and reaching for her hand.

She glanced at their reflection in one of the mirrored walls across the room. The vision was surreal. The two of them looked like they belonged in a scene from an old-fashioned movie. "Thanks. So do you." She motioned to Shanayze. "Is it okay if we take a picture for my mom?"

He leaned close, brushing his whiskers on her ear. "I have a surprise for you."

Feeling Hakim's breath on her neck sent shivers over her skin. She raised a brow in question.

Hakim smiled but didn't say any more.

They walked through the entrance hall and joined the Sheik who wore a traditional gold robe with black edging over a simpler white robe. The wide sleeves and the silk fabric whisked around him as he moved. On his head he wore a white *keffiyeh* held in place by black rope.

Shelby thought it made him appear even more Sheik-like and intimidating.

He glanced at Hakim's tuxedo and, for a quick second, a spark of disapproval flashed in his eyes.

Was his father disappointed Hakim hadn't dressed in robes, too? Shelby felt a jolt in her chest at the realization that Hakim had chosen to dress like *her* and not his father. Did he want to make her more comfortable? To send a message to his father? Shelby hated being the cause of bad feelings between Hakim and his father. She worried the Sheik felt as though his son was turning his back on his culture and Khali-dar, too. She resolved to talk to Hakim about it later.

The Sheik leaned his cane against a pillar, placed his hands together, and bowed a greeting.

"*As-salaamu 'alaykum.*" Shelby bowed her head as she used the formal salutation.

"You look very beautiful tonight, Shelby Walker."

"Thank you." She cast her gaze downward. How could he say such nice words and still make them feel like an insult?

Hakim stepped between them and wrapped his arm around her waist. He led her past the entry and toward the ballroom.

Shelby was immediately comforted by his closeness, and at the same time, her pulse sped as the heat from his arm warmed her through her dress.

From her short glance outside as they passed through the entrance hall, Shelby saw the first cars arrive. Some were limousines with little flags on them, while others were shiny luxury cars. Shelby thought it looked like a parade. The palace swarmed with security.

Guards spoke into the two-way radios on their wrists as they scanned the grounds and the guests. She saw Nasir, wearing a tuxedo and keeping a close eye on everyone, especially Hakim.

Hakim seemed unable to take his gaze from her. The way he regarded her made her feel beautiful, and she stood a little taller and her anxieties started to melt away. No matter what happened tonight, she would make him proud.

The reception was held in the grand ballroom. A colonnade of elegant pillars stretched down the two long sides of the large rectangular room, appearing to support a high, barrel-vaulted ceiling. Arabian-shaped archways rose between the pillars. The ceiling was the actual focus of the room. Soffits of arches were decorated with sculpted designs and the panels in between stood out, painted with geometric patterns in beautiful, bright colors. Massive gold chandeliers shaped in minarets gave the room a beautiful glow. The floor was a dark, almost black wood. The same intricately carved wood separated the wall panels on the two shorter sides of the room and framed the large entry ways. They had come in through one arched door. The other was closed, and an exquisite cloth mantle hung across it.

Hakim and Shelby took their place next to the Sheik at the ballroom entrance.

Shelby smiled and shook hands as she was introduced to ambassadors and heads of states. Many hailed from countries she'd never heard of. The memory of telling Hakim she was good at geography on the day they met made her grimace.

Hakim introduced her as his friend. Most of the

visitors greeted her politely, but a few raised their eyebrows or gave him a knowing look. Hakim, gracious as ever, maintained a polite smile. They were guests in his house, after all.

As Shelby watched the endless line of visitors, she noticed Hakim stiffen. She glanced up and saw that he still smiled, but his face seemed tense. "You okay?"

He gave a terse nod, glancing to his left at the people speaking with his father.

Shelby leaned forward to observe three people that she assumed were a family.

Exchanging bows with the Sheik was a middle-aged man dressed in traditional Arabian clothing. He was tall and slightly overweight, but something about the way he carried himself drew her gaze. He was obviously used to commanding attention. Two women, one middle aged and one much younger, accompanied him. Shelby assumed they were his wife and daughter.

As she observed the man, Shelby felt the sensation of somebody watching her. She looked at the daughter. The hateful glare coming from her dark brown eyes caused Shelby to suck in a quick breath. She stepped back until Hakim blocked her view.

The man stepped toward them and took Hakim's hand. They spoke in Arabic for a few moments.

Hakim turned and flashed her a tight smile. "Shelby, I would like you to meet Samir bin Kareem Abul-Rahman. He is the patriarch of an important family in Khali-dar." Hakim turned to the man and continued in English, "And this is my friend, Shelby Jo Walker, from the United States."

Samir bin Kareem Abul-Rahman squinted his eyes and lifted his chin as he watched Shelby with an appraising look.

She put her hands together and bowed. *"Ahlan wa sahlan."* She hoped she wasn't expected to remember his entire name.

"Ahlan wa sahlan," he replied, though his expression carried none of the warmth of the greeting.

"I would also like to introduce you to Samir's wife, Ramah, and his daughter, Ghaniyah."

Both women were very beautiful, and they knew it. Shelby felt disapproval flowing from them like poisonous gas. Up close, she saw the details on their gowns and their elaborate jewelry. Both wore headscarves. Hanging from her scarf, medallions of gold with gemstones and pearls brushed Ghaniyah's forehead. The gold contrasted strikingly against her dark skin. Her eyes, lined in black, gave her a fierce appearance.

Shelby couldn't help comparing her to Aaliya. Their features were similar, but where Aaliya's face showed kindness, Ghaniyah's displayed a sharp haughtiness. Shelby offered her hand to the women, but they both ignored her gesture. Her face colored as she saw the loathing in their eyes. Was their reaction because she was American? Or because she was with Hakim? Or both?

Luckily, she was spared any future discomfort as the women saw friends they knew and hurried away.

"I'm sorry, Shelby Jo," Hakim whispered in her ear. "I did not expect such a discourteous reaction."

"Ouch. Was that your ex-girlfriend or something?" She struggled to shake off the sick feeling Ghaniyah's reaction produced.

Hakim answered slowly. "I believe if things had

worked out the way she and her parents had intended, Ghaniyah would be the one standing beside me tonight."

"Oh." Shelby stole a glance over her shoulder.

They had greeted guests for nearly half an hour when Hakim squeezed her hand. "Your surprise is here," he whispered.

Shelby glanced around but couldn't see anything out of the ordinary, until she looked closer at the man speaking with the Sheik. With a start, she recognized the President of the United States.

The President put his hands together and bowed a greeting to Hakim.

"Welcome, President Mannen, Mrs. Mannen. I would like you to meet Shelby Jo Walker. She is a citizen of your country and a dear friend of mine."

"Pleased to meet you, Miss Walker." The President shook her hand.

Shelby stood frozen in shock. Recovering quickly, but not quickly enough, she sputtered, "You're…" She shook her head. *Smooth, Shelby.* "President Mannen. It's a pleasure to meet you. And Mrs. Mannen. How do you do?" *Where is Shanayze with my camera?*

"We are so pleased you could attend this evening." Hakim bowed as he shook their hands. "Please, make yourselves welcome."

"Thank you, Prince Hakim." The President and the First Lady moved into the entrance hall and followed the ushers into the ballroom.

Hakim turned with a grin.

"Go ahead and laugh." She gave him a little shove. "I was so surprised I didn't know what to say. What if he finds out I didn't vote for him?"

Jennifer Moore

Hakim laughed out loud and spread his hand toward the doorway. "Come. All of the guests have arrived."

Shelby walked next to him, and they joined the crowd in the ballroom.

Hakim was still chuckling.

Crisp white cloths draped over the round tables throughout one side of the room. Hakim led her to the head table. Out of nowhere, a man in a server's uniform slid back an intricately carved dining chair to seat her next to the First Lady.

"Will you be all right if I leave you for a few minutes?" Hakim asked. "There are people I feel I must speak to."

"Sure. I'll be fine here." She fingered a blue glass goblet, pretending to be admiring the gold detail, and hoping she didn't appear nervous as he left her. Shelby noticed how straight and tall Hakim walked and wished some of his confidence would rub off.

Another server, this time a woman, filled Shelby's glass with water.

The President continued to mingle, while his wife remained seated at the table. She leaned over to Shelby. "I am so glad you're here. It's not often I have someone to chat with at things like this."

Shelby studied the First Lady. Shelby had always considered her pretty. Her short, blonde hair had started to gray, but this only added to her sophistication. She wore a black formal gown with long gloves that came up past her elbows. A strand of large pearls hung around her neck.

"Prince Hakim is very handsome," Mrs. Mannen said. "How did you two meet?"

214

"We met skiing in Denver."

"How romantic, and now here you are, dressed like a princess, with him unable to take his eyes off you."

Shelby followed the woman's gaze across the room to where Hakim stood, speaking with someone. His gaze met hers, and heat tickled her cheeks.

"What about you?" Shelby asked, eager to take the attention away from herself. "How did you meet your husband?" She realized she knew hardly anything about Mrs. Mannen. After the way she had reacted when the Sheik didn't know the name of the tapestry weaver, she felt embarrassed she was guilty of the same thing.

"We met in college. We had an Art History class together, of all things. The two of us just hit it off right away. And now here we are, thirty years and two kids later…"

"Sitting in a ballroom of a Middle Eastern Sheik's palace," Shelby finished.

"If there's one thing I've learned, it's that life is unpredictable." Mrs. Mannen bent her wrist, waving off her small laugh. "So, tell me about yourself, Shelby. Where are you from?"

"A small town in Colorado. Culver Springs. My parents have a ranch there. I live in Denver, now."

"And how long are you staying in Khali-dar?"

"I'm not sure." Shelby shifted in her seat, biting her lip. "I guess you could say it's complicated."

The President, Hakim, and the Sheik made their way back toward the table.

As they got closer, Shelby could hear Hakim speaking in a serious tone.

"We believe if we could just find the headquarters and the leader, we could quell this uprising."

Jennifer Moore

"Well, you know the US will support you in any way you need."

"Thank you."

The men sat, and the Sheik gave a speech welcoming the guests, thanking them for their support. Then he sat at their table next to the President.

Shelby surveyed the room, fascinated. People from all nationalities wore costumes and gowns covering the entire fashion spectrum. She kept her gaze from traveling to the table where the Khali-dar families, and specifically Ghaniyah, sat. She hadn't thought before about the kind of society that must exist here. These were people Hakim interacted with on a regular basis. How would she fit in with this elite group? A part of her wanted to win them over, but the more practical side of her knew no matter what she did, how long she stayed, or how hard she tried, she would never be one of them. She'd always be an outsider.

The conversation at the table centered on the *Nahl* group and the threats against the Khali-dar government. Shelby listened, her insides tightening in worry and at the same time warming with pride. She had no idea the United States took such an interest in the welfare of Khali-dar.

President Mannen turned toward Shelby. "So, Miss Walker, what do you think of Khali-dar?"

Shelby nearly choked on her drink. "Please, call me Shelby, Mr. President." She set down her glass and clasped her hands on her lap so he would not see how they shook. "Khali-dar is incredible. I've hardly ever been more than a few hundred miles from my home town, and so I feel really lucky to be here. Especially tonight at such an important event."

"Yes, this country is one of my favorite places to visit. I never fail to be astonished by the beauty of this palace." President Mannen tipped his head back and let his gaze travel to the ceiling. "It's as if the room is glowing."

"It's mica," Shelby said before she could stop herself.

"Pardon me?"

Shelby noticed some of the other people at the table had stopped their conversations to listen. The blood rushed to her cheeks. "Mica mixed into the plaster gives the walls their sheen. It also repels dust and keeps away spiders and hornets." *Why can't I stop talking?*

"What a fascinating bit of trivia. How is it that you know so much about the components of plaster?"

"I don't." She paused, wishing people would just go back to their own discussions and swallowed over her dry throat. "I read it in a book about Khali-dar." *Great, now I sound like Hermione Granger.*

"I'd love to hear more about the palace." Mrs. Mannen set down her fork and turned her attention to Shelby.

"I only know what I've read. And some things Hakim told me." She glanced at Hakim.

He nodded and gave her an encouraging smile.

"Let's see…The palace was built here because there is a natural water source, an oasis, under the ground. At one time, a moat surrounded the palace to keep out invaders. The walls surrounding the property are between twenty and thirty feet high from the outside, but from the inside, they never exceed fifteen feet. That way it doesn't feel like they are looming over you. What else...?" Shelby let her gaze travel around the room, settling on the south doors. "I do know a pretty interesting story, if it's all right for me to share it." Raising an eyebrow in question, she looked at Hakim who nodded his permission.

"The Khalid family has ruled Khali-dar for nearly eight hundred years. This ballroom was part of the original palace built in the fourteenth century. Sheik Abdul Muhsi had the doorways built large enough for an elephant carrying a loaded riding carriage to fit through." Everyone at the table turned their attention to the massive doorways, and Shelby knew they were all trying to picture a fully-laden elephant sauntering inside.

"Flash forward about a hundred years to the 1480s. The reigning Sheik had no heir. The people feared the Khalid dynasty would end, so the Sheik sent for the wise man of the village to advise him. The wise man told him the south doors, which were the main entrance to the palace at that time, must be sealed. As long as they stayed sealed, the Khalid family would have a suitable heir. The Sheik immediately had the doors sealed, and within a year, his son was born. So, the doors remain sealed to this day, and the line of rulers has never been broken." Shelby realized the entire table of twelve had gone quiet to listen. She felt her ears heat and glanced toward the Sheik, wishing she could read his expression.

"You can see, perhaps, the obligation the prince has to his people. He must not only produce an heir, but also make an appropriate alliance in order to ensure that it is the *proper* heir," the Sheik said.

Hakim tensed.

Although the Sheik's voice seemed amiable and conversational, beneath his polite words, the meaning was crystal clear to Shelby. He did not consider her appropriate. Tears burned the back of her eyes, and she lowered her gaze, hoping no one noticed.

Under the table, Hakim squeezed her hand.

"There is such a rich history here, isn't there?" Mrs. Mannen said. "Receptions like this are always official business, and I'm afraid we don't get to hear as much about the culture as we'd like."

During Shelby's story, an army of servers had silently filled the tables with trays of food. The rich smells made her stomach growl. The plates looked too fancy to actually put food on. Exquisite gold chargers lay under richly painted bone china. Golden silverware and deep blue goblets finished the beautiful settings. Her mouth pulled in a fond smile as she remembered how excited her mom was when they had all pitched in to give her six sets of matching stoneware for Christmas last year.

Dinner was wonderful. Most of the dishes were unfamiliar, but she was surprised by how delicious everything tasted.

Hakim was attentive throughout the meal, identifying the different foods and watching to see her reaction as she tasted them. She was touched by his actions and could tell he was making an extra effort to distract her from his father's rudeness. He pointed out different men and women in the room, telling her about them, and she was astounded by the important people who had all gathered here in support of Khali-dar and the Sheik. Not only important rulers and heads of state, but businessmen, political activists, bankers, and diplomats. The room buzzed with energy around all these influential people.

After the servers cleared away the last plate, the Sheik stood again, leaning on his cane. "I thank all of you for coming tonight and for your continued support of Khali-dar. In our country, guests are blessings, gifts from Allah." He dipped forward his head as his guests applauded. "I invite you now to join me at the other end of the ballroom, for the entertainment portion of the evening."

Hakim escorted Shelby to the rows of chairs facing a large empty section of the dance floor.

They were seated, and when the audience quieted, two lines of men filed into the room and stopped, linking arms and facing each other. They all wore traditional Arabic costumes: white *dishdashas* and their red checkered *kheffiyas* were tied to their heads. All of the young men stood with their shoulders pulled back and their heads held high.

"This is a traditional folk dance," Hakim told her. "It is called the *Ayyalah*."

Soon, a drum began to beat a slow, steady rhythm, then more drums joined in. The men swayed back and forth to the beat of the drums. They brandished swords from their belts, and each side took turns calling to each other in challenge.

The entire room was silent, their gazes focused toward the performance. Shelby almost believed she was watching a battle that would break out any moment. When the performance ended, she realized she had been mesmerized by the beat and the chanting. Shelby blinked and looked around the room, noticing the same reaction on the faces of the other people in the audience.

As she passed her gaze over the section where Ghaniyah sat, she felt the icy glare again and tensed. Not just from Ghaniyah and her mother, but now from other people who sat around them. They apparently had serious influence on their friends. Shelby turned away, trying not to let it distract her from enjoying the evening.

More dances were presented. Her favorite, *Na'ashat,* was performed by women, swaying slowly to a beautiful haunting melody played on a flute, accompanied by a tambourine. The women placed their right hands on their hearts, and their long black hair swung hypnotically back and forth.

Shelby was disappointed when the program ended. People moved around the room, mingling. Servers weaved between them with trays of drinks.

Hakim excused himself for a moment to go speak to someone, leaving Shelby sitting alone, observing the people interacting throughout the room.

After a few minutes, a small group approached, led by Ghaniyah.

Shelby stood and smiled. This was not the time to appear unsure of herself.

"I hope you are having a lovely evening, Shelby Walker." Ghaniyah spoke a little too loudly.

Shelby could hear the sarcasm dripping through her thick accent.

Some of her friends snickered.

"Thank you for asking, Ghaniyah. I am having a wonderful time." Shelby kept her voice light, ignoring the condescension in Ghaniyah's tone.

"I am always amused by who Prince Hakim

chooses to spend his time with." Ghaniyah placed her hand on Shelby's arm and leaned close, as if to confide. "Such is the way with men, I suppose. Choosing to keep themselves entertained temporarily." Her dark eyes bored into Shelby's. "In the end, he will do what is right for his kingdom and make a proper alliance."

Shelby kept up her head, hoping the hurt she felt at Ghaniyah's words didn't show on her face. *I wouldn't be surprised if Ghaniyah and the Sheik are working together.* "It was nice meeting you, Ghaniyah. I hope you enjoy the rest of your evening." Shelby turned to go.

Ghaniyah's fingers tightened on her arm. "Prince Hakim and I have been promised since birth, Shelby Walker. I come from the wealthiest family in the country, and you are nothing but a poor American. I hope you do not think his immature fascination is anything more than a game. You are not the first of his bad decisions, but I hope you will be his last."

Shelby didn't trust herself to respond. Instead, she breathed deeply and clenched her trembling hands as she left the group and went to stand next to President and Mrs. Mannen.

Hakim hurried over and led her to a side of the room away from the crowd. His brows were pinched together. "I saw you speaking to Ghaniyah. I am sorry—I did not mean to leave you alone with her."

"I'm fine." Shelby swallowed hard against the lump in her throat.

"What did she say to you, Shelby Jo?"

His eyes swam with a mix of anger and concern, but Shelby couldn't think of anything light to say to ease his worry. "Let's talk about it later, okay?" she said. "I don't want her to ruin my night."

Hakim looked unconvinced and led her back to mingle with the crowd. For the remainder of the evening, he did not leave her side.

Chapter Sixteen

Sheik Rashid, Prince Hakim, and Shelby Walker watched as the last guest left through the entrance hall, appearing on the surface to be a perfectly happy family. Hakim's heart felt heavy, and he wished the image wasn't merely a façade. If only his father could see how much he cared about Shelby and wanted her to be a part of their lives.

The Sheik hadn't been pleased when Hakim had wanted Shelby at his side to greet their guests. But Hakim had insisted. Shelby was not a secret. He was not ashamed of her, and he wished his father felt the same.

Everyone had enjoyed themselves, and Hakim and his father had strengthened valuable alliances. *The night was a success.* He smiled when he thought of Shelby making sure Shanayze took her picture with the President and the First Lady. The Mannens had both hugged her before they left, and Hakim had seen her wipe her eyes when they spoke about their flight home to the U.S. He knew Shelby was homesick and wished he could make everything perfect here.

After a curt farewell, the Sheik retired to his rooms, leaving them alone, and Shelby and Hakim walked toward the staircase.

When they stopped, Shelby stepped out of her shoes. Limping to a nearby couch, she sat and rubbed her ankle. "Sorry, not too lady-like, I know. I guess this is when I change back into little cinder Ella." She crossed her legs and rotated her ankle with her hands to stretch it out.

Hakim had nearly forgotten about her injury and scrutinized her scars. Unable to stop himself, he allowed his gaze to trace the curves of her calves while her skirt was pulled up. Catching himself, he looked away and rubbed the back of his neck.

She put her feet flat on the floor, leaned back and closed her eyes. "I need a sec to gear up before I tackle that staircase."

Hakim sat on the couch, wanting to scoot close, but not sure how Shelby would react. She hadn't been the same since speaking with Ghaniyah, but he didn't know how to broach the subject. What had Ghaniyah said? He could only imagine. She was such a shallow, spiteful woman. Over the years, he'd come to resent suggestions the two of them would be a good match.

Shelby opened her eyes and raised her eyebrows. "What are you thinking?"

"Truthfully, I was thinking about Ghaniyah." The expression of shock and hurt on Shelby's face was like an arrow in his chest. "No, Shelby." He took her hand. "I was wondering what she said to you. I can tell it upset you."

Shelby swallowed before answering. "It wasn't anything, really. She told me the two of you were promised to each other, and you are always showing up to things like this with a different girl. Just that kind of stuff."

Hakim sat straighter. He could tell Shelby downplayed the incident. She spoke in a light voice but couldn't conceal her hurt. And she wasn't telling him everything. He knew what Ghaniyah was capable of, and anger flared in his chest. He was trying so hard to dispel any kind of uncertainty Shelby may have about him and their relationship. To re-earn her trust. Of course, Ghaniyah would try to ruin it. *Between her and my father, it is a wonder Shelby is even speaking to me anymore.*

"I…" He hesitated, rubbing the soft skin on the back of her hand with his thumb. "Shelby Jo, I hope you do not believe Ghaniyah."

"I won't lie, the things she said hurt, but girls are mean, whether you're in a palace or a high school bathroom. Ex-girlfriends are even meaner. Especially ones who think they still have a chance." She smiled, but lowered her eyes. "You don't have to explain everything you've ever done or everyone you have ever dated. That doesn't matter. What matters is the future. Not the past."

"Those are wise words, Shelby Jo." Hakim was not convinced she meant what she said, based on the way she avoided his gaze.

"I don't have any right to be hurt by Ghaniyah. I mean, you and I have never really discussed what the future might hold." Shelby studied their joined hands, turning over his and running her fingers along the lines in his palm.

"I cannot imagine a future without you in it." He tipped his head looking into her eyes, hoping to find confirmation. He saw hope. And doubt.

"A relationship is a lot to think about, isn't it?" she murmured.

"Yes."

"Hakim"—she stood—"I had a wonderful night. I went to a royal ball with a handsome prince—I got to meet the President! I won't allow one spiteful girl to ruin it."

He stood and cupped her cheeks in his hands. The feel of her soft skin made his heart trip. "I had a wonderful night, too. You were perfect. Beautiful, charming." He rubbed his thumbs over her cheeks. "However, since you were so kind as to offer me advice after my first date, allow me to return the favor after your first 'royal ball.'"

"All right…" Shelby squinted.

His wink produced her smile and his heart warmed. "Let's just say, a girl agrees to attend a party with a guy, even though she is undoubtedly uncomfortable, and she enchants an entire table full of diplomats, while shining as the most beautiful woman in the room— proving to the guy and everyone that met her she is every bit as amazing as he knew she would be. If that is the case, he will probably expect her to kiss him."

Without waiting for Shelby's response, he bent to meet her lips. His hands slid down her neck and arms. He pulled her closer, moving his mouth on hers.

Her hands brushed up his chest, wrapping around his neck, and she sighed. Then Shelby broke the embrace.

The moment ended too soon, making him worry that she wasn't entirely unaffected by Ghaniyah's words.

"Well, I'd better go to sleep." She picked up her shoes. "See you tomorrow?"

Hakim drew her close once more. His pulse pounded in his ears. He gave her a soft kiss and whispered, "Goodnight."

Hakim was still standing at the bottom of the stairs when Nasir joined him.

"Every guest has left, and the property is secure," Nasir said.

"Thank you." Hakim walked through the entrance hall, deciding on a stroll in the gardens before retiring to his chambers.

Nasir followed. "Your Highness, I am concerned. *Nahl*'s silence worries me. For months, we had reports of continual chatter on the internet, attacks were planned and carried out. Then, the search for Miss Walker, and suddenly...nothing."

"You are worried because the kingdom is *not* under attack?" Hakim glanced up at the lit windows of Shelby's room.

"It is their sudden silence that is troubling," Nasir said. "It is as if they are holding their breath. Or biding their time."

Hakim loosened his tie and unbuttoned his collar. The terrorist group had been the topic of nearly every conversation that evening, but he wondered if they were as dangerous as they'd thought. "Perhaps, *Nahl* was not the threat we perceived them to be. The lack of action on their part could be due to poor funding or support. The rebellion could have died out."

"It makes no sense, Your Highness. In my gut, I feel as though something big is coming."

They crossed the bridge and strode down a gravel path bordered by gardenia trees.

"The reception tonight would have been the perfect opportunity to make some sort of statement, but it was uneventful. Do you think they would attempt something at the Derby in a few weeks?" Hakim breathed in the heady smells of the blossoms, hoping the fragrance would calm his anxiety.

Nasir was silent for a moment before he answered. "No, my instincts tell me they believe their cause to be a matter of national pride. They would not take the fight to foreign soil. Although we will ensure extra security measures are in place while you travel."

Hakim nodded, turning down a path which led back to the palace.

"It seems that as soon as Miss Walker was safely at the palace, the entire *Nahl* faction relaxed. As if they have a plan in place, and we are unaware of it."

Nasir's measured tone indicated he was choosing his words carefully. Hakim stopped below Shelby's balcony, staring at the lights glowing behind the curtained windows. He could not bear the thought of something happening to Shelby, but he had faith in his security. Nasir and his team were the best money could buy. The safety measures they had put in place left no room for error. If they could not keep Shelby safe, nobody could.

****

Shelby ran her hand along the railing as she limped up the stairs, lost in thought. What in the world was she doing here? Had she really rambled on about plaster and wasps in front of the President of the United States? And how could she forget the Sheik's not-so-subtle hint that she was the wrong person for his son? Shelby's throat thickened as she remembered the conversation with Ghaniyah. The woman was spiteful and horrible, but was there truth to what she said? Shelby hadn't known Hakim for very long. Did she believe him?

Could she trust him? Thinking of his smile, his fathomless eyes, Shelby felt her heart scream, "Yes!" But that could just be the aftermath of his amazing kiss.

Why did she have these doubts? What was his motivation? She believed he cared about her, but why all the lavish gifts? Was he trying to buy her affection? And what about his dad? The Sheik had basically told her Hakim would snap out of it and dump her when he figured out his duty to his country.

"What am I doing here?" Shelby wondered out loud. She opened her door, and the smell of hot chocolate drifted toward her. She breathed out a sigh. *Thank you, Aaliya!* She poured herself a cup and sat at her desk, bringing the cup to her nose. A wave of homesickness washed over her, making her eyes burn.

Mom would love the pictures from tonight. She turned on her laptop and when she opened her Inbox the first thing she saw was a note from Xan. She sighed, clicking on it. Of course, he was upset she'd left so suddenly. He missed her and hoped she'd hurry home. From the sound of it, her old job would be waiting when she returned. Good old practical, uncomplicated Xan. Life with him would be so simple and comfortable. Not to mention normal.

A small knock sounded on the door, and Shelby looked up from the computer.

"Did you have a nice evening?" Aaliya moved close and clasped her hands in front of her.

Shelby shook her head. She lifted her hands and dropped them. "Honestly, I don't know. At times, it was romantic and magical, and then other times, I wished the floor would open up and swallow me."

"That is unfortunate, Miss W—Shelby. Would you

like to talk about it?"

"No. Yes. I don't know."

"I have been told I am a good listener."

Shelby thought about it for a minute. Having someone to talk to would be so nice. "Sure." She stood and when she put weight on her ankle, a jolt of pain caused her to wince. "Let me pour you some cocoa."

"Shelby"—Aaliya crossed the room in an instant and led her back to the chair—"Are you injured?"

"No, I had surgery a few months ago, and my ankle kind-of stiffened up in those heels tonight."

Aaliya knelt on the floor, lifting and studying Shelby's leg. "You need a massage to loosen your muscles."

Shaking her head, Shelby pulled back her leg and crossed it over the other one. "No way will I sit here and make you rub my ankle, Aaliya."

"I will call a masseuse to work on it while you tell me about your part lovely, part disastrous evening."

Shelby sat straight. "It's the middle of the night, nobody…"

Aaliya pulled a small radio out of her pocket and spoke in Arabic, and then listened when a voice answered. "She will be here in a few minutes. I think you may prefer to change out of your gown into something more comfortable." Aaliya slid the radio back into her pocket.

Of course, there is a masseuse on call at all hours. Shelby didn't think she would go a day at the palace without being surprised.

With Aaliya's help, Shelby removed all of her formal wear and put on pajamas. She washed her face, put her hair in a ponytail, and wrapped up in a luscious bathrobe. She had only sat again for a few seconds before Aaliya opened the door, letting in a small woman with smile lines around her dark eyes and streaks of gray in her long braided hair.

Aaliya introduced her to Shelby as Fatima.

Although Fatima was small and timid, her fingers were deft. As the woman kneaded and stretched Shelby's ankle, the stiffness melted away.

Shelby described her evening to Aaliya. When she came to the part about Ghaniyah, she saw the other girl's face darken. "Do you know her?"

"Ghaniyah is my cousin." Aaliya looked down at her folded hands.

Shelby pressed her palm against her chest. "Oh, I'm sorry. I shouldn't have…"

"Ever since she was young, Ghaniyah has been obsessed with her goal of becoming Queen. She has unsuccessfully sought Prince Hakim's affection and manipulated situations in order to be noticed by him, but her efforts have been in vain, and she has become very spiteful." Aaliya swished the liquid around in her teacup. "The two of us were very close before she went away to attend the University."

"Didn't you go to college, too?" Shelby asked.

"No. And I believe this is part of the reason ill feelings exist between us. You see, Ghaniyah hated school. She fought her parents' decision to send her to the University. While I…" Aaliya lowered her gaze.

"You wished you could go."

"Yes. I was told in school that I have a natural aptitude for languages. I had the top scores in my classes. In Secondary school, I learned English and German and wished to learn more. It was my dream to be a teacher. But my parents could not to afford to send me." Aaliya spoke matter-of-factly.

Shelby envied her ability to speak about herself so confidently. "I'm sorry. But it's not too late. You could still save up and go, right?"

"I am very fortunate to have been selected for this job. I trained as an assistant under Shanayze before you came. It is quite an honor to be your assistant now."

"But this job isn't what you want." Shelby's stomach felt hard at the unfairness of her situation. "You're smart, Aaliya. You speak better English than I do. You have excellent taste. You're organized. You're the kind of person that colleges love. You should do what *you* want, instead of what other people want you to do."

"It is difficult for you to understand." Aaliya spoke without raising her gaze. "But in Khali-dar, that is not our way."

Shelby was overwhelmed with sympathy for Aaliya. "I know someone who could use a great language teacher." She touched Aaliya's arm. "I have some books I found in the library. Would you teach me Arabic?"

Aaliya looked up and her face brightened. "I would love to, Shelby."

Chapter Seventeen

Shelby couldn't believe she had been in Khali-dar for a week. She spent every morning riding *Al-qamar*. A few times, Hakim had joined her, but often she rode alone. She didn't mind the solitude—she even looked forward to it. Having time to herself was nice. In the palace, or the gardens, people were everywhere.

This morning as she rode back to the stables, she saw Kadir waiting. He wore the cowboy hat she'd given him. Luckily, Aaliya had known where to find one. He waved and held the reins as she dismounted. "Howdy, Miss Walker," he said, his smile shining.

"Howdy, Kadir the skater." She knew he didn't understand much of what she said, but he laughed when she rhymed his name.

They entered the stable together, brushed down the mare, and made sure she had enough to eat and drink.

A few days ago, Kadir would have insisted on doing the jobs himself, but by now he knew Shelby liked to work with the horses, and she could tell he enjoyed her company. He especially liked using the new words Shelby taught him.

Once they had finished, Shelby walked toward the stable door. "All right, Kadir. I'll see you tomorrow."

"*Adiós, muchacho!*" he called back.

Shelby was still chuckling when she closed the door behind her and stepped outside into the sun.

Aaliya was waiting. "Good morning, Shelby."

"Morning, Aaliya. What's up?"

"The prince had to leave this morning while you were riding. He asked me to deliver a message. Tonight, the *Al Nuaim* tribe is hosting a traditional Bedouin dinner party, and some of the guests have decided to make an outing of it. Prince Hakim would like to take you on a desert safari."

When she thought of leaving the palace and seeing something new, Shelby felt her heart soar. "I have no idea what a desert safari is, but I totally want to go."

"You will ride horses through the desert to the Bedouin camp. The men will take their falcons and hunt along the way."

Perfect. She wouldn't mess this up. This sort of thing was right up her alley. "So, are you coming, too?"

"No."

"Oh, I can ask Hakim."

"I will come…if you desire it." She left her sentence hanging like she wanted to say more.

"But with me gone, you can finally do something you want to do, right?" Shelby only had to glance at Aaliya to know she had hit the nail right on the head. Not waiting for Aaliya to continue, Shelby stopped and turned to look her right in the eyes. "I would love to have you there, but I know you hardly ever get to do anything else. Take the night off and hang out with your family or friends, or whatever you want. My feelings won't be hurt by the fact that you have a life besides taking care of me, okay?"

Seeing the gratitude in Aaliya's expression, she realized how much of a sacrifice this woman's job demanded. Shelby wrapped her arm around Aaliya's small shoulders and gave her a squeeze as they walked through the palace entrance.

****

Combing her hair after her shower, Shelby entered her bedroom. When she saw the clothes Aaliya had set out, she stopped short. A few minutes of maneuvering were needed to make sense of the different pieces. All the clothing was made of black silk. She put on a pair of wide-legged trousers that looked like a long, flowing skirt, and a blouse with gold embroidery on the cuffs. A knee-length sleeveless jacket finished off the ensemble. More of the intricate embroidery decorated the collar, flowing down the front.

Aaliya helped her tie a sash around her waist and showed her how to wrap the scarf over her head and loosely around her neck.

Shelby could lift it up to protect her nose and mouth if the wind blew sand in her face. A pair of gold earrings completed her outfit. She loved the feel of the cool silk against her skin.

"What do you think?" asked Aaliya.

"I love it," she replied. "Plus, I look a little bit like a ninja."

An hour later, Shelby practically floated as her light clothes swishing around her. When she saw Hakim waiting in his usual spot at the bottom of the stairs, she did a double-take, catching her breath.

His clothes were similar, although with less embroidery and more masculine pants. On his head, he wore a black head dress with the scarf pulled down under his chin.

"You look so handsome." The words spilled out of her mouth before she could think of anything smooth to say.

"And you look like an Arabian Princess." He brushed a kiss over her lips.

Hakim held Shelby's hand as they strode through the entrance and down the long walkway. A slight breeze blew the mist of the fountains over them with a refreshing coolness. He touched his hand on the small of her back, guiding her to the passenger side of a shiny black military-style luxury SUV where Nasir had opened the back door.

"Thanks, Nasir," Shelby said.

Nasir closed the door and strode to the other side of the vehicle to open the door for Hakim to slide into the back seat next to Shelby.

"You don't have to sit back here by me."

Instead of answering, Hakim put his arm around Shelby's shoulders and pulled her close.

Shelby snuggled into his shoulder as she surveyed the inside of the luxury SUV. Like everything else Hakim owned, this automobile was top-of-the-line. The interior was black leather and shined like someone just finished polishing it. Of course, it had all the available features. She could imagine how Chet would love it. He would have definitely wanted to ride 'shotgun.' She smiled when she thought of him saying something like, "This ride is totally tricked out."

As the vehicle neared the gates, Hakim squeezed her shoulder, then pulled away his arm and sat straight. He scooted a bit closer to the door.

Shelby looked up, studying his expression. *Did I do something wrong?*

He squinted and then caught her gaze, raising his brows and motioning with his lifted chin toward the gates.

Shelby recognized the apology in his gaze and remembered Shanayze's warning about showing any affection in public. She thought back to the reception and the way Hakim hadn't touched her, aside from squeezing her hand beneath the table, until they were alone. The idea of acting one way in public and another in private grated on her, like she was putting on a show or assuming a pretend façade. But she knew the behavior was important to Hakim and smiled to reassure him that her feelings weren't hurt, and then scooted toward the other door.

Nasir drove through the gates and into the city.

Shelby darted her gaze around, searching for any sign they were being followed, but after a few tense minutes, she took her cue from Hakim and relaxed, enjoying the ride. As much as she loved life at the palace, Shelby was overjoyed to be doing something new. She tapped her fingers on her leg as she stared out the window to watch as the city went by. She didn't want to miss anything. Leaving the skyscrapers behind, they drove past winding streets and crowded, narrow alleys. She saw market stalls and small storefronts. Clotheslines hung high above them. She pictured Aladdin jumping through the high windows and running over the flat rooftops.

Getting closer to the outskirts of town, the houses were spaced farther apart. Although all the buildings seemed to be made from the same tan colored stone, decorative carvings or window shape made each house unique. Palm trees and hanging plants on the various levels softened the boxy appearance of the buildings. "What are those enclosures on top of the roofs?" Shelby pointed to the wide towers with open windows that perched on nearly every rooftop.

"They are wind tunnels." He dipped his head to look up at the tops of the buildings. "Built to capture the moving air and funnel it down inside the house to cool it, although most are purely decoration since the invention of air conditioning." Hakim adjusted the rear vents. "Speaking of air conditioning, how is the temperature? Are you too hot?"

"No, I'm good." Shelby adjusted the scarf around her neck.

"These clothes…" Hakim smiled. "They complement you very well."

"You can thank Aaliya for that." Shelby paused, thinking for a moment. "So, do you know Aaliya at all?"

"Rather distantly, I'm afraid. She is a relative of…" He stopped, widening his eyes and pressed his lips together.

"I know. She's Ghaniyah's cousin."

Hakim nodded.

"Aaliya's really smart. She speaks a bunch of languages and had one of the highest scores in her class." Shelby glanced at Hakim before continuing. "But she didn't go to college, because her parents couldn't afford to send her."

"Yes, this is a common difficulty for families with daughters, because there is no women's university in Khali-dar." He glanced with his brows pulled together. "Does this trouble you?"

"It seems unfair. Aaliya would love to attend the University, but can't afford it, and then girls like Ghaniyah, who don't even want to go, get to because their parents have more money."

He stroked his chin and frowned. "Is it not the same everywhere?"

"Well, yes, sort of. But what about scholarships or student loans? What about the girls who have local jobs or are taking care of their families? If they want to stay in Khali-dar, there aren't any other options. No other school they could go to that was closer and more affordable. Like a community college or something." When he didn't answer, Shelby said, "I hope you don't think I'm criticizing. It's really none of my business."

He shook his head and turned in the seat to face her directly, then laid his hand on hers where it rested in her lap. "Shelby, you must feel free to tell me anything. I appreciate that you are concerned for Aaliya and for my people. Asking questions is not the same as being critical. This is a discussion my father and I have had before—about women's education. But, you are right, the situation has not been resolved, and I am afraid it has slipped from my mind while other matters have taken its place. I am glad you reminded me."

She was grateful Hakim hadn't been annoyed. Shelby looked around for something to change the subject. They drove on a straight road between dunes that were dotted sparsely by scrawny plants. "Why aren't the roads covered with sand?"

"The roads are cleaned off a few times a day by road sweepers. Vehicles equipped with a system using GPS so the driver can locate the pavement when the sand obscures it."

Nasir veered off the road and parked. He opened Hakim's and then Shelby's door.

They both climbed out, and Shelby studied the

surrounding desert. She was overwhelmed by the sameness, and the endless, peanut butter-colored sand, as far as she could see. Even the city had disappeared. Dune after dune faded into the distance. Everything felt exposed without the mountains she was used to. *How does anyone keep track of directions out here?*

She walked a few feet, studying the dunes, and bent over to grab a handful of sand, letting it pour through her fingers. *Soft and fine. Perfect for a sandbox.* She brushed her hand on her pants while she turned to see what Hakim and Nasir were doing. A hissing sound caught her attention. She looked for the source and discovered Nasir was using a tool to let air out of the tires.

Shelby gasped and darted her gaze to Hakim for his reaction. *Is this okay? Does he know what Nasir is doing?*

Hakim's expression was calm.

So she relaxed and studied him. He stood a few feet away from the vehicle. Gazing out across the sand with the breeze ruffling his clothes and blowing the thin fabric of his headdress, he looked like he belonged in a movie. *All he needs is a sword and an ancient map.*

Hakim turned toward Shelby with his eyebrows raised.

Her heart sped up, and her breath caught. "I don't know whether you are aware, but your friend is sabotaging our ride." Shelby strolled toward Hakim. "Are you planning to abandon me in the middle of the desert?"

His expression grew thoughtful. "Let me see. You are dressed to endure the arid climate—there is food and even water to be found if one knows where to look.

I think you would survive." He put his arms around her. "Although, I am afraid I would spend the rest of my life in fear, watching over my shoulder and waiting for Shelby Jo Walker to take her revenge."

"Good." She nodded, pretending to be serious, but inside, she was enjoying his teasing.

He lifted her chin and ran his thumb across her bottom lip. Bending, he touched his lips to hers.

His touch sent tremors down her spine. Warmth spread through her insides, and she wrapped her arms around his neck, pulling him closer. She sighed, feeling her body melt into his.

Hakim pressed on her back with one hand and cradled her head with the other. "Shelby," he whispered into her ear.

Chills skittered down her back. "Hmmm?" she sighed.

"Perhaps I will not leave you in the desert today. I will allow you to join us."

Shelby lifted her head and swatted at his chest.

Hakim grinned and led her toward the vehicle where Nasir waited.

This time, Nasir held the driver's door for Hakim and led her to the passenger side. Nasir climbed in the back.

"I give up. Why are the tires flat?" Shelby asked after she closed the door.

Hakim adjusted the mirror and flashed a white smile. His gaze flicked to something over her head.

She glanced at the handle on the ceiling above the passenger window.

Hakim stepped on the accelerator, but instead of pulling back onto the road, he turned and drove straight into the desert.

Shelby gasped and grabbed onto the handle as they tore over the sand.

Hakim drove to the top of the dunes, cresting them or swerving at the last minute to slide, sending out a wave behind the tires. He pushed a button on the console and loud music blasted from the speakers. A wide grin lit his face as he turned the volume even louder.

More than once, Shelby was certain they'd roll as they drove up a particularly steep hill. The momentum tugged her toward the middle of the vehicle, and she held onto the handle with both hands.

At the last second, Hakim somehow managed to twist the car into a slide. Scaling another dune, the front of the car dipped suddenly.

Shelby felt her stomach fly into her throat. "You're driving like an animal, but you can't even drive a stick shift?" she yelled over the music.

Hakim laughed, and they plummeted over another steep hill, barely turning in time to keep from rolling. The rear of the vehicle fishtailed all over the place. The ride was more like a jerky, bumpy roller coaster than a trip through the desert in a luxury SUV.

Seeing Hakim relax and enjoy himself was worth the stomach rolling and white knuckles. Disoriented, Shelby wondered if he was headed in any particular direction. Her question was answered as they climbed to the top of another dune and she saw trucks and horse trailers at the bottom of the hill. A small company of people milled around, apparently waiting for them.

Hakim parked the car.

Shelby pried her fingers off the handle.

The three got out—Shelby a little wobbly—and joined the group. At first, she didn't recognize any of them, but as she got closer, she realized Ghaniyah was among them. *Lovely.* Shelby greeted Sheik Rashid and a few of the other people Hakim introduced her to.

The party made their plans in English for Shelby's sake, although Ghaniyah had no qualms about speaking in Arabic, apparently relishing the fact Shelby couldn't understand. They split into two groups to give the falcons a wider hunting area. The parties would meet at the Bedouin camp. Hakim would travel with one group and his father with the other.

The nickering of a horse caught her attention, and Shelby turned to see Kadir leading *Al-qamar* out of a horse trailer. She excused herself and walked toward the boy. "Whass-up, Kadir-gator?" When she drew close, she gave him an exploding fist-bump.

Kadir grinned.

Al-qamar nuzzled her, and Shelby greeted her in a quiet voice, stroking the mare's soft nose. She felt the gazes of the group on her and realized all of the other horses were already saddled, but Kadir knew she preferred to take care of her own horse. *They'll just have to wait.*

Kadir handed Shelby *Al-qamar*'s blanket.

Although the group was waiting, Shelby didn't hurry. She didn't want to work too quickly and make a careless mistake that would result in the saddle rubbing against the horse in the wrong places and irritating her skin. Shelby took the bridle from Kadir and slid the bit into the horse's mouth and the bridle over her head, double-checking the buckles to make sure the mare would be comfortable.

Shelby glanced behind and saw the Sheik watching her. Her skin tightened, and she turned back to the horse. Not for the first time, she wished she could read his expression. If only she could impress him. She glanced at Ghaniyah, whose face was twisted in its usual sneer. Shelby looked away quickly and let her gaze travel around the group until she found Hakim.

He was speaking with another man who held a large bird on a thick leather glove. Hakim waved for her to join them.

Shelby handed the reins to Kadir, and then strode over the soft sand, enchanted by the sight of the hooded falcon.

"Shelby, this is *Laiqa*," Hakim said. "She is a six-month-old peregrine falcon."

"She?" Shelby watched the bird tip its head when it heard her voice.

"The males are much smaller. Females are the best hunters."

"She's beautiful."

Laiqa was reddish-brown. Black specks marked her white chest like spots of ink. The bird was silent and still. Small twitches of her head were the only indication that she was real.

"Can I touch her?" Shelby asked.

"Yes, however, it is wise to stay out of range of her beak."

With two fingers, Shelby stroked the soft feathers on *Laiqa*'s back. "Why is she wearing this mask?"

"A falcon relies mainly on sight. Covering her eyes with the hood takes away eighty percent of her senses. Being unable to see helps to keep her calm, and she will be alert when it is removed," Hakim said.

"What if she doesn't want to hunt today?"

"She will. She has not eaten since around this time yesterday." Hakim spoke to the bird handler for a moment and then lifted a hand toward the group, motioning for Shelby to accompany him.

"What does she hunt? Little rabbits?" Shelby asked as they walked toward the horses.

Hakim shook his head. "A peregrine falcon is the fastest animal in the world. She can fly at speeds of up to 320 kilometers per hour, too fast to hit an animal on the ground, so she hunts other birds. Her favorite food is pigeon, but today, we hope to find something larger."

"I can't wait." Shelby grinned.

Hakim rubbed his palm on the back of his neck. "Shelby Jo, women in my country do not typically hunt. They accompany the men, but only to observe."

Shelby pulled back her head. "Oh. I didn't know." She felt her stomach start to sour.

"I'm sorry. I know you are fully capable, and if it were only the two of us..."

"Of course. I completely understand." The stinging behind her eyes surprised Shelby. The homesickness she hadn't felt for days returned with a surge. But she wouldn't let Hakim know. If she cried, he would feel guilty, and the others would think she was throwing a childish fit.

"Are you all right?" Hakim touched her fingers and bent his head to the side to catch her eye.

Shelby reached deep and found a smile, though she couldn't imagine it was very convincing. "Sure. Let's do this." She hurried to the other side of *Al-qamar* and took a deep breath, pushing away any emotions that would embarrass both her and Hakim, and then mounted the horse. She waved goodbye to Kadir as he and the other stable workers climbed back into the pickup attached to the horse trailer.

The groups split up. The younger people followed Hakim, and a group of older men accompanied the Sheik. In each party were two falcons and ten people, beside the falcon handlers and bodyguards.

Hakim rode ahead with the men in their group.

Shelby hung back, not wanting to keep him from enjoying time with his friends. She also didn't want to get too close to Ghaniyah's group as Ghaniyah made a point to glare at Shelby before turning to her friends and laughing. The surge of emotions returned again, constricting her throat. She looked between the two groups and realized that she didn't fit in either one. The thought made the backs of her eyes prickle and she forced back any tears. *What am I doing? I don't belong here.*

After a few miles, Hakim left the men and brought his horse to ride beside Shelby. "Are you all right, Shelby Jo?" he asked. "I am sorry I have neglected you. And..." He looked back at Ghaniyah and her group.

Shelby put on her brightest smile. "I'm doing great. I love this. Go ahead and ride with your friends. Guys sometimes need 'guy time.' I don't feel neglected." At least part of her statement was true. She did love riding the horse and the amazing openness of the desert. But even more, she loved seeing Hakim so happy, and would never want him to know how lonely and uncertain she felt. She pointed toward the other men and flicked her wrist. "This is your safari, so get up there and lead the way."

He studied her face for a moment then a smile

spread over his face. He winked then spurred his horse forward to join the men.

Shelby allowed her smile to fade. Life in Khali-dar was more different than she could have ever imagined. Would she ever find a place where she fit into this culture and could be the person Hakim needed her to be? Or would she lose herself trying?

They rode for nearly half an hour. Shelby was grateful for her light clothing. The silk moved, keeping her cool even though beads of sweat rolled down her back. But she wasn't complaining.

Although the entire landscape was the same golden color, the desert didn't lack interesting details. Shelby marveled at the patterns in the sand. The wind blew it into ridges like ripples in water. Some of the dunes hung over at the top like tidal waves where the sand had slid down beneath.

Riding alone gave her a chance to think. She watched Hakim talking and laughing with the other men. Occasionally he would catch her gaze and smile. She glanced back at the group of women chatting amongst themselves. *This is how life is here.* Men and women's worlds were separate, and Shelby was an outsider to both. Could she ever be happy in Khali-dar?

One of the falcon handlers urged his horse forward to catch up with Hakim. He said something, pointing at the sky, and the men stopped.

The women watched, still talking and giggling.

Shelby rode a little closer before reining in *Al-qamar* and leaning forward in the saddle.

Hakim flexed his fingers in the thick glove before the handler placed the bird on it. He muttered in a soft voice, stroking the bird's feathers and then removed the leather hood from the bird's eyes.

Laiqa looked around, stretching out her wings and tail feathers.

Hakim motioned for Shelby to ride closer. "Are you ready?" His expression lit up in an excited smile. "She will fly with her back to the sun in order to make herself invisible to her prey." He held out his gloved hand. "Hup, hup," he said loudly.

The falcon stretched out her wings and lifted off. She circled, gliding close a few times before gaining real altitude.

The handler pointed, speaking in an urgent tone.

Hakim yelled something in Arabic, and then urged his horse into a gallop in the direction the bird had flown.

Nasir and the other men were right behind him.

Al-qamar strained to follow them, but Shelby kept a tight hold on the reins.

The women maintained their leisurely pace as they followed the cloud of dust left behind by the hunters.

Shelby could hear the men calling to one another as they galloped after the bird. She looked back at the women.

A few appeared to be admiring their friends' shoes, others looked completely bored, and one was even texting on her phone.

Finally, Shelby couldn't stand it anymore. She leaned forward in the saddle and urged *Al-qamar* into a gallop. In the distance, she saw the men point at the sky, and Shelby followed their line of sight, finally spotting *Laiqa* soaring high above.

Without warning, the falcon dove toward a larger bird Shelby hadn't even noticed, picking up speed until the falcon hit it like a bullet. The impact sent out a cloud of feathers. *Laiqa* glided to the ground, a limp mass of feathers in her talons. Shelby approached the men where they had stopped but rode slowly forward.

Hakim had already dismounted and hurried toward where *Laiqa* perched on top of the other bird tearing chunks of skin and feathers out of the carcass with her beak. He knelt near her and coaxed the falcon away from her kill, offering her a piece of meat. His patience paid off as *Laiqa* hopped onto his glove and tore into whatever Hakim had given her. He slipped away the dead bird and gave it to the handler.

Some of the men darted strange glances at Shelby. But Hakim, intent on the falcon had not seen her yet.

Should she return to join the women? Shelby looked back the way they had come and saw the group, a little over two hundred yards away, approaching at the same steady pace. She turned *Al-qamar* toward them, but twisted around when she heard Hakim's voice behind her.

"Did you enjoy hunting, Shelby Jo?" Hakim reined in his horse to ride next to her.

He didn't look angry, but she still felt a sickening guilt roll through her stomach at the idea that she had embarrassed him. "I'm sorry. I know I should have stayed with the other women. They were just going so slow, and I wanted to see—"

Hakim reached to place his hand on hers. "Do not apologize. I should have known the excitement would be too much for you to resist." His lips twitched.

"I hope I didn't embarrass you in front of the other guys."

"I imagine they were most likely impressed by

your horsemanship." His smile turned serious. "I know our customs seem strange. Especially for an independent western woman." He glanced toward the approaching group. "I want you to be happy here, more than anything." He lifted her hand and pressed a kiss on her fingers.

His affection should have dispelled her worry, but a tension still lingered, and the air between them felt heavy. "What kind of bird is that?" Shelby hoped to change the mood with a lighter topic. "It sort of looks like a long-legged, skinny chicken."

He studied her expression for a moment before answering. "It is called an Arabian Bustard. We will deliver it to the Bedouin tonight. They are always grateful for extra meat."

The hunt was repeated, this time with Hakim's friend's bird.

Shelby watched from a distance, although the sight of racing horses and the sounds of excitement pulled at her sense of adventure, and she held herself tightly to resist the urge to gallop, whooping across the desert. She didn't ride with the women or the men, but remained somewhere in between, which she thought was fitting. The sun sank lower in the sky, and Shelby's stomach growled. She hoped they were close to their destination.

They rode for another half hour, and the shadows of the dunes stretched. The sunset colored the sand a deep red-gold.

Hakim joined her and the uncomfortable silence hung like a shadow between them. "Are you upset, Shelby Jo?"

"No. I was just thinking about how much fun my

dad and Chet would have chasing these birds over the dunes."

"You miss your family."

Shelby nodded, swallowing over a lump in her throat.

"I am sorry."

Again Shelby nodded, and they rode in silence for several minutes.

Hakim leaned forward and patted his horse. "We are nearly to the camp. Are you tired?"

"No." She turned toward him and studied his expression. The planes of his face were shadowed by the setting sun, and the cloth from his head wrap blew in the wind, making him look like the hero in an adventure movie. Shelby's heart skipped at the sight. Lines pulled at the corners of his mouth and eyes and she realized he was worried about her. "I loved today, Hakim. I loved riding with you and seeing the desert and the birds hunt. Even if we didn't spend every second together. Please don't be worried about me."

"I will always worry about you, Shelby Jo."

They climbed another rise, and a small camp spread out below them. The cluster of tents was surrounded by a woven fence. If they had ridden a hundred yards to either side, they would have missed it among the dunes. The gates stood open, and the party dismounted before Hakim led them in.

A group of men approached and led away their horses.

When she was faced with a man stepping up to take *Al-qamar,* Shelby held onto the reins. "Hakim, will you ask him if I can take care of *Al-qamar* myself?"

The man listened, nodded, and indicated for Shelby

to follow him toward a small fenced-in corral.

"I will come find you after I speak to the tribal Elder," Hakim said.

Shelby removed *Al-qamar*'s saddle and bridle. While the mare drank, Shelby rubbed her down with an old brush she found. After making sure *Al-qamar* had something to eat, she climbed out of the corral and rested her forearms on the fence to watch the horses in the dwindling light.

"Shelby Walker."

Shelby turned to see the Sheik approaching her with another man.

"As-salaamu 'alaykum," she said as she bowed to Sheik Rashid.

"May I please introduce Malik bin Bazyli al Fattah Al Nuaim? He is the Elder of the *Al Nuaim* tribe."

"Ahlan wa sahlan," she said.

"Ahlan wa sahlan, Shelby Walker," the Elder replied. He spoke her name with a thick accent. He turned and spoke to the Sheik in rapid Arabic.

"Elder Malik would like me to tell you *Al-qamar* is very special to his tribe, and he is pleased to see you treating her so well."

"Shukran," Shelby thanked him.

The Elder stepped closer to the fence, and *Al-qamar* trotted over, nuzzling him as he spoke.

Sheik Rashid continued, "It is believed by the Bedouin that sharing a tent with an Arabian horse guarantees no evil spirit will enter. They have a deep love for their animals."

The Elder spoke again and Sheik Rashid translated. "He said *Al-qamar* is happy. She is grateful for the care you give her."

Shelby couldn't tell what the Sheik was thinking. Was the Elder serious? Was he some kind of horse whisperer, or was this one of the Sheik's little tests? She chose her words carefully. "Please tell him I am thankful for the opportunity to spend time with such a remarkable animal, and *Al-qamar* is special to me, too."

After listening to the Sheik, the Elder gave Shelby an appraising look and a smile. He seemed as if he were about to say more when Hakim arrived.

Hakim bowed to his father and to the Elder. Then Hakim and Elder Malik bent toward each other and briefly touched noses.

Shelby gave a start. *What was that?* She glanced at the Sheik to see his reaction, but he didn't act as if anything out of the ordinary had happened.

Elder Malik and Hakim spoke together for a few minutes, and Shelby heard her name and *Al-qamar*'s.

"What the heck was that nose bump thing you did?" Shelby murmured to Hakim as they followed the two leaders toward the tents.

"It is a traditional greeting between men. An exchange of breath," he explained.

"Oh," said Shelby, still feeling a little awkward. "I thought you guys were going to kiss."

Hakim chuckled, and his hand found hers in the dark. He leaned close and whispered, "I plan to save my kisses for you."

Chapter Eighteen

Lanterns came to life throughout the camp, illuminating circles of light in the near pitch-blackness as Shelby and Hakim walked between the tents. Each structure was made of brightly colored woolen fabric, and was constructed around one or two wooden poles supporting the ceiling and the sides. Ropes ran from the corners attaching them to stakes driven into the sand. Most of the tents were closed and dark.

Shelby shivered and rubbed her arms, surprised by how fast the temperature had dropped as soon as the sun went down.

At the end of the common area, a large tent shone, lit with more lanterns that hung from the ceiling and sat on the tables. Delicious smells and the sounds of voices and laughter drifted toward them. As they got closer, Shelby saw thick woolen rugs covered the ground under the tent. Cushions were spread haphazardly on the rugs around short tables. The room looked and smelled welcoming when she entered.

A young girl bowed to Hakim and offered them a drink.

"*Shukran*," Shelby thanked her. She took a small sip and tasted fruit juice. The beverage was cold and sweet, and delicious.

"*Sharab*." Hakim gestured to her cup. "Given as a welcome to refresh weary travelers."

Shelby gazed around as Hakim led her to a seat. Ghaniyah and her friends had already arrived, and she looked fantastic as usual. Apparently, she had found time to freshen up after the sweaty horse-ride. Another face was familiar, and Shelby tried to remember where she knew him from. She finally recognized him as the man who'd delivered *Al-qamar* to the palace. The man whose face drooped on one side. *What was his name— Usman?*

For a moment, she attempted to catch his eye, but when she remembered how he had avoided her gaze when they'd met before, she gave up.

At the far end of the tent, Shelby sat next to Hakim at Elder Malik's table. In the light, the Elder looked much older than the Sheik. He wore a white *dishdasha* and, on his head, a checkered *kehfiya*. His dark and wrinkled skin spoke of someone who spent a lot of time in the sun. Although his eyes seemed sunken and heavily lidded, Shelby saw a lively spark in them.

His gaze darted around as he watched the people in the room.

Hakim introduced the others at the table as the Elder's wife and older children.

Shelby shifted on the floor, experimenting with different positions, and finally sat cross-legged.

Many of the men lounged, resting on cushions while they ate, but the women all sat straight.

Hakim sat with his legs crossed, leaning on his hand which rested on the ground slightly behind Shelby. As he translated the conversation at the table, he leaned close, his breath flowing warm on her cheek.

Shelby shivered and reminded herself more than once to sit straight, instead of resting against him.

Dinner on the floor felt so comfortable and intimate.

Young girls served the meal in steaming bowls. The food was delicious and simple. Dancers entertained them, their beautiful costumes and jangling jewelry shining in the lantern light.

Shelby felt their genuine hospitality as Elder Malik and his wife spoke in halting English. With Hakim translating, they asked her about her family and her home. Elder Malik seemed especially interested when she told him about her father's cattle ranch. He asked questions about the weather in Colorado, how it affected the animals, and how her father kept track of such a large herd.

"Well, we brand the calves when they are new. That is how a rancher like my dad identifies his animals if they wander. Hakim can tell you about that. He was there this year for branding."

Hakim translated using hand gestures and speaking in an excited voice.

The Sheik pulled back, his eyes growing wide.

Elder Malik threw back his head as he laughed. "You will make Prince Hakim to be a cowboy, Miss Walker."

Shelby smiled at the Elder and risked a glance at the Sheik, expecting a scowl of contempt, but his expression was contemplative as he studied her. How she wished she knew what that man was thinking. Shelby avoided looking at Ghaniyah, although she still felt her glares boring into her throughout dinner.

The meal ended and the Elder stood and spoke to the group. "My friends, I am pleased to have your company here, in my home. It is good to strengthen the bonds between our people. Although our lives are very different, when we meet, we discover we are very much alike. We all share a love for this land, and our cooperation will make Khali-dar strong. It is essential to strengthen ties with our old allies, as well as make new friends." As he said this, his gaze lit on Shelby, and he gave her a fatherly smile.

Hakim squeezed her hand under the table as he translated the Elder's words. "It seems you have won the approval of the Elder," he whispered.

Shelby smiled and inclined her head in a small bow to Elder Malik.

Hakim turned. "Shelby, traditionally after dinner, men and women separate for a short time. Jawahir will take you to the women's tent." He raised a hand to indicate one of the Elder's daughters.

The young woman smiled and gave a small bow.

"Separate? Why?" *Not this again.*

"It is simply a tradition." The corner of Hakim's mouth twitched in a teasing smile, and he bumped her with his arm. "And we have manly topics to discuss."

The women began to stand, and Shelby chewed on her lip. She was really starting to hate the "women's role" thing going on here.

Hakim raised his brows and nodded his encouragement.

"Okay, I'll see you in a few." Shelby followed Jawahir and the other women to a nearby tent.

One of the women held aside the blanket covering the doorway for Shelby to step through.

Shelby found this tent to be a smaller version of the one they had just left. Close to twenty women sat or stood throughout the space, and Shelby noticed they stayed separated in two distinct groups: the Bedouin women and the city women. Shelby sat next to Jawahir.

"Shelby Walker, it's good to see you where you belong, among the farmers' daughters."

Shelby turned to see Ghaniyah standing behind her.

"Don't worry, they won't judge you." Her cold voice pierced the warmth of the tent. "They prefer their own kind—filthy, poor girls who smell like horses. I'm sure they envy your position as a diversion for a rich man."

The Bedouin women remained silent, keeping their heads lowered. Some of their faces were flushed.

Why weren't they saying anything? Did they understand Ghaniyah?

The women sat with shoulders hunched, their eyes shifting. They avoided Ghaniyah's gaze and some fiddled with their hands to appear busy, while others clenched their fists.

Shelby stood and took a deep breath to get herself under control. Yelling would solve nothing. "Ghaniyah, you're right. I do belong here. I'm proud to sit with these women. How dare you insult them this way? You're their guest." She tried to speak calmly, though her voice trembled with rage. "That's the problem with people like you. You believe having a big house and a rich daddy makes you better than everybody else. The Sheik listens to Elder Malik and considers him an important ally. How would he react if he heard that you thought a member of a respected family in his kingdom wasn't good enough? Prince Hakim would be disappointed and ashamed to hear how you treated these people. He'd never want a partner who acts so disrespectful."

"You have the gall to consider yourself 'his

partner'?" Ghaniyah spat out the words. "Do you really think the two of you have a *relationship*?"

"Frankly, Ghaniyah"—Shelby spoke just as softly, hoping her trembling voice didn't betray her anger— "it's quite clear Hakim prefers spending time with me to spending time with you. He isn't looking for a spoiled brat who worries more about her appearance than being his friend. He wants to be with someone who keeps up with him, races horses, talks about important things, and likes the things he likes. Someone who loves him, not just his title."

The silence stretched through the room like a thick mist, pressing down on them until Shelby thought she could actually feel it. The women from both groups stared open-mouthed as Shelby again sat next to Jawahir. She ignored the tension, and instead, asked the Bedouin women about their camp. Most were able to answer her in halting English. A few of the city women looked interested in the conversation, so Shelby scooted over, making the circle bigger.

Ghaniyah remained standing in the same spot, apparently considering her options. She didn't storm out to stand outside in the dark by herself. After a few moments, she sat—although, she remained on the other side of the tent, as far away from Shelby as possible.

One of the women asked Shelby about her home, and the conversation turned toward her family and life on the ranch. Shelby had just finished explaining about some of the different rodeo events, and relating one of Chet's more hilarious adventures in bull-dogging, when they heard men's voices outside their tent.

The women gathered their things and said their goodbyes.

Jawahir and her mother stood next to Shelby. "Thank you, Shelby Walker." Jawahir took Shelby's hand and slipped a bangle bracelet onto Shelby's arm.

Shelby ran her finger over the bracelet. It was made of small threads of metal woven together into an intricate pattern. Coins and colorful beads and jangled when Shelby moved. "Jawahir, this is beautiful. *Shukran*."

"You are a good friend to my family," she said in a heavy accent.

Her mother lifted Shelby's other hand.

Shelby hugged both of the women and turned to find Hakim, Sheik Rashid, and Elder Malik watching her from the tent entrance.

Both Hakim and Elder Malik smiled.

An expression flashed over the Sheik's guarded face, and Shelby wondered if she'd imagined it. Was it approval?

Hakim held Shelby's hand as they followed the Sheik and Elder Malik through the darkened camp to the gates. Her tinkling bracelet was the only sound in the darkness.

When they arrived at the fence surrounding the camp, the group stopped.

"*Shukran*" Shelby placed her hands together and bowed to the Elder. "Thank you for a lovely evening."

He smiled, the lines around his eyes showing even in the darkness. "You will always be welcome here, Shelby Walker. Please return."

"I would love to. And I will bring *Al-qamar* to visit."

The Elder nodded his head and bid farewell to Hakim and his father.

Nasir waited outside the lantern light to lead them to their vehicle and drive them back to the palace.

Shelby didn't realize how tired she was and remembered nothing after Nasir closed the vehicle door behind her.

"Shelby." Hakim brushed her hair back from her face.

She sat up, lifting her cheek off his chest. Sometime during the ride, he had pulled her into his lap and held her as she slept.

"Wake up. We are home."

His words jolted her out of her sleepy stupor, and warmth spread through her chest. *We are home?* She liked the sound of that.

****

"*Sab'a, thamaaniya, tis'a*...um,... '*ashra.*" Shelby finished counting.

"Excellent," Aaliya said.

The two sat poolside, dangling their feet in the water.

"Now," she continued, "What color is your dress?"

Shelby looked down at the blue sundress she'd pulled above her knees and tucked under her legs. "Let's see..." She bit her lip as she thought. "*Zarqaa'*."

"Perfect! You even remembered to use the feminine form." Aaliya smiled and nodded. "You are learning quickly."

"Yeah, but everything I know is like Arabic Sesame Street. Colors, numbers, a few animals." Shelby lifted a date out of the bowl between them and chewed on it before she spoke again. "What about this?" She held the half-eaten fruit. "What is this called?"

"*Balah.*"

"And the sandwiches we had?" Shelby waved toward the blanket behind them where only bits of the delicious meat, vegetables, and flatbread remained from their picnic.

"*Shawarma.*"

"*Shawarma* is possibly my new favorite food." Shelby patted her stomach, her Bedouin bracelet jingling.

Aaliya laughed. "It is one of my favorites, too. My mother makes it when we have extra meat."

"You haven't told me much about your family. Do they live close?"

"My parents live in the city."

"Do you get to see them often?" Shelby bent forward and scooped the cool water onto her legs.

"Yes. I visit them once a week at least."

"Do you have brothers and sisters?"

"Yes. One younger sister who lives with our parents." Aaliya pulled her feet out of the water. She turned toward Shelby, sitting cross-legged. "Your younger brother is named Chet?" When Shelby nodded, she continued. "Do you miss him?"

"Yes." She was surprised at the lump in her throat and the tears that threatened to spill over. "Aaliya, I don't know what will happen."

"No one knows the future, Shelby."

"I feel…suspended—trapped in mid-air or stuck in mid-motion. You know what I mean?" She clenched her fists in frustration. "I don't know how long I'll be here or what my role is in this world. Hakim has alluded to a future together, but if I were to stay, how would I fit in?"

"In my opinion, you are becoming a woman of Khali-dar. You are speaking the language, enjoying the food, and yesterday, you looked the part beautifully, wearing the clothes."

"We both know I will always be an outsider."

Aaliya squeezed Shelby's hand. "Not to Prince Hakim, and not to me. This bracelet you wear shows the wonderful impression you made on Elder Malik and his family. You must not worry. You make friends easily—you are special. And if you continue to be yourself, you will find your place here."

****

Shelby's life at the palace fell into a comfortable routine. Every morning, she hurried down to the stables to ride *Al-qamar*. She never forgot to bring Kadir a treat, and the two spent time together, joking around and taking care of the mare. Much of the morning, she occupied herself by reading in the gardens, or practicing Arabic with Aaliya on her balcony. She ate lunch, and every sound caused her heart to skip. She expected Hakim at any time, and the rest of the day always belonged to him.

She knew he worked hard, attending various meetings with his father, and she was determined to give him the space he needed, which was why she was surprised to see him waiting one morning when she left the stables. She had just returned *Al-qamar* after their morning ride.

Hakim was speaking to the trainers and security guards near the racing entrance. He and one of the men strode over to join them. "Shelby, this is Sayyid. He is the head trainer of our racing horses."

She noticed Kadir had walked over to stand next to

Sayyid. "*Al-salaam alaykum*, Sayyid."

"*Wa alaykum e-salaam*, Miss Walker," he responded, bowing.

"Sayyid is the boy's father," Hakim told her. "His family has raised and trained racing horses for my family for generations."

"And now, he's teaching Kadir," Shelby said.

Hakim nodded. "We have been making the final preparations for the race horses to be sent to Kentucky to qualify. The Derby is in two weeks."

Hakim spoke a few words to Sayyid before taking Shelby's hand and walking along the path to the palace.

"Later, Kadir!" Waving, Shelby called to the boy. "See you tomorrow."

He smiled widely as he waved back.

Sensing that Hakim had a lot on his mind, Shelby remained quiet. She didn't want to disturb his thoughts.

When they reached the garden, Hakim led her down a new path. It opened into a small clearing surrounded by high hedges. In the clearing stood a wooden gazebo. The windows were carved intricately—their arches rose to a point. A bench ran around the walls. Hakim held her hand as they stepped inside. "This was my favorite place to play as a child," Hakim said. "I still come here when I wish to be alone."

"Do you want to be alone?" Shelby asked. He'd spoken as if he was distracted.

"No. There is something I would like to speak with you about."

Shelby sat next to him.

He put his arm around her. "Are you happy here?" He kissed the top of her head.

"Yes." Shelby sighed and rested her head against

his shoulder.

He was silent.

Shelby knew he was waiting for her to continue. "Everything is perfect, and everybody is so nice. Well, almost everybody. I have loved spending time with you and, even sometimes, your father. These weeks have been the best of my life."

Hakim took a deep breath and looked into her eyes. "Would you like to stay here with me?"

Shelby was silent, considering the meaning of his words, but before she could speak, he continued.

"Shelby Walker, will you stay here in Khali-dar and be my wife?" He took her hand in his, and slid a beautiful ring on her finger.

A gasp escaped, and Shelby's heart raced. Her throat went dry. Holding up her hand, she admired the gold band with a large ruby set between two diamonds. The ring was the most beautiful she had ever seen, and this moment was exactly what she had hoped for. She was in love with Hakim, and he was in love with her. And their love had seemed like enough.

Yet, seeing the ring, the ruby, something started to tickle her subconscious, pushing its way up until it burst out. Shelby's mind reeled. What would this mean? Could she live here forever? They had spoken generally about the future. Just not in any detail. Suddenly, those forgotten details loomed up and pressed in on her.

What about her family? Would she be able to see them? She didn't think Hakim would keep her from visiting, but the terrorists might. Could she give up her family?

Ghaniyah, her friends, and who knew how many other people in Khali-dar hated her. Would she have to endure their looks, their spite forever? And what about children? Would the other kids of Khali-dar hate her kids because she, an outsider, was their mother? How would she even go about raising children in a palace? She knew Hakim had been educated by tutors—so did that mean their kids wouldn't even get to go to school? Or play football? Or have friends?

She looked from Hakim to the garden outside the gazebo as thoughts continued to fill her mind. She worried about the whole issue with his dad. Did the Sheik know Hakim's plan to marry her? What would he say? Even worse, what would he do? Hakim was risking the disapproval of his father, but what if the Sheik forbade it? Disowned his son? Was Hakim really willing to give up everything to be with her? She couldn't let him do that. His father was the only family he had. Hakim had been prepared since the day he was born to be the next Sheik. He would be the best Sheik Khali-dar ever had. She couldn't let him sacrifice all that for love.

She set her hands in her lap, and looked back at him, through eyes full of tears. "I don't know, Hakim. I don't know if I can marry you."

Hakim's shoulders slumped. He moved his head from side to side, and the skin around his eyes tightened.

"I love you," she continued, "and I want to be with you, but I don't know if I can live this life. I'm living here like I'm on a cruise ship. I sleep in, people make my bed, and my days are filled with doing whatever I want." Shelby reached for his hand, but thought better of it and clutched her elbow. "I'm a taker. I don't have a role here. I don't feel as if I am contributing to the world in any way. And I don't know if I can do that forever."

Frowning, Hakim opened his mouth to say something.

She held up a hand to stop him and shook her head. "I'm sorry. I know I sound selfish after all you've done for me, but I need to do things for you, too. Not just bask in your affection and gifts, rewarding you with a smile and a kiss. I need to feel like I have something to offer—not only to you, or your father, or to Khali-dar, but to myself as well." She curled her hand into a fist on her knee. "Otherwise, I'll lose who I am, pretending to be someone I'm not."

"Shelby."

"I know, I'm talking crazy." She shook her head. "But I can't do this, Hakim. I can't love you honestly if I'm not true to myself."

"Is this because of my father?" Hakim's voice was thick. His eyes shined over-bright and his expression flitted between disappointed, desperate, and angry.

"Partly. You know how he feels about me." She pointed to herself and then let her hand drop. "He will never consent to this. But he's not the only one, Hakim. Most of your people don't approve of us. Of me."

"Those are people who have not met you, yet. You will win their hearts as you did Elder Malik and his family. I know you will." His breath hitched and he stared with a crinkled brow.

"Your whole country is depending on you to be the Sheik." Blinking hard, Shelby looked at the ring again, sliding it off her finger. "Sheiks don't marry poor American cowgirls." Saying those words made her stomach churn. Her mind reeled, and she knew she had to leave. Seeing the pain in his eyes made her heart feel like it was shrinking. He looked so vulnerable. She wiped her dripping nose on her sleeve and stood, placing the heavy ring into his hand.

"I just need time to think, all right?" She ran from the gazebo, following the same path they had taken, back to the stables. Shelby ran past a bewildered Kadir, re-saddled *Al-qamar*, and spurred her into a gallop. She rode in a daze before she reined in the mare and considered where she was. Luckily, *Al-qamar* had followed their regular path into the forest. At least the horse seemed to know which way to go. She prodded the mare forward, letting her set her own pace.

Shelby's mind raced. *Had that just happened?* What was she doing? Was she giving up the greatest thing that had ever happened in her life? She knew the answer was "yes," but she also knew in a place deep down, a place she often wished never existed, that she had been honest with Hakim. Being raised on a farm, working hard her entire life, she couldn't deny her existence would be a fake if she wasn't true to the part of herself that understood the need to contribute to the world, instead of just seeing what she could get for free. She wasn't paying attention to the path, and when she noticed two men ahead of her, she startled.

They wore the uniforms of the gardeners, but instead of going about their business, they scrutinized her.

Her scalp tightened. Usually, Shelby felt annoyed that people were everywhere at the palace, never allowing her to be truly alone. But, after she darted her gaze around, she realized for once, no one was near to help. She was in danger. Heart pounding, Shelby dug her heels into *Al-qamar's* side to spur her into a run, but the action came too late.

One of the men had moved fast, grabbing the reins and halting her horse. The other, larger man yanked Shelby from the saddle, clamping his hand over her mouth to keep her from screaming.

Shelby bit down, and the man grunted in pain. In her panic, she struggled, swinging her arms and legs as hard as she could. She felt the satisfaction of her foot making contact a few times before she felt a cloth pushed against her face and smelled the acrid tang of chemicals. Shelby sank into darkness.

Chapter Nineteen

Hakim sat where Shelby had left him, rotating the ring around and around in his fingers—his gaze focused on nothing. He heard a noise and looked up to see Nasir running down the path toward the gazebo.

"Your Highness." Nasir spoke between panting breaths. "I have bad news."

When he saw the expression on Nasir's face, Hakim jumped to his feet. "Has there been another attack?"

Nasir hesitated for a split second. "Your Highness, Miss Walker has been kidnapped."

Moments later, the two men strode down the hall. Nasir briefed Hakim on the information they had so far.

"Her horse wandered back to the stable alone. Following the animal's usual path, we found signs of a struggle. Miss Walker's bracelet was discovered and, nearby, a bottle of chloroform." Nasir handed Hakim a piece of twisted metal.

Hakim recognized it as the Bedouin bracelet Shelby loved, and his stomach hardened into a rock.

"Based on our intelligence," Nasir continued, "we believe this kidnapping was orchestrated by *Nahl.*"

"What intelligence?" Hakim fought to control the panic threatening to engulf his thoughts. *How long has it been since Shelby left me? Twenty minutes? Half an hour?*

"It was posted in a chat-room forum. The person claimed the 'prince's girlfriend' was the prisoner of *Nahl*."

Hakim knew Nasir chose his words carefully to spare him further pain. The kidnappers had undoubtedly called Shelby something worse than his "girlfriend. "Were we able to trace the user?"

"No, Your Highness, the IP address was untraceable."

"How did this happen? We have the best security possible." Hakim vaguely registered shock that his heart was capable of hurting worse than it had when Shelby had rejected his proposal. But thinking about what the terrorists would do, could be doing, to Shelby, even now…

His breath came in short gasps, and he knew he needed to calm himself. He pressed a hand against a wall and evened out his breathing.

Nasir stood by the prince and continued his update. "After reviewing video from the security cameras, we believe three men in gardener's uniforms were able to conceal Miss Walker under a large pile of branches which were hauled out of the forest roughly a half hour ago."

Hakim could barely believe what he was hearing. He rubbed his forehead as he tried to make sense of what Nasir was saying. "And they just drove through the gate?"

"Yes, Your Highness. The truck and its cargo were found abandoned a few blocks from the palace where Miss Walker was apparently transferred to another vehicle."

A million thoughts tumbled through Hakim's mind.

How had these men obtained entrance to the grounds? Were they actual gardeners? How had they escaped without being searched? Why wasn't Shelby being guarded? Who had let this happen? All of these questions would be answered, he knew, but right now, Shelby's safety was his highest priority. "What is being done?" He tried to keep his voice from rising or shaking.

"We are attempting to identify the men, and technical analysts are searching the internet for any further information."

Hakim nodded. His stomach was roiling.

"There has undoubtedly been some negligence in our security." Nasir's face colored. "You may be assured the people responsible will be dealt with."

Hakim nodded again, his mind far away.

"Your Highness." Nasir placed his hand on the prince's shoulder.

Hakim saw uncharacteristic concern in his face as he considered his bodyguard. This was the first time he had seen a different side of Nasir other than pure professionalism. He sensed true sympathy and realized how much he depended on this man. How much he trusted him.

"Based on their previous patterns, it is likely *Nahl* will try to use Miss Walker as a bargaining chip. Which means for now, anyway, they will keep her alive."

Hakim felt some small relief when he heard this, at first, but then his mind wandered. They could do worse than death, and the images that filled his head made his heart pound and his lungs constrict to the point that he gasped. He pushed away the thoughts, realizing he would be no good to Shelby if he could not pull himself together. "Nasir, please find her."

Nasir swallowed and nodded.

****

Shelby awoke in the dark and assessed her situation. She sat with her back against a hard wall. Right away, she felt pain. Her legs were bent in an awkward position that made her bad ankle throb. Her arms burned from being bound behind her. She struggled and strained for a few minutes to un-cramp her screaming muscles and finally gave up. Then, she noticed muted noise. Somewhere close by, strangers carried on conversations she couldn't understand. She blinked her eyes and willed herself into a hazy consciousness.

She was squashed on a cement floor in a small, dark room about the size of a closet. In fact, that's probably exactly what this room was. The only light came from a strip under the door. As Shelby's eyes adjusted to the dark, she saw the room contained nothing except for dust, spider webs, and a round drain in the center of the floor.

The small room was too small for Shelby to stretch her legs out all the way. She managed to stand, which required a bit of work with no hands and a groggy head, and noticed her boots had been taken, leaving her wearing socks. She backed up to the door and twisted to the side, lifted her arms, and tried to turn the knob. She wasn't surprised to find it locked. Leaning forward, she used her left heel to bang on the door and yelled, "Hey! Open the door!"

Her screaming silenced the voices in the other room and earned her a shove, as the door flew open.

She was pushed down hard. "Let me out," she

screamed, turning around on her knees. "I'm an American citizen!"

The man who had pushed her only laughed.

Shelby recognized him as the large man who had pulled her from her horse. The one she had bitten. She flicked her gaze to his right hand which rested on the door frame. She felt a twinge of satisfaction to see nasty red tooth-shaped marks. She also noticed this man's thick dark hair grew down on his forehead, almost to his eyebrows. He reminded her of a large, hairy monkey.

He held the door partly closed so she couldn't see any of the other people behind him.

"Listen, you need to let me out of here right now or you'll be sorry when Prince Hakim and the Sheik find you." Her voice shook with rage and fear.

The man laughed again and said something over his shoulder in Arabic.

Shelby gritted her teeth and wished she could understand more of the language.

He turned back, sneering, and said, "They will not be a threat to us for long." Then he slammed the door.

Shelby kept kicking and yelling until the door jerked open again, and a bucket of ice cold water was dumped on her. The door slammed and she screamed, pounding on it with her stockinged feet—the pain in her ankle feeding her anger.

After being drenched by three more frigid buckets of water, she stopped shouting and collapsed against the wall. Her body felt exhausted. She was soaked and freezing. The closet was too small for her to lie down, and Shelby wouldn't have lain on the cold, wet ground anyway.

Over the next hours, pain screamed through Shelby's shoulders. The ropes dried, becoming tighter around her wrists. Terrified, she wondered what would happen. Would they let her live? She assumed she would be used as a bargaining chip to force Hakim to do whatever *Nahl* wanted. What if he refused? Was Khali-dar's policy on terrorist negotiations the same as the United States'? How much time would they give him? Would they send him her severed fingers in the mail to make sure he knew they were serious? Would they beat or torture her? Would she ever see her family again? She couldn't imagine any scenario in which this turned out well. Her mind was reeling out of control, and surges of panic shot down her arms and legs.

She breathed deeply and struggled to focus. As she willed her mind to relax, she found another, more pressing issue. As scared as she was, she couldn't keep her focus from centering on her physical discomfort. Had her captors not considered the fact that she would eventually need to use the bathroom? Even if she did abandon all humanity and used a drain in a closet floor, she could not make that work in her current situation.

The door opened, interrupting her thoughts. Shelby squinted, suddenly blinded by the brightness. She glanced up, expecting to see Mr. Hairy, but she saw, instead, the silhouette of a nervous-looking smallish woman. Shelby wondered if she was afraid she'd get a mouth-shaped welt on her hand, too? The thought made her smile a little.

The woman motioned for Shelby to get up and follow her.

As she stood, Shelby moaned. Her body was stiff from being crunched in such a confined space. She winced when she put weight on her right foot. She gazed around as she followed the woman and realized she was in a house. They walked through the main room which served as a kitchen, family room, and office. Dark curtains covered the windows, keeping out the sunlight. *Is it night or day?* She looked for a door that led outside, but her heart sank when she saw two men standing in front of it. She recognized Mr. Hairy's companion from the woods. Shelby did her best not to limp. Unable to stop herself, she glared.

He sneered back.

Shelby wondered if this was the shy woman's house. *Is she married to Mr. Hairy? Who are the other guys? Are they members of* Nahl?

The woman stopped in front of a door and opened it, displaying a small bathroom which only had a toilet and a sink. Motioning for Shelby to turn around, the woman liberated her swollen wrists and stepped aside, allowing Shelby inside the bathroom.

Her arms burned in protest as she rolled them forward and rubbed her shoulders with a suppressed moan. Shelby searched the tiny room for something she could use as a weapon, or something to pick a lock. A bobby pin, anything. But her search was in vain. She was glad for the chance to use the facilities and wash her face and hands. Opening the door, she found the timid-looking woman outside. Shelby followed her back into the closet where a small bowl of soup and a slice of bread sat on the floor.

She smiled at the woman, shot a glare of defiance at the men, and stepped through the door, relieved that she didn't have to pretend to be brave anymore. The lock clicked behind her, and even though she had expected to hear it, she still jerked and her heart sank. Tears burned her eyes.

The only thing that changed in the small room besides the food being replaced while she used the bathroom was the light shining under the door. It dimmed, brightened, and sometimes went out. Shelby tried to figure out how long she had been there based on the illuminated strip, but the light appeared inconsistently, and after a while, she lost track of time all together.

At first, Shelby was nearly paralyzed with terror. Every little sound caused her to jump, but as time passed, she grew numb and her fear lessened. Even her desperation to escape, to have answers, to know what was being done about her absence yielded to plain old boredom.

Knowing she needed something besides self-pity to occupy her mind, Shelby gave herself small tasks. She measured the room. Her grandma had once told her the space between the second and third knuckles on her pointer finger is approximately an inch. She multiplied to calculate feet, divided to calculate percentage of a mile, converted to metric, figured the volume in liters, milliliters, cubic centimeters... She recited in her head the lyrics to every song she could think of, and then recited them backward, in Pig Latin, mixed every other word with another song... Anything to keep herself from falling to pieces.

But no matter what she occupied her mind with, she couldn't keep her thoughts from wandering to Hakim. *When did he discover I was gone? Is he panicked? Will I ever see him again?* This last thought brought a lump to her throat, and the feelings she had repressed since the morning in the gazebo burst out of her mouth in sobs.

When she thought of the last thing she had said, she cringed. *She needed time to think?* Well, now she had it. She might as well use it. *How did my life come to this? Am I seriously so selfish that a* prince *wasn't good enough?* But that other side of her brain kept reminding her that her happiness wouldn't be found lolling around in beautiful dresses, eating all the hummus she could get her hands on. There needed to be more to her life. More to do, more to focus on besides herself. Finally, she collapsed into a fitful sleep.

Shelby spent her first few days of confinement in relative silence, but after what she guessed to be two or three days, she noticed movement in the house, and her heart pounded. Something was happening. As the time passed, she heard more and more voices. Most of the voices belonged to men, although she heard women, too. One woman in particular yelled in a shrill, loud voice. Shelby hoped *she* was Mr. Hairy's wife.

Twisting herself into a more comfortable position, Shelby found she could hear the people in the room almost perfectly with her ear against the door. She understood some words, and even a few sentences, and listened as closely as she could.

****

A knock sounded on Hakim's door. "Your Highness, I am sorry to wake you."

"Please, come in, Nasir. I am not asleep." Hakim sat on the couch in his bedroom—his father on a chair beside him. The room was bathed in a dim lamplight.

"I am sorry, I didn't know you were here also, Your Majesty." Nasir bowed.

The Sheik nodded and indicated a chair near them.

"Thank you, Your Majesty, but I only came to bring news. Our sources indicate an internet video will be released in two days detailing the demands of the kidnappers."

"Two days?" asked Hakim. Two days seemed like an eternity. "Why are they waiting so long?"

"It is a game, Your Highness. At that time, five days will have passed since Miss Walker was taken. They hope to have you in such a state of desperation that you will be willing to give them anything they ask for."

"It is a good plan," Hakim said. He rubbed his eyes. "There is nothing I would not give if it would ensure Shelby's safety."

"My son," the Sheik said in a gentle voice. "The *Nahl* will not ask for money. That is not what they seek."

Hakim leaned back in his chair and rubbed his eyes. *How can I choose between the welfare of my country and the woman I love?* He was exhausted. Every time he closed his eyes, he had to jerk himself back into consciousness. The last three days had been the longest of his life. The hours after Nasir had brought him the news about Shelby's disappearance had passed in a blur. Hakim insisted on being involved in every aspect of the investigation. He rode with Nasir as the grounds were searched. He was present as employees were interviewed. He watched over the analysts' shoulders as they examined security tapes and searched the internet. He oversaw the dispatch of every available officer and listened to each of their reports as they failed to find any trace of Shelby. He pushed his soldiers, desperately trying to think of something— anything they had overlooked.

With each failure, Hakim became more frantic. He felt so helpless. He should be doing something! He wanted to drive around the city, searching, but Nasir convinced him that he would serve Shelby better if he waited in the palace. The kidnappers would eventually make contact.

After two days, the frantic energy fueled by adrenaline began to be replaced by fatigue, and Nasir and the Sheik convinced Hakim to rest. However, sleep brought no relief. Each time he closed his eyes, he was plagued by images of Shelby imprisoned, or being beaten, or tortured, or worse.

He had no one to blame but himself. If he hadn't been so arrogant, so convinced he was the only one who could keep her safe... And how could he have been so selfish to think she would give up everything to stay in Khali-dar? This was not the life for a lively, independent woman. These thoughts continued to haunt him as he stared out the window of his bedroom, with nothing but his own pain to keep him company.

That evening, Hakim paced back and forth across his father's office then sank into a chair in front of the Sheik's desk. "I can't put them through this, Father. She is their only daughter. How can I tell them?"

The Sheik leaned on his cane as he walked around the desk and sat in a chair next to him.

Hakim could tell his father was hurt at seeing his son so distressed.

He put his hand on Hakim's shoulder. "If you were in danger, I would wish to know."

"I know. It is my responsibility, but..."

"But you are afraid. You are afraid to cause Shelby's parents the same pain you feel. You do not want them to agonize day and night over her safety as you do. As a father, I must insist that you call them."

Hakim nodded. He knew his father was right. It was only a matter of time before Shelby's parents or the media picked up an internet transmission and learned about Shelby's capture. "I will call."

The Sheik exited the room to allow Hakim privacy.

He scrolled through the contacts on his cell phone, his pulse pounding so hard that his fingers ached.

"Hello?"

At the sound of Shelby's mother's voice, Hakim's throat went dry and he swallowed hard. "Hello, Debbie. It is Hakim."

"Oh, hi, Hakim. I'm so glad you called. I haven't heard from Shelby in a few days. The two of you must be having so much fun that she hasn't had time to call or email."

Guilt slammed hard, and Hakim pressed his eyes shut. "Debbie, I…"

"Is something wrong, dear? Is Shelby okay?"

At the sound of her last question, Hakim heard her voice lose its levity. He cleared his dry throat. "Debbie, I am so sorry. Shelby has been taken."

Silence stretched across the line before Debbie responded. "Taken? I don't…what do you mean?"

A knot twisted in Hakim's stomach. "We believe she was kidnapped by a terrorist group that—"

"Kidnapped! How? No. It can't—not my Shelby—" Debbie's voice dropped from a scream to little more than a whimper.

"We are doing our best to locate her, but—" Hakim

heard movement on the other end of the line.

"Who is this?" Burke said into the phone.

"Burke, it is Hakim."

"Hakim? What's happening? Where's Shelby?"

"I am so sorry, Burke." Hakim coughed as he pushed the words through his constricting throat. "But Shelby has been kidnapped." He could hear Debbie crying in the background as he told Shelby's father what had happened, and what they knew.

Burke was devastated. He pleaded with Hakim for details, grasping at straws, trying to think of different avenues the security team may have missed. There must be something they hadn't tried. Burke wanted to come to Khali-dar immediately and help in the search, but Hakim convinced him to wait. He would keep them informed of any new developments and send a plane within the next few days

As the call ended, Burke spoke in a choked shaking voice. "Please, Hakim, please find my girl."

"I promise, I will not rest until she is safe."

Chapter Twenty

Hakim opened the door and stepped inside. Any other time, his presence in Shelby's room would be completely inappropriate, but he felt desperate to be near anything that would make him feel close to her.

Her old laptop sat on the desk. Hadn't he told Shanayze to get her a new computer? Shelby had probably refused. He pulled out a picture from where Shelby had tucked it into her mirror frame. Shanayze had taken it on the night of the reception. Shelby looked radiant. He remembered how nervous she had been and how he had kissed her goodnight. That night seemed so long ago. He put back the picture and picked up another, smiling when he saw Shelby and Kadir. The stable boy wore a cowboy hat, and the two stood outside the stable, pointing their fingers like pistols at the camera. Hakim lifted a framed picture of Shelby's family.

Seeing her mother's face, Hakim felt pain pierce his heart, remembering the grief in Debbie's voice on the phone. Through the entire conversation, Shelby's parents had never blamed Hakim. Although he thought it would have been easier to endure their anger rather than their anguish. He swallowed the lump in his throat as he thought of the pain Shelby's family was enduring.

Hakim carefully replaced the pictures and continued around the room. A stack of books stood on the table next to her bed. Arabic, Khali-dar history. Thumbing through them, he found the letter he had written on Shelby's first morning in the palace. She must've been using it as a bookmark.

As he passed her closet, he spotted the Arabian clothing she had worn to the desert. She had looked so beautiful and happy. His Arabian princess. He remembered how he had joked with her about leaving her in the desert and how her eyes had shined when Elder Malik complimented her. He touched the blouse, feeling the soft silk between his fingers, and thought about how Shelby's body had molded to his as she slept on the ride home. He let go of the shirt and tried to remember what she had been wearing the last time he saw her. Jeans, a blouse, and of course, her red boots.

With a groan, he sank on the small sofa and rubbed his eyes with the heels of his hands. The same questions that had plagued him for days pounded in his brain. Was she warm at night? Was she comfortable? Hungry? In pain? How were they treating her? Would he ever see Shelby again? Hakim had never felt so desperate, angry, and helpless in his life.

****

When the timid woman came again, Shelby found the entire outer room filled with people. For some reason, the sight felt ominous, and Shelby shook with fear.

The room was small, and the people packed there made it even smaller. She counted at least twenty. Men wearing *dishdashas* lounged on cushions on the floor. A group of women dressed in traditional black *abayas* and headscarves, and even some wearing full black *burqas*, were crowded together near the kitchen.

Shelby had to walk close as she passed. She looked into each of the women's eyes, searching for the smallest sign of pity. There was none. As her gaze moved toward the men in the room, Shelby felt a jolt of recognition. Even though he turned away and covered his face, Shelby couldn't mistake the drooping eye. *Usman.* What was he doing here? She kept her face neutral, as if she hadn't seen him, stifling the impulse to run and beg him to get her out of here. Instead, she concentrated on the different people. Trying to figure out the dynamic of the group. Who was the leader?

All of the people watched as Shelby walked past.

She knew from the expressions on their faces that she was being displayed.

Mr. Hairy and company were showing off. A few of the men laughed.

They spoke words that she didn't understand, but knew must be insults. *Cowards. They wouldn't dare talk like that to me if I wasn't a prisoner.* However, she gave no sign that she heard or understood them. Chin lifted high, she marched to the bathroom, ignoring them all. She closed the bathroom door and leaned against it, trying to calm her pounding heart. Instinctively, she'd known not to show any fear. She breathed deeply and splashed water on her face. When she came out, she heard some of the men talking.

"Two days." One man typed on a laptop.

Shelby thought he looked like a typical techie, even though he wore a *dishdasha* and *keffiya* instead of a Sci-Fi T-shirt and ripped jeans.

Usman stood near him, his face turned away.

Shelby couldn't understand what the other men said. The only phrases she understood were: "Prince

Hakim," "valuable," and "won't refuse."

She returned to the cold closet with all the dignity she could muster. After she closed the door, she wondered what they were talking about. But only a second passed before she knew with a sinking heart that *she* was valuable. *She* was what the prince would not refuse. *She* would be used to force Hakim into doing what these people wanted. And *she* had just two days to figure out what to do about it.

Hearing voices outside, Shelby leaned her ear against the door, listening closely. One word was repeated over and over. She didn't recognize it, but she knew it was important. Even the shrill-voiced screaming lady was saying it. *Al-Khalija.* They talked about things happening 'at' *Al-Khalija* or going 'to' *Al-Khalija.* She wished she understood more. Besides the talk about the big deal going down with the prince, she also heard talk about a major event happening on May first.

May first. The day of the derby. Shelby felt a heaviness in her heart. She imagined how it would have been to wear a big hat and sit next to Hakim as they cheered for his horses. *There is always next year, right?* But she was pretty sure there wouldn't be a next year. Even if she got out of this prison, she had no idea what the future would hold for their relationship.

She had done the right thing. She couldn't keep living a life that didn't belong to her, one where she was being someone else. But thinking about leaving Hakim caused such pain it took her breath away.

With her wrists untied, Shelby worked the aches out of her shoulders and made sure to switch position often to keep her muscles from stiffening. She didn't have high hopes that there would be a chance to escape, but if the opportunity did present itself, she wanted to be ready. As she listened through the door over the next few days, Shelby often heard what she thought was one side of a phone conversation. Sometimes, she heard more people talking in the outer room, but they never strayed far from their regular topics. May first. *Al-Khalija.* They appeared to be spreading the word. Letting everyone know their plan. She blew out an agitated breath, wishing she could figure out a way to warn Hakim.

Shelby was woken suddenly from her sleep and yanked out of her prison. Someone forced her hands behind her and tied her wrists together. A bag was crammed over her head, and she was half-led and half-dragged into the main room where she was pushed down onto her knees.

She heard men speaking, but the movement around her prevented her from hearing anything clearly until the bag was torn off. Looking around disoriented, she saw the men all wore scarves, concealing their faces. They held guns, pointed at her.

She wanted to scream, but suppressed it. Her breath came fast. She could feel her heart pounding so hard that thumps sounded in her ears. She darted her gaze around. A red light caught her eye, glowing from the top of a video camera sitting on a tripod.

After days of waiting, finally some action was being taken. They were filming her and trying to make her appear as vulnerable as possible for Hakim. For his sake, she knew she must show no fear.

****

Hakim sat at Shelby's desk, holding the picture

from the reception as he had so many times before when he heard a noise outside the door.

"Your Highness!" Nasir burst into the room. "A video is being streamed onto the internet. It is Miss Walker."

Hakim and Nasir ran to the security office where the Sheik and various security agents waited. They all stood around a large computer monitor as the technical analyst pulled up the grainy image.

Six masked men wearing military clothes and holding automatic weapons stood shoulder to shoulder in a cement room.

Nasir squinted and leaned closer to the screen. "M249 military-issue automatic machine guns," he said. "Probably close to twenty-five years old, cumbersome, with an exposed hot barrel. They look impressive, but these weapons haven't been retrofitted with the latest upgrade, and see how the men are awkwardly holding the sharp edges against their bodies. They have no experience with these guns. Amateurs."

Even with a cloth bag on her head and her arms tied behind her back, Hakim recognized Shelby as an unidentified masked man led her into the room.

He shoved her roughly to her knees and uncovered her face.

Hakim grasped the back of the analyst's chair.

Shelby was thinner, her hair was wild, and for a moment, she appeared as though she would completely succumb to her panic. However, composing herself, she lifted her chin and gazed at the camera with an expression of confidence.

Nasir nodded and muttered, "Good girl. Do not show them any fear. Doing so will only increase their power over you."

Hakim stared at the screen and vaguely registered Nasir and the other security agents discussing the images.

Nasir pointed toward the screen. "The windows are covered to prevent any type of location analysis based on the sun or surrounding buildings." He moved his finger, indicating the men. "They stand too close together and hold their weapons nervously. Obviously, they are not soldiers, making the situation all the more dangerous for Miss Walker."

One of the masked men stepped close behind Shelby as he spoke. "And so you see, dear Prince," he spat out the word. "*Nahl* has something that is very valuable to you." He stroked the side of Shelby's face with the barrel of his gun.

Trembling, Shelby closed her eyes.

Hakim's breathing came in gasps—his knuckles turned white as he tightened his grip on the chair.

The man continued, "We have a few simple requests. The current government is corrupt and allying itself foolishly with Western countries. The ways of our Fathers are being forgotten in favor of modernism. This must end!" He pointed his finger at the camera.

The men behind him cheered.

"We demand Sheik Rashid and his son Hakim leave the country and never return. They will be replaced by men who believe in the Traditions of Khalidar. Alliances with Western countries will be cut off, and the kingdom will be returned to its former self-sufficiency and glory. We also demand our brothers who have been wrongfully imprisoned be freed immediately. They are innocent and should be regarded as heroes of Khali-dar for attempting to rid the kingdom of corrupt leaders."

Hakim felt his chest tighten. He glanced at his father and saw the Sheik's face was pale and his eyes hard.

"Now," he spoke in English as he knelt and put his face next to Shelby's. "I would like for Prince Hakim's consort to add her voice to our cause."

Although his accent sounded thick, the taunting tone came through loud and clear. Hakim cursed between clenched teeth.

"Go ahead, Shelby Walker. Tell your prince to do as we say. Plead with him to save you." As he spoke, he curled his fingers around her neck.

Shelby took in a deep breath. She looked directly into the camera and held up her head. "Hakim." She spoke in a loud voice.

The men behind her chuckled.

Ignoring their cruel laughter, she squared her shoulders. "If you do what these vile men say, they will destroy the country you love. Do not give in to—"

The man next to her thrust his hand over her mouth to silence her.

She bit down and jerked her head to the side, smashing into his face. Shelby faced directly at the camera and yelled, "Stay strong, Hakim! Don't—"

Glaring, the man backhanded her across the face, and another slammed the butt of his rifle into her forehead.

Shelby crumpled to the ground.

Hakim drew in a sharp breath, and his body tensed.

He raised his gun to strike again, but the man with the broken nose yelled through a mouth full of blood.

"No, we must follow orders. We will wait until tomorrow at sundown." He turned his bloody face to the camera. "And then, *Prince* Hakim. We will make this woman an example of your foolish western ideology. She will pay the price, painfully, for the choices you have made."

"No!" Hakim screamed as the screen went blank. He picked up the computer monitor and threw it across the room. It slammed into a giant plasma screen with a spray of sparks. "Nasir. We must find her," the prince pleaded.

"Yes, Your Highness. We are doing everything we can."

The Sheik placed his hand on Hakim's back, leading him away from the computer terminal. "Come, son. You have not slept in days. You must eat." He softened his voice. "And you must again call Shelby's family."

Hakim shook. His throat constricted, and he clenched his fists. Knowing his legs would no longer support him, the prince sank into a chair, wrapping his arms around his stomach to try to ease the ache.

****

Shelby regained consciousness slowly. She tried to move her head and moaned as pain throbbed. Her arms were still tied, and she was too weak to struggle with the rope. She laid still, her memory returning in flashes.

Her face had been covered. She saw the men with weapons, their faces hidden. Mr. Hairy mocking her, insulting Hakim. Biting his hand. *That was disgusting.* Smashing his nose. *Kind of awesome.* And after that, pain had exploded in her head, blinding her. She wondered vaguely if she was bleeding. She was too tired to lift her head and check.

The house was silent, and Shelby was grateful. She didn't want to listen any more. She should have blurted out *Al-Kalija* instead of saying anything else. For days, he had been planning to get that information to Hakim. She had her chance, and she'd blown it once she'd seen the camera and thought of his face watching. He needed to know everything was all right. That she didn't blame him. Why had she felt the need to comfort Hakim instead of giving him the clue that might unravel the terrorists' plans?

Shelby was almost too tired to feel disappointed in herself. She was pretty sure *Nahl* wouldn't be releasing her now. A hostage who didn't do what you wanted wasn't valuable. So, they would kill her.

Wasn't she supposed to feel desperate? Afraid? Her mind was too fuzzy to hold onto anything for very long. She did feel a pang of regret when she thought of Hakim. She had never told him how she felt about him. That they could work out their differences and figure out a way to be together. Is this what it took to realize a life with him was what she wanted? She heard the door to the outside unlatch and gave a little start. It sounded like shrill-voice-lady was home.

Memories of riding *Al-qamar* with Hakim, looking into his eyes, watching him laugh, eased Shelby back into unconsciousness.

****

Hakim did not know how long he sat in the security office after he talked to the Walkers. He had never felt so useless. Shelby was out there somewhere, and she needed him. Yet, he was powerless to do anything.

Nasir, the head of security, and his father had all taken turns checking on him. Someone even left food on the table, but each recognized his desire to be left alone.

He must have dozed off and woke suddenly when the sun began to shine through the glass door ushering in the day he knew would be Shelby's last. Hakim heard arguing and stepped through the doorway to investigate. There in the hall, he saw the stable boy. *What is his name? Kadir.* The sight of him brought a lump to Hakim's throat. He thought of the picture of the two in Shelby's room.

Kadir argued with the guards who held his arms, pulling him away.

"Wait." Hakim held up a hand.

"Your Highness, I am sorry this boy has disturbed you," a guard said, bowing.

Hakim silenced him with a look. He put his hand on the boy's shoulder, meeting the boy's eyes. "Kadir, what is wrong?"

Kadir gazed up at Hakim, his dark eyes wide. "I think I know where Miss Walker is."

Hakim breathed to calm the racing of his heart, knowing it would only lead to more pain if he allowed himself to hope. "Tell me."

"I was carrying a bag of groceries for my mother home from the *souq* when a woman stepped onto the sidewalk in front of me, and we collided, spilling both of our bags. I could not see the woman's face beneath her *burqa*, but she yelled in a high voice as I hurried to gather our spilled food." Kadir glanced at the guards.

Hakim squeezed his shoulder to regain his attention. "Please, continue."

"She bent to pick up her bags, and I saw the woman was wearing Miss Walker's red cowboy boots." The boy twisted his fingers together. "I followed her, staying far behind so she would not see me. She went into a house, and I hid behind a car and waited to see if she would come back out."

Hakim leaned closer. This was the first hint they'd found of Shelby's location. "Tell me about the house, Kadir."

The windows were covered with heavy curtains, and while I watched, more people came and left. But I did not see the woman again."

Hakim summoned Nasir and asked Kadir to repeat the story.

Some of the guards whispered to each other, shaking their heads and rolling their eyes.

"Could you find this house again?" asked Nasir, glaring at the other men, ending any further cynicism.

"Yes." The boy gave a vigorous nod.

Twenty minutes later, a convoy of armored vehicles sped through the city. Once the decision had been made, the police force was mobilized.

Nasir drove the lead vehicle with Kadir and Hakim in the back seat. Nasir had simply nodded when Hakim refused to remain at the palace.

When they reached the house Kadir indicated, Hakim grabbed the door handle.

Nasir cleared his throat. "Your Highness, I know you are anxious to get in there and find Miss Walker. However, I must insist you remain where it is safe."

Hakim opened his mouth to argue. His stomach clenched, and adrenaline shot like electricity through his veins. He needed to get into that house and see if

Shelby was inside.

"We do not know what we will find." Nasir shook his head. "There are too many variables, and your safety must be our primary objective."

"I will wait. But not for long." Hakim sat back and clenched his hands into fists.

Nasir exited the car and walked to the other side, leaning against the door, his weapon drawn, and his gaze glued on the house.

Soldiers burst from the other vehicles and surrounded the small house, breaking down the door and storming through.

Hakim could see a flurry of movement through the open door. The curtains on the windows shifted, and he strained to see inside. His heart pounded as more soldiers were waved in, and then everything was silent. Hakim's mind churned with questions. Had they found the right house? Was Shelby inside? Were they too late? He glanced to his side at Kadir.

The boy stared wide-eyed at the house, his hands clenched into tight fists that made his knuckles white.

The prince patted the boy's knee, catching his gaze and giving what he hoped was a reassuring smile, although it felt strained and probably appeared more like a grimace. He turned his attention back to the house, the silence stretching until he could not stand it any longer and he pushed opened the door.

Nasir took in a breath as if he would protest, but at that moment, an officer appeared at the door, giving the "all-clear" signal.

Heart racing, Hakim bounded from the car and followed Nasir into the house, his heart in his throat. He could hear snatches of conversation around him.

"…we were met with no resistance…"

"…confiscated their cache of weapons…"

He paused in the doorway as his eyes adjusted to the dim light of the house. He saw officers in various stages of arresting the five men and two women. As Hakim's gaze swept the small space, he recognized heavily curtained windows and an area cleared of furniture with a camera on a tripod.

More officers swarmed the small home, searching through drawers and unhooking computers to confiscate for evidence. On the far side of the room, a small medical team crowded around a doorway.

Hakim gasped and rushed across the room. "Shelby!"

Dried blood spread over Shelby's forehead, and her lip was split. She was conscious and trying to sit up. She looked toward Hakim with eyes that didn't seem to focus.

One of the medics attached a device to her finger to measure her oxygen level, while another shined a light in her eyes. The medical team made room for Hakim to kneel by Shelby's head.

He held her hand and brushed the back of his fingers across her cheek. "Everything will be all right now, my darling," Hakim whispered. "Just rest."

"I knew you'd come," she murmured, closing her eyes.

"We must be sure she is stable and safe to move, and then we can get her to the ambulance," one of the medics told him.

Hakim nodded, glancing behind her at the small concrete closet that Shelby had apparently just been pulled out of. His relief at finding her was replaced by anger. He stared back at the group that had kept Shelby prisoner. What Kadir had told them was true. One of the women wore Shelby's boots on her feet. He had to squeeze his eyes shut and breathe as a red-hot fury clouded his vision. He listened to the conversations around him.

Nasir spoke with one of the officers. "Did any resist?"

"Only Miss Walker. When I opened the door, I got a kick in the…you know…"

A shadow of a smile crossed Nasir's face.

Hakim looked back down at Shelby and cradled her cheek in his palm.

The medic poked an IV into her arm, causing Shelby to stir.

"Do not worry, Shelby Jo. You are safe, now," Hakim murmured through a dry throat.

Shelby's eyes snapped open, and she blinked a few times. "Hakim, I need to tell you something."

"It is all right. You—must rest."

"No, it's really important."

"You can tell me later. Rest now."

The medic filled a syringe and inserted it into her IV tube. "I'm giving her morphine. Some of her ribs are most likely broken. A doctor will need to assess her for internal damage."

"Listen, I heard them," Shelby continued, struggling to speak. "I didn't understand much, but I heard them say *Al-Khalija*. They said it a lot. *Al-Khalija…*" Shelby's blinks grew longer, the morphine starting to take effect. "The horse guy, with the droopy face. And May first. Something…bad…May first," she slurred. Her body relaxed, and her head dropped to the side.

Hakim watched as the medical team loaded Shelby into the ambulance. His memory flashed back two months before where this same scenario took place on a cold mountain. But, this time, his anger at the people responsible threatened to overshadow his feelings of helplessness and worry. When the door closed, he turned to Nasir. "Please have somebody retrieve Shelby's boots."

"Yes, Your Highness." Nasir spoke to a passing soldier and then turned back to Hakim. "And now, is it your wish to follow Miss Walker to the hospital?

"It is, but there is something I must do first." Hakim pulled his cell phone out of his pocket and smiled as he scrolled through his contacts. He imagined the pain Shelby's parents had suffered over the past few days and was thrilled to call with good news. After he hung up the phone, Hakim climbed into the car next to Kadir.

The boy's eyes were wide, and he twisted his fingers together. Obviously watching armed soldiers invade a house and lead out cuffed prisoners at gunpoint, then seeing his friend taken away in an ambulance was a lot for a boy to handle.

"Kadir, I am indebted to you. You have saved Shelby's life and helped the police to discover the identity of men who are plotting against Khali-dar. You are a hero. I do not know how to ever repay you."

"I just wanted to help Miss Walker. Will she be okay?"

"Yes." Hakim's voice caught, and he swallowed. "She will live, thanks to you."

Kadir breathed a sigh of relief.

Hakim and the boy sat quietly for a moment. The prince rubbed his eyes then heard a soft knock, and looked up to see Nasir standing next to the car holding Shelby's boots. He rolled down the window, reached for the boots, and handed them to Kadir. "I am entrusting you with these boots. They are very special to Shelby, and I would like you to keep them safe and return them when she is healed. Will you do that?"

Kadir took the boots from Hakim. He ran his hands over the embroidery on the leather. "Yes, Your Highness." He spoke in a solemn voice accepting the assignment. "You can trust me."

"At this time in Khali-dar, there are few men whom I can trust. I am grateful to count you as one, Kadir." Hakim pressed his hands together and bowed to the boy who returned the formal gesture.

Hakim and Kadir got out of the car, and Hakim motioned for the captain of the guard to join them. "Please see to it that Kadir is taken home discreetly. I do not want any repercussions from his involvement today to fall upon him or his family. Also, I would like to meet with Kadir's parents next week. Please set up an appointment." He bowed once more to Kadir and watched the soldier lead him to an unmarked car to take him home. Hakim sat in the passenger seat as Nasir drove toward the hospital.

"Your Highness, I couldn't help overhearing what Miss Walker said to you."

"She must have been confused. *Al-Khalija*? The Bay? There is no bay in Khali-dar."

"Perhaps *Al-Khalija* was a mispronunciation." Nasir spoke in a slow voice. "When I was young, I often spent the summers helping my uncle on his farm in the northernmost region of Khali-dar. There is a section of the mountains the locals refer to as '*Al-Khaliya.*'"

"The Beehive," Hakim said.

"Yes, it is apparently riddled with tunnels. Isolated, unexplored. Strategically, the location is a perfect one to headquarter a terrorist movement."

"Nasir, I trust your intuition. This must be investigated immediately."

Chapter Twenty-One

Shelby woke to the beeps of a heart rate monitor. When she opened her eyes, she saw the blinking lights of the machine and an IV bag dangling above her. Feeling an uneasy sense of *déjà vu*, she lifted her head and looked around.

Hakim sat in a chair next to her bed. His hand covered hers, and he was fast asleep.

At the sight of him, she felt her pulse race. Allowing her gaze to travel around, she realized the room was nothing like any hospital she had ever seen. The floor was carpeted for one thing, and beautiful drapes hung at the windows. A sofa sat against a wall across from the foot of her bed beneath a beautiful painting. Although she still lay in a hospital bed, the bedding was tasteful and comfortable.

She returned her gaze to Hakim and felt her heart swell. She had been sure she would never see him again. The last few days had taken a toll on him. His beard, un-trimmed, looked scruffy, and his clothes were rumpled. His face appeared thinner, and drawn. She squeezed his hand.

Hakim jerked up his head and opened his eyes.

"Hey," she whispered.

His features relaxed and he bent forward, cupping her cheek. "How do you feel, Shelby Jo?"

"Awesome. But that probably has something to do

with the painkillers."

He smiled and rubbed his eyes with his other hand.

"I missed you," she whispered.

"Shelby Jo, when I found out you had been taken, I…" He swallowed and leaned forward to lay his head on her shoulder.

Shelby inhaled his familiar smell as she wrapped her arm around him and stroked his hair. "Everything is okay, now. I knew you would find me."

Hakim lifted his head and smiled. "It was Kadir who found you."

"Kadir?" *Kadir found me?*

"He saw a woman wearing your boots and followed her from the market. He was able to lead us to you."

"Man, I love that kid."

"As do I." He rested his head back on her shoulder, and she continued to run her fingers through his hair until she fell back asleep.

****

Three days later, Shelby sat up in bed, eating a meal that was the polar opposite of hospital food.

Aaliya sat on the chair next to her.

"Mmmm." Shelby spread more hummus on her flatbread. "This is just what the doctor ordered." She took a bite and chewed. "So, how much longer do you think I have to stay here? I feel pretty good. Just sore." She had seen the doctor a few times when he had come to check on her, but he hadn't given her any information, preferring to speak directly to Hakim.

"I don't know, but I'm sure Prince Hakim will not take any chances with your health. He will keep you here until he is satisfied that you are completely healed.

Persuading him to leave your side for a few hours so I could help you shower and change your clothing was difficult."

Shelby kept eating. She hated being cooped up in a hospital bed, but treasured the alone time she had spent with Hakim.

He had told her about the raid on the northern border and how the information she'd overheard led to the discovery of the *Nahl* headquarters. Numerous weapons and explosives had been recovered, and a terrorist attack planned for a local shopping mall was prevented, saving an untold number of innocent lives. Unfortunately, Usman the Bedouin, and mastermind behind *Nahl,* had escaped. From what Hakim told her, Elder Malik was furious and horrified that one of his trusted people had led the rebellion. He pledged his tribe's full cooperation as the manhunt continued.

At the sound of a knock, Aaliya rose and opened it, admitting Hakim.

Shelby grinned when she saw him, but her smile faded when she saw his face. Hakim's brows were drawn and his expression serious. He rubbed the back of his neck in a gesture that Shelby recognized as him being nervous.

Hakim glanced at Aaliya and then down at the paper he held in his hand.

"Is everything okay?" Shelby asked.

"Yes. Shelby Jo, I have something to talk with you about."

Aaliya excused herself with a bow and closed the door behind her.

Hakim sat in the chair next to the bed and took Shelby's hand. "Shelby Jo, before…when I asked you…" He darted his gaze to hers and returned it to their joined hands. "When I asked you to marry me…"

His voice was low so Shelby squeezed his hand for encouragement.

He let out a breath. "You told me you did not feel as though you could remain here in Khali-dar, without contributing, that you needed a role, or you would not feel as though you were being true to yourself." Again, he lifted his gaze.

Shelby saw the vulnerability had returned to his face. His lips were tight and there were lines around his eyes. She nodded. "I remember."

"I have made a proposal to my father which he has accepted. We would like to offer you a position as one of the Sheik's advisors."

Shelby grabbed a handful of blankets. "You can't be serious. What use would I be as a Sheik's advisor?"

"Shelby Jo, my father and I agree you would be very valuable. You are loyal to Khali-dar. You have shown us there are people in the kingdom who deserve to be heard, and we would like you to be their voice." His voice grew stronger as he spoke. "We need a person with vision and passion to organize and manage the building, staffing, and running of a women's university." He handed her the paper and held his breath.

Heart pounding, she looked from him down to the document in her hand. The letter was typed in English, and below in the swirling script of the Arabic language. Shelby raised her gaze to Hakim's. She did not know how to answer. She was flattered and stunned and extremely nervous. A lump grew in her throat as she thought about Hakim speaking to his father. His words demonstrated such confidence in her abilities, and the faith he showed was overwhelming.

He leaned forward and pointed to the bottom lines. "Here, next to my father's signature is the Minister of Education's name as well. We know you can do this, Shelby Jo."

She opened her mouth to reply.

Shaking his head, Hakim held up a hand. "Do not answer now. I will give you time to consider." He stood and began to walk to the door, but stopped and turned. The lines around his eyes deepened. "And while you are considering... Shelby Jo, I love you. I would do everything in my power to make you happy."

"I know." The ache in his expression tore at her. She blinked at the moisture in her eyes.

Shelby sat back against her pillows and looked at the paper again. An advisor to the Sheik.

Could Hakim's father have actually agreed to this? The entire situation seemed unreal, but the alternative was painful. Could she really leave Khali-dar? Leave Hakim? Remaining in Khali-dar would be difficult. She would have to sacrifice so much. Besides missing her family and friends, she would also give up her security and much of her freedom.

But, she realized, she wasn't the only who would have to make sacrifices. Why hadn't she seen how hard this situation would be for Hakim? He would be forced to give up some of the peace in his country, traditions, and the respect of many of his people who were against the idea of an American woman being their queen. His marriage proposal demonstrated he had been willing to sacrifice all of this.

When she thought of her future, she knew without

Hakim, it would never be complete.

Shelby shifted on the bed, wincing at a stab of pain. She put her feet on the floor, and Aaliya helped her stand and get into the bathroom. Shelby insisted she would be fine taking a shower by herself, but Aaliya remained close in case Shelby should need her.

Shelby was all right as long as she kept one arm pressed against her side. Washing her hair one handed was a little tricky, but she managed. When she came out of the bathroom, she saw Aaliya's eyebrows knitted together.

"What's up?" Shelby asked.

"Sheik Rashid will be here to meet with you in half an hour."

"With Hakim?"

"No, apparently the Sheik has business he would like to discuss with you alone." Aaliya shrugged. "That is all I know."

Aaliya helped Shelby into clean pajamas and a robe and then combed and blow-dried her hair.

A knock came at the door and Aaliya answered it, bowing when the Sheik entered. She stepped out into the hall, giving Shelby an encouraging smile before closing the door behind her.

"Your Majesty." Shelby stood and gave an awkward and painful bow to the Sheik. "Please come in." She chewed her lip, unsure of what to say. "Um…would you like to sit down?"

"No, thank you, Shelby."

She gave a little start. His voice almost sounded kind, and this was the first time he'd called her by her first name.

"However, I insist *you* sit down." The Sheik gently

held her elbow and escorted her to the couch.

Shelby was speechless. The Sheik had never shown her any kind of consideration before. What was going on?

For a long moment, Sheik Rashid was silent, his gaze traveling around the hospital room.

Shelby wondered what he was thinking about. Was he here to rescind the offer Hakim had undoubtedly convinced him to agree to? She shifted uncomfortably.

"I have not been in this room for many years," he said in a soft voice. He walked closer to the bed and stood silently for a moment. He stepped back and moved away from the bed, and began to pace, using his cane. "It will come as no surprise to you that I was very much against my son's relationship with you."

Ouch.

"I assumed his infatuation was temporary, and he would tire of you quickly. As a father and a Sheik, I felt becoming involved with an American woman was unwise. The first night I met you, I was appalled by your boldness and self-importance." The Sheik stopped pacing and stood in front of Shelby.

Hearing his statement made her wince, and she felt like shrinking under his intimidating gaze.

"However, Shelby Walker"—he paused—"my opinion has since changed."

Shelby gasped and looked up, not believing what she was hearing.

"What I had mistaken for Western arrogance was in reality, confidence, and what I had assumed to be smugness was actually dignity." The Sheik's expression softened. "As I have observed you for the past weeks, I have seen you show the same kindness to everyone from stable boys to heads of state. You have not put on airs in an attempt to impress. Allah has blessed you with a gift. The ability to relate to all people."

Stunned, Shelby stared with her mouth open. He was complimenting her?

"I hope to add my plea to my son's and ask you to become an advisor to the kingdom."

"Are you offering me a job because I'm your son's girlfriend? Did Hakim talk you into this?" She wouldn't have the Sheik or anyone give her something she didn't deserve.

"I put Hakim in the difficult position of choosing between his heart and his duty. Between you and Khalidar. I am afraid my prejudices run deep. I did not give you a chance." The Sheik paused and regarded her before he continued pacing. "I was wrong to think that by choosing you he would betray his country. Hakim's heart and duty should not conflict. I believe you are what our country needs, Shelby Walker."

After studying her expression, he joined her on the sofa. "Shelby, I sat in this same room twenty years ago, helpless, as my wife's broken body finally failed. This past week, I have seen the same pain I suffered on my only son's face." The Sheik rubbed the back of his neck with one hand. "He told me you were leaving. That you had refused to marry him, and he told me why. I wanted to ensure you considered all of your options before making a decision. I will tell you truthfully the position will not be easy. Many of the people of my country are as prejudiced as I have been. But I believe you are the right person to help break down these barriers."

"Your Majesty," Shelby began, unsure of what to say. She knew how hard this must be for the Sheik. "I don't want you to bribe me to keep me here. I don't want a job that I didn't earn."

"Shelby, do you think I earned my job?" The Sheik turned his body toward her and lifted his chin.

Shelby blinked. She hadn't expected the question and had no idea how to answer him.

"I was born into my job. I am the Sheik because my father was the Sheik and his father before him. Hakim will one day replace me. Did he earn this? Do we deserve this job?"

Considering her answer, Shelby pulled her brows together. "Before I came here, I would have said no." She tipped her head to catch the Sheik's gaze. "But I have seen how much you and Hakim work and sacrifice and care for Khali-dar."

He nodded, the corners of his mouth turned down. "Yes, Shelby. My position has taken me a lifetime to earn. I believe you have also earned your place in our kingdom, and when it comes to work and sacrifice, I would expect no less of you."

****

The next day, Shelby dressed, and in spite of Aaliya's protests, left the hospital room for the first time in nearly a week. She walked through the gardens toward the stables, hoping she would find Hakim. He hadn't come to see her the night before, wanting to give her time to think. Shelby knew her family would be landing in Khali-dar within the hour and she wanted to speak to Hakim before they arrived.

She turned down the path that led toward the stables, but the sight of a person on another path startled her. She let out a relieved breath when she recognized Nasir.

He stood with his arms folded but raised a brow and motioned with his head, indicating the pathway behind him.

Shelby flashed him a grateful smile and turned in that direction. She knew where Hakim was, and wondered why she hadn't thought to look there first.

When Hakim saw her enter the clearing near the pond, he jumped up from his seat in the gazebo and hurried toward her, taking her arm and leading her to sit on a bench "Shelby Jo, you should not be out of the hospital."

"I wanted to talk to you."

"You should have sent for me. Is something wrong?" Hakim hooked a finger beneath her chin, his gaze searching hers.

Shelby shook her head. "Nothing is wrong. I…" She felt suddenly shy, unsure of the words to say what was in her heart. She shifted around to lean against him, resting her head on his shoulder.

"Your family will be here soon. They are welcome to remain at the palace as long as they like. The Gulfstream will be ready to return to Colorado whenever they…you…are ready."

Shelby nodded her head, rubbing it against his shoulder. "Thank you."

"What are you thinking about right now?" Hakim asked in a quiet voice, sliding his arm around her.

"I was just thinking about that story. You know the one with the bird and the ruby?" She spoke without facing him. "That little bird was so brave. She knew what she wanted. She must have been scared, right? Not knowing what to expect. But she still did it. She followed the unknown path, with no guarantees, nothing." Shelby blew out a heavy breath. "It's what you would have done. I was a coward."

"Shelby Jo, in the few months since I met you, you have repeatedly proven to be the bravest person I know. In fact, Nasir called you a warrior, and he does not give such praise lightly."

"Then, why was I so afraid?"

"Fear and courage are not opposites, Shelby. Bravery is acting in spite of your fear."

Shelby turned and studied Hakim's face. The sadness in his eyes made her heart ache. He looked defeated, but was still willing to let her go if doing so made her happy. "Sitting in that stupid cement closet for so many days gave me plenty of time to think." She saw his face tighten, but didn't pause. "I thought about my parents and Chet and Lacey, and worried I would never see them again. I was really scared. But when I thought of you..." Her voice caught, and she swallowed, looking down at her hands, "When I thought I'd never see *you* again, I hurt. My heart hurt so badly I didn't think I would be able to stand it. It hurt worse than anything they could have done to me." She still couldn't meet his gaze.

Hakim grasped her shaking hand.

"I chose the wrong ruby," she said in a soft voice, then raised her gaze to meet his.

Hakim blinked his eyes. His mouth moved.

He looked as though he wanted to say something but didn't even know what question to ask. "Hakim, you aren't my ruby. I don't want you to be. I don't want to give you up."

"I am not your *ruby*?"

"You know, like in the story. The bird sacrificed

her ruby."

He raised his eyebrows and tipped his head back as understanding dawned on his face. "Shelby Jo, what are you saying?"

"I'm saying I don't want to leave. I love it here." She blinked against the tears forming in her eyes. "I love the palace and Aaliya and even your dad, but mostly, I love you. I don't want you to be my ruby." Hakim's face broke into the smile she loved.

With a quick move, he pulled her onto his lap.

A burst of sound that was a combination of laughter and tears burst out of her mouth. She wrapped her arms around his neck, ignoring her aching ribs as, her heart swelled until she thought it would burst. Another laugh/sob eeked out, and she buried her head in his shoulder.

He chuckled. "Shelby Jo. Somehow with that strange sentence, you have managed to simultaneously astonish, delight, and confuse me." He eased back and lifted her face, then brushed his lips across hers and whispered, "I refuse to be your ruby, and I promise you will never be mine."

Epilogue

Seven years later

With quick steps, Sheik Rashid strode up the stairs and down the palace hallway—his sheer robes billowing around him. The University Dedication ceremony had taken longer than he had expected, and he had a promise to keep.

His daughter-in-law, Shelby, had been eloquent and dignified as she gave her speech—her Arabic flawless.

Hakim had watched her with adoration shining in his face, and the Sheik himself had felt a swelling of pride at the way Shelby represented Khali-dar and the work she had done to make her dream of the Women's University a reality.

She had spent years researching, consulted with countless experts, overseen every decision herself, and had established a world-renowned establishment other countries were now striving to emulate.

He had nearly reached his goal when a woman sitting outside the door stood and bowed.

"Am I too late?" he asked.

"I put her to bed not twenty minutes ago, Your Majesty."

He nodded and opened the door slowly. Moonlight shone in a wide strip through the sheer curtains, over a

The Sheik's Ruby

cowboy hat next to a golden tea set, and onto the beautiful child who sat up in her bed as soon as she saw him.

Her face was a blend of her parents—Hakim's high cheekbones, Shelby's flashing eyes—and at times, he even caught a glimpse of his wife, whose name she bore.

"Grandpa! I knew you would come."

"Shh, Kalila, you are supposed to be asleep," he whispered, stepping into the room.

"But I am not even sleepy."

"If you do not get proper sleep, how can we battle the hungry hippopotami tomorrow?"

"Hungry, Hungry Hippos, Grandpa," she corrected him, yawning.

"Yes, I would be sorry if we could not play because you were too tired."

She laid her head back on the silk pillows. "Will you tell me a story, Grandpa? Like you promised."

"Of course, my princess." He pulled up the sheets around her, brushing her dark hair off her face. Settling into a chair, he took a deep breath before he began. "Long ago, before the time of the great waters, while genii roamed the earth and magic still thrived, there lived a songbird…"

A word about the author...

Jennifer Moore is a passionate reader and writer of all things romance due to the need to balance the rest of her world, which includes a perpetually traveling husband and four active sons, who create heaps of laundry that are anything but romantic.

Jennifer has a B.A. in Linguistics from the University of Utah and is a Guitar Hero champion. She lives in northern Utah with her family. You can learn more about her at: authorjmoore.com